PhDs, Pornography and Premeditated Murder

by

JL Wilson

PhDs, Pornography and Premeditated Murder

COPYRIGHT ©2009 by JL Wilson

Cover Art by *Kim Mendoza*

The Wild Rose Press
PO Box 706
Adams Basin, NY 14410-0706
Visit us at www.thewildrosepress.com

Publishing History
First Crimson Rose Edition, 2010
Print ISBN 1-60154-638-6

Published in the United States of America

**I paused to order my thoughts and
Sloan didn't pressure me. He just waited.**

It was very soothing. I struggled to make him understand without making it look as though I was hoping for a reassuring compliment. "I've always known I'm not the type of woman—" I stopped and started again. "I don't make men—" I stopped again. "I mean, I'm not terribly sexy. Toby was very sexy and sophisticated. When he paid attention to me, I was so flattered. And I was unsure about my future. I was starting a new job, but wasn't sure if it was the right career path for me. Toby lied to me. He told me he'd be deported unless I helped him. He told me he was here on a graduate student visa and..." I looked at Sloan, expecting to see pity at my stupidity.

Instead I saw compassion. It gave me the courage to continue. "Then, a few days after we got married I found he was sleeping around. Maggie— you met her? She saw him with another woman. I confronted Toby about it but he just laughed it off." I ran a hand through my hair, tugging at my curls in agitation. "It mattered a lot to me. I trusted him."

"I can understand how that must have made you feel," Sloan said quietly. "You trusted him and he threw it in your face."

I looked into his eyes but didn't see a hint of condescension or laughter at my naiveté. This was a man who understood trust and the converse of that—violated trust.

I believe it was at that moment that I decided to convince Marcus Sloan to introduce my virgin body to the joys of sex.

Reviews

for CANDY, CORPSES AND CLASSIFIED ADS:
"This story delivers a heady romance, a well written mystery and a great ending, which you will have to read to find out!"
~Verbena, Long and Short Reviews

for AUTOGRAPHS, ABDUCTIONS AND A-LIST AUTHORS:
"...A wonderfully fun and tongue-in-cheek look at the world of author conventions.... Need a quick, entertaining, feel-good story with suspense and murder adding an intriguing twist? Then you will enjoy AUTOGRAPHS, ABDUCTIONS, AND A-LIST AUTHORS!"
~Stephanie B., Fallen Angel Review Chatters

Dedication

To Scott, Grace Ann, Ted, George, Bob
and the cast of characters who populated my time
at the University of Northern Iowa's
English Department.

Chapter 1

Of all the people on the planet who deserved to die, my husband had a premier spot at the top of the hypothetical hit list. But that doesn't mean I killed him.

Someone else did me that favor.

It was a pristine August evening in Minnesota. The temperature was in the low 70s, there was a gentle, fresh breeze blowing, and the mosquitoes had been eliminated, at least temporarily, probably by the spraying of some noxious chemical. I chose not to concern myself with the possible toxic side effects that came with exposure and instead enjoyed a buzz-free night.

"Jane, Jane—look over there," Kathy said, pointing with her corn dog to a young couple entwined together on a bench.

I was at the Minnesota State Fair with my friend, Kathy Sylvester. We were meeting another friend, Maggie Carlson. I looked where Kathy pointed. The boy's hand was—and the girl's was—"Lord, that's illegal, isn't it?" I asked.

"Only if she has an orgasm."

I laughed, nearly spilling my beer as the crowd

jostled me. Kathy plowed ahead, short and solid like a small all-terrain vehicle. She was the office manager for the English Department of The University of Saint Paul (TUSP), where I was an Associate Professor of American Fiction. She and I had spent the afternoon enjoying the culinary delights of the fair, people-watching, and strolling through the swine barn to inspect the World's Biggest Boar. We had a good chuckle at that, since everyone knows the World's Biggest Bore is Jim Crowndorf, an Associate Professor of Renaissance Prose in our department at the University.

Kathy and I soon reached the grandstand where I spied Maggie, looking as always pert and petite. Even her buddy, Peg—Maggie's name for her prosthesis—didn't detract from Maggie's prettiness. Maggie looks rather like Jane Pauley with short, tousled dark hair and a direct, unwavering gaze. I, on the other hand, look like a short Jane Curtin with curly red hair and slightly more weight.

"I brought my handicapped sticker," Maggie said, waving her cane. "This'll get us good seats. I can't believe they're doing general seating for this concert."

"I don't think the grandstand has quite the same cachet as a Broadway play at the Orpheum Theater," I said, looking at the three tiers of bleachers behind her filling with rock and roll fans, some of whom were in full costume.

"We'll get front row seats," she said confidently, maneuvering into the crowd flowing onto the staircase leading to the seating.

"It pays to have a gimp for a friend," Kathy said, elbowing her way next to Maggie. Kathy was an enormous help to me when Maggie fled Pittsburgh four years earlier. With Kathy's assistance, I got Maggie a job, her boys into schools, and the family into a house and a new life. It was the least I could do for a friend who endured what Maggie suffered. Kathy, bless her big heart, agreed.

Conversation was curtailed as we inched our way with the other ZZ Top aficionados into the patio in front of the grandstand, then finally ascended the steps to the first concourse. Maggie limped when it served her purpose and used her cane in well-placed jabs to secure us good positions in the slow-moving line. She was correct. When we got to the grandstand, the guards took one look at her prosthetic leg, then ushered us to three seats in the second row, center, reserved for Handicapped. The seats in front of us were removed for the wheelchair-bound. This truly was Rock Star Seating. We sank down with a happy sigh and ordered beers from the roving beer vendor.

"I need to show you something," Maggie said as soon as we relaxed back in our metal seats. She handed me her beer to hold so she could rummage in the fanny pack she wore. On most people a fanny pack looks like a cancerous growth. On her it was a stylish fashion accessory. She pulled an envelope from the pack, thrusting it at me. "I got this. It was forwarded on to me, from the mail box we rented."

I pulled a letter from the envelope, scanning it in the dimming light of the Minnesota sunset. The handwriting was spiky and angular, reminding me of the soldier-straight rows of corn to be seen now in Minnesota fields.

Dear Phire: I am so pleased to finally write to you at your real address. It's taken me time to find you. I respect your privacy and won't advertise who you are. I've been an ardent fan since I read Literary Lover. Your depiction of how people feel during sex is so intuitive, so realistic. I can only imagine what you are like in real life. Women like you surely only exist in dreams, don't you?

I just wanted to tell you how much I appreciate

you. I look forward to your next book. I hope you'll have an autograph signing someday I can attend. I would love to meet you in person.

It was unsigned. I inserted the paper back in the envelope. "How did they get the mail box number? All my fan mail goes to my publisher and they forward it."

"More to the point, how'd they know my name?" Maggie flipped the envelope over in my hands, tapping it significantly.

I looked at the name on the front above the mail box number. *Maggie Carlson.* "Oh no."

Kathy took the letter from me. "What mail box?"

"When I was running away from my ex-husband Jane rented me a mail box at one of those Mail Box Unlimited places," Maggie explained. "I used it until Pat was convicted, then I turned the rental over to Jane."

"I use it for..." I gave them a meaningful look, lowering my voice lest anyone hear. "You know...things."

"Huh?" Kathy looked up from the letter she was skimming.

"Research," I said.

"Oh, you mean dirty movies, porn books, sex toys, whips, and leather?"

I looked around anxiously but the crowd was ignoring the three forty-something-year-old women in the second row. "Research," I said. "For my books." In the six years since Kathy had dared me to write 'a sexy book', four of my books were published under the pen name "Phire Foxe". I'd read copiously of the erotic literature available then jumped wholeheartedly into the genre, the result being a modest success.

In fact, I was such a success my publishers wanted me to produce a trilogy with one of my main characters, a paid female assassin, as the cohesive link between the books—and they wanted it in a year. I could do it but not while I taught four University classes, managed dissertation projects, volunteered for the literary council, and served as community liaison for the department. Oh, and don't forget I needed to pen some esoteric scholarly articles on William Dean Howells, Henry James, or Edith Wharton.

That's why I wanted the promotion that would soon be voted on in my department. Jim Crowndorf and I were competing for the Full Professorship with its pay increase, better teaching opportunities, and a yearlong sabbatical starting in January. I hoped to use that uninterrupted year to plot four or five books. Then I would do the expected research on an American novelist and return to my teaching job refreshed and invigorated. I'd be secure in the knowledge I had bankrolled some erotica, to be pulled out of the hat, voila, like a miracle.

"Sex toys." Kathy went back to the letter, finished it then handed it to me. "Sounds like a hottie. Do you get these often?"

"Surprisingly enough, yes, I do. The people who read my books apparently believe I live as exciting a life as my heroine." I examined the letter. "The only address anyone has for me is my publisher. How did this person obtain the mail box address?"

"And my name?" Maggie looked at me. I could see the fear in her eyes.

"It's not Pat," I said immediately. "It isn't."

"He's still in jail, isn't he?" Kathy asked, her eyes wide with apprehension.

"For at least another month," Maggie confirmed. "And he's not supposed to leave Pennsylvania when he's released." She drew in a long, ragged breath. "No, I'm sure it's not Pat."

She didn't sound confident but I didn't blame her. Five years ago, her ex-husband had driven their car off the road in a fit of rage when she demanded, yet again, a divorce. Maggie survived the accident but lost a leg. Pat finally got the prison sentence he so richly deserved. In the years since then Maggie had made a new life for herself, but the ominous specter of Pat The Bastard was always in the background.

Who could have sent this letter? My secret identity as Phire Foxe was known to only a select few: my editor, my family, Kathy, Maggie, and one or two other erotica writers with whom I exchanged email. I wasn't ashamed of my books but it wouldn't help my campaign for the Full Professorship to be known as "the hottest writer of unwilling stranger seduction available for download today." TUSP was a stodgy, private college. The English Department was possibly the stodgiest of the stodgy, excepting perhaps Library Science where they still bemoaned the loss of paper card catalogs and big oak file cabinets to house them.

"What should I do?" Maggie asked.

Maggie and I have been friends since grade school, in Boston. I could see the worry in her dark blue eyes. "Let me keep this." I stuffed the letter into the bulging sack I got at the Home Improvement building, adding it to the other effluvia I collected during my outing at the fair. "I'll devise a plan. I'll talk to Robbie. Maybe he'll have an idea. He's coming here next week." I waggled my eyebrows at Maggie. "For his annual visit."

She rolled her eyes. "I wish you'd quit trying to be a matchmaker. I was in love with him in eighth grade. I haven't seen him since high school."

"Robbie's such a catch. He's cute, he's rich, he's single..."

"It's the last bit that has me worried," Maggie said with a laugh. "Any man who gets to his fifties and isn't married, divorced, or jilted at the altar is a concern. He's too set in his ways to change now." She tapped Peg the Leg. "And I've got a few deficits to deal with."

"Your brother knows you write erotica?" Kathy asked, propping her feet up on the guardrail in front of us to wiggle her Keds at passersby.

"Robbie knows all," I said. He even knew my Deepest Secret, one not shared with anyone else in the world. If there was one person I could trust, it was my big brother Robbie. "There must be some logical explanation for—"

The lights dimmed precipitously. At the same instant I felt the subtle touch of a hand on my neck. I knew what that meant. Someone was watching me. My sixth sense was sporadic but infallible when it occurred. It was an inheritance from my Rom grandmother, who had made an excellent living as a fortuneteller before being targeted by Hitler and his minions. I knew from experience it would do no good for me to try to observe the person who was focusing on me. I closed my eyes, letting the feeling engulf me.

I couldn't center on the sensation. I knew it was a man and someone known to me, but that was confusing. Few men I knew would attend the ZZ Top concert at the Minnesota State Fair. I had a brief impression of straight black hair, cut stylishly. I drew in a sharp breath. I *almost* recognized that face...

My eyes snapped open. I was surprised by how dark it had become. We were in a typical outdoor fairground venue with the bleachers overlooking what served as a racetrack during the day. The concert stage was on the infield with large video screens alongside. A bank of floodlights lit the space as roadies bustled on stage, performing arcane musical tasks.

The sun was nearly down and with the lights

off, the track in front of us was just a murky oval. My eyes were drawn to two people, seated to the right. One person sat forward, talking over the back of the chair of the man in front. The man in front was looking over his shoulder—at me. He was in shadow so I couldn't discern his features, but I knew he was watching me. I felt his gaze as effectively as if a spotlight was highlighting me.

Then he turned his attention to the person behind him. It was hard to tell in the murkiness what was happening but it appeared they were arguing. His eyes kept returning to me. It was unnerving.

"Press," Kathy said, pointing to people walking in to sit in the prime seating in front of the grandstand. "And Princess Kay."

I jerked my attention from the man on the track to Princess Kay of the Milky Way, the reigning Dairy Princess. She and her court of six other wholesome young women were regular attendees at Fair events. I watched the seven young women, all wearing blue jeans, T-shirts, and tiaras, take their seats.

I barely noticed. My mind was trying to decipher how someone sent a letter addressed to Maggie, meant for me, to her old mailbox address. I applauded the warm-up band at the appropriate times, tapped my feet with the rhythm and swayed to the music while evaluating what happened. No one in my 'real life' knew I rented that mailbox. I ordered items under my initials, J. P. Renard. The credit card I used for my erotic purchases was billed to that mailbox. Why had someone associated Phire Foxe with Maggie, at that mailbox?

I attempted to put my unease aside as ZZ Top took the stage, breaking into "Sharp Dressed Man," one of my personal favorites. I vowed to call Robbie when I got home to discuss the situation with him. If anyone could assist me in unraveling this mystery, my brother could.

It was while Billy Gibbons, Dusty Hill, and Frank Beard were launching into "Legs" that I felt the cold breeze on my neck again. I closed my eyes, letting the feeling wash over me. It was that man. He was someone connected to me from my past. He was staring at me. It was—

I opened my eyes, looking down at the darkened track. Princess Kay and her court had left, probably to grace some other event with their royal presence. The chairs were now sparsely populated with a few groups of people spread widely apart.

He was watching me again. He'd turned in his seat and was peering up into the darkened bleachers. I felt...beseeching, perhaps? Or was it fear? Or anger? Some powerful emotion was washing through the crowd and up the stand to ooze around my bare legs and twine up my denim shorts, sneakers, and University of St. Paul T-shirt. I sensed he needed me for some reason, wanted to speak with me. He was anxious I—

His attention turned to the person behind him, still speaking to him over the back of his chair. The man appeared engrossed in whatever the person was saying, nodding in agreement several times. Then their conversation seemed to change and the person behind him appeared angry. At one point that person stood up abruptly then sat down just as quickly, burying his or her face in raised hands.

The band was deep into their set when the person in the 'behind' row of seats got up and left, vanishing into the dark shadows at the far side of the track. The man who'd been staring at me remained in his seat, facing forward to watch the band. He didn't turn to gaze at me again, but something about his posture pricked me with unease.

"Look at that man," I said to Maggie in between "Tush" and "Cheap Sunglasses." "Is something odd about him?"

She peered down at the track. "What kind of odd?"

"I don't know." The feeling was annoying. I was almost certain something was out of order. I considered the environment around me. Security guards were pacing on the track and I thought I saw two uniformed police officers, near the infield. "I'm going to check on it." Before Maggie could protest, I slipped out of my seat, sliding forward to stand between two wheelchair patrons seated in front of us. Making hasty excuses, I descended the stairs leading downward to the cinder track.

I timed it perfectly. A security guard was striding away from the stair area while the uniformed patrol officers were facing the stage. As I stepped onto the track, I established my bearings then started toward the man in the chairs on my right.

"Hey!"

I looked back. The guard who'd been leaving was now returning. He was short and powerfully built, his white State Fair Security shirt highlighting his tanned skin and his salt-and-pepper hair, which was thick and cut short. He was attractive in a muscular, bodybuilder sort of way. Not at all my type, but he had an interesting, although angry, face.

"You're not allowed down here."

I smiled in what I hoped was a placating fashion. "I think that man is ill." I gestured to the man in the chair about thirty feet away. I started to sidle in that direction.

"How do you know?" He glanced to where I pointed.

I used his distraction to shuffle closer to the man on the track. I didn't want to get into a discussion of psychic phenomena so I fabricated a believable lie. "I thought I saw him vomit. Perhaps he's drunk."

As I expected, the mention of intoxicated behavior got the guard's attention. He walked carefully through the rows of chairs, coming up to the seated man from the right. I lagged behind, alternating my attention between the guard and ZZ Top as they pounded out "Tube Snake Boogie" to the roar of approval from the crowd.

"Sir?" The guard reached the man then bent over, shining his flashlight on the ground.

That's foolish, I thought. The flashlight should be on the man, not the... Then I saw what the guard had already seen. There was a pool of some liquid on the ground, under the man's chair. I edged forward.

The guard pulled out a radio appliance from his belt and spoke rapidly into it. I was now less than five feet away as the guard touched the man's shoulder then moved his fingers up to the man's neck. Even I knew what that meant. I've watched my share of detective shows on television. I recognized the gesture as a check for the man's vital signs.

"Is he hurt?" I asked, staying well back from the suspicious looking puddle.

The guard looked over his shoulder at me. "How did you know about this man?"

I didn't like his accusatory tone of voice. I started to edge backward but a chair blocked my path. "Know what?"

"He's injured."

"Injured?" Curiosity got the better of me. I leaned forward, trying to get a glimpse of the injury. "How?"

The guard swung his flashlight. For the first time the seated man's face was illuminated. "Oh God." Even in the flickering light I recognized that long, handsome face with the thick, full mustache. His hair was still black, barely touched by gray.

"What?"

"My God. It's Toby."

"You know him?" the guard demanded, swinging the light from the slumped man to me.

My legs were suddenly too weak to support me. I dropped down, almost missing the chair behind me. "It's my husband. I mean—he was—is—my husband." I looked up at him, bewildered. "I mean, I think he was my ex-husband. Maybe."

Chapter 2

I leaned forward but the security guard put up an intervening arm. "It's Toby," I stated.

"He's your husband?"

"I thought he was my ex-husband." I didn't have time to further explain my remark. Suddenly men were teeming around us. I sat, frozen with surprise and disbelief, as police, paramedics, and security people converged on the spot. Within minutes there was a wall of live bodies hiding Toby's presumably dead body from anyone's view.

The security guard who'd found Toby approached me. "The police need to talk to you. They have an office here, at the Grandstand. You have to go with them."

I looked up at him, confused. "I can't. My friends are here. I have to—"

"There's been an accident on the infield," the loudspeaker blared. I belatedly realized the music had stopped. "We're going to ask folks to leave as orderly and quietly as possible. There's no danger to anyone, but we need you to clear the area."

"The murderer," I said, standing up to peer at the large crowd that was, even now, moving like the tide toward the exits. "He's getting away."

"You saw the murder?" It was hard to read the guard's expression even though the infield lights had been lit. He had a rough, craggy face with white eyebrows, piercing pale blue eyes and a nose that looked as though it was broken at one time. I thought his expression was curious and sympathetic but perhaps that was wishful thinking on my part.

"I saw something," I said, tearing my gaze away from his to look at the crowd. Maggie and Kathy were standing outside the ring of men, peering at me. I waved.

"You can't go." He put up a hand as though to stop me.

"But my friends—"

He motioned to a policeman nearby. "They'll be escorted to the office. You need to tell the police what happened."

"Aren't you the police?"

"I'm just fairground security."

I looked at the hard-faced men around me. "Can't you come with me?" I whispered. This man wasn't friendly, but at least he wasn't a police officer. I was nervous with the large amount of testosterone-laden law enforcement surrounding me.

He must have heard the earnest supplication in my voice. He exchanged a look with a police officer, who nodded. Before I could protest, I was whisked away, guided along the track to a door in the bottom of the bleachers. We entered a long hallway that appeared like what I'd seen of locker room tunnels on TV shows. I glanced behind me. Maggie and Kathy, two policemen flanking them, followed. They waved energetically and I attempted a similar greeting in return. We soon came to a door. The security guard opened it, gesturing me to go in.

Several desks, TVs, computers, and a bank of phones cluttered the gray, airless room. I sat down in an orange vinyl chair next to a battered grey desk and looked up at my security guard, who'd perched himself on the edge of a similarly well-used desk. A large man wearing a white golf shirt, similar to my security guard's but with a different logo on the pocket, conferred with my guard in a low voice. Then he appropriated a chair to sit near me.

"Detective Sloan said you saw this man in the infield?" the large man asked me.

"Detective? He said he wasn't with the police." I looked at my guard, who nodded.

The new man shot my guard a look that I thought was perhaps...disgust? Anger? "He was with the police. He's retired."

"Who are you?" My voice sounded shrill but I knew my constitutional rights. This man had to identify himself. I knew I had a right to know who was interrogating to me. Or, rather, I *thought* it was a constitutional right, but I wasn't sure because legal matters were not my field of expertise. I suddenly wished Robbie, my brother, were with me. It was often useful to have an attorney in the family.

The man sat back. "I'm sorry." He pulled out a wallet with a badge in it then extracted a business card. He handed both to me. I turned my gaze to my security guard in expectation. He looked surprised then he, too, handed me a card. I read his first. *Marcus Sloan, Security Consultant, J A K Enterprises* followed by several phone numbers. The police card read *Lt. Sam Sloan, SPPD.*

"You're related?" I asked, putting the two cards in my effluvia bag then handing back the surprisingly heavy badge in the worn wallet.

"Brothers," Lt. Sloan confirmed. "Now about the man in the chair. You said he was your husband? Why wasn't he sitting with you?"

Oh, this was going to be awkward. I decided to go on the offensive. "How did he die?"

The two men exchanged a look then Lt. Sloan said, "We can't release that information at this time. Could you answer my question? Why wasn't he sitting with you?"

"I didn't even know Toby was here."

"Here at the concert?" It was the other brother, Marcus Sloan, who asked. His brother looked peeved. Apparently it wasn't acceptable for non-law enforcement personnel to ask questions. I filed that little nugget of information away for later study.

"Here in town," I corrected. The brothers exchanged a puzzled look. "St. Paul," I added, in case they'd forgotten where we were situated.

"He's your ex-husband?" Lt. Sloan asked. Unlike his brother, the Lieutenant was taller but also solidly built with dark hair graying around the ears and dark blue eyes. Again, he was not unattractive but was not my type.

"No, not really." I twisted the handle of my Home Depot bag nervously. "I mean, I thought he was my ex-husband."

This seemed to stump the good detective. "How long has it been since you've seen him?"

I considered that question. How long had it been? Let's see, Mom had still been alive. She passed on almost twelve years ago, so...

"How long?" Lt. Sloan prompted.

"I heard you. I'm thinking." I tallied the time, mentally double-checking to make certain I was correct. "Fourteen years."

He tried to hide it, but I noted his astonishment. "You haven't seen your husband for..."

"Fourteen years." I waited for the rest of the questions. I was accustomed to this type of amazed reaction to my bizarre story.

"Let's start at the beginning," Lt. Sloan, pulling out a notebook. "I need to get some information about you."

16

I rooted in my effluvia bag for a reciprocal business card, but couldn't find it among the brochure for gutters, a sample of vinyl siding, a cube of pressed fertilizer, a map of the fairground, a souvenir squeezy stress pig, the tiny blue panda I won at the shooting gallery, and the other items pressed on me during my fair outing. I gave up the search and at his prompting, provided my name (*Dr. Jane P. Renard*), address (*RFD 3, Chaska, Minnesota*), and my occupation (*Associate Professor of American Literature, TUSP*).

"And your husband's name?" he asked, pen poised over his little notebook.

"Toby Considine."

"Do you know what his occupation was?"

"Gigolo."

My security guard, the one called Marcus, made a strangled noise. I glanced at him and thought I spied a grin on his face then his impassive, calm demeanor appeared once more. Lt. Sloan looked bewildered. "I beg your pardon?"

"Toby was a lady's man," I said. "He attracted women, used them, extracted money, and then moved on. That was his profession."

"How long have you been separated?" It was Marcus Sloan asking the question. I eyed Lt. Sloan, who appeared unable to speak.

I fidgeted. This was always awkward. "Twenty-two years."

Lt. Sloan looked at me incredulously. "Say again?"

"You heard me. Twenty-two years."

"How long have you been married?" This was Marcus Sloan.

I glared at him. He was too intelligent by half. "I thought it was four months. But it might have been twenty-three years. Almost."

His brother appeared unable to speak. Marcus

Sloan carried the conversational ball. "So you got married then almost immediately separated."

I nodded, running my hand through my hair. It was a humid day and my curls were responding with their customary vigor. "I considered an annulment, but Toby had already absconded. I didn't have the funds to track him down. So I filed an in-absentia divorce. I recently discovered the legal paperwork of the divorce might have not been properly filed. So we may, technically, still have been married. Perhaps." I sat back. It sounded believable. Almost.

The Sloans exchanged unreadable looks. "But you saw him fourteen years ago?" Lt. Sloan prompted.

"Saw is the operative word. Toby and a woman were talking at a café in Boston, near where my parents lived at the time."

A man came into the room to hand something to Lt. Sloan. Marcus Sloan watched as his brother examined what looked like a man's wallet. Lt. Sloan looked up at me. "Did you know your husband—your ex-husband—was living in Florida?"

I shook my head. "As I said, I had no idea where Toby was." I prayed my lie would pass police inspection.

Apparently it did. Lt. Sloan looked at his brother. Some unknown fraternal message was passed. "We'd like you to stay here while we check your story," Lt. Sloan said, standing up.

"What story? I'm an innocent bystander." Marcus Sloan slid off the desk where he'd been sitting and started to walk toward the door. "Where's he going? He can verify what I said." I almost said 'verify my story' and stopped myself in time, lest I sound like I was prevaricating.

"We'll get his statement and yours, Miss— Mrs.—Renard."

"Doctor," I snapped. "I'd like to see my friends.

They're probably worried about me."

The Sloans exchanged another look then Lt. Sloan nodded. "We'll need you to give a statement then you'll be free to go. Just a few more minutes." He and his brother exited, leaving me with a roomful of men, computer equipment, and my worries.

A woman police officer came in. I repeated my story, struggling not to embellish it and to keep my lies consistent. "...I saw this man and thought he was ill; it was something in the way his shoulders slumped..."

She showed no indication about the plausibility of my story, just took down every word I said, typing at a computer almost as fast as I could talk. Then she printed it, I read it, made a few minor notations to correct some typographical, grammatical, and punctuation errors, then signed it. As suddenly as I arrived, I was escorted to the door.

Kathy and Maggie were waiting in the hallway. "What the hell is happening?" Kathy demanded, almost pouncing on me. "They asked us a bunch of stuff about where you were tonight then they refused to talk any more. Assholes." She glared at a tall, young-looking man in a police uniform who had a stoic, pained look. I could imagine what Kathy subjected him to while I was inside.

"Where's my security guard?" I asked, looking down the gray hallway.

"Your security guard?" Maggie asked, leaning on her cane. She looked exhausted. I felt immediately guilty.

"The security officer who can corroborate my story," I said. "Short, white hair, white shirt, black jeans..." I didn't see him anywhere. "Where is he?"

Maggie shook her head. "People have been coming and going like crazy. What happened? Why did they question you? Why'd they question us?"

I gestured Kathy closer then leaned next to

Maggie to whisper, "It was Toby. He's dead."

"What?" Kathy almost fell over in amazement.

I grabbed her to drag her nearer. "It was Toby. He was killed down there on—"

"Dr. Renard, there you are."

My head snapped up so fast I heard something go *pop*. I'd probably have a neck injury in the morning. My security guard was striding down the hall toward us. "There you are!" I glared at him, hands on my hips. "I hope you explained to your brother that I didn't kill Toby. I was there when you found him. You know perfectly well I had nothing—"

"I've got a golf cart here. I can take you and your friends to your cars." He looked pointedly at Maggie.

I had a complete reversal of opinion. What a sweet and thoughtful man. "Oh, thank you. We're out in Ostrich Lot. Or was it Raccoon?" I glanced at Kathy.

"Raccoon," Kathy confirmed. She and I had ridden together, parking in the lot with the quaint designations, undoubtedly so-named to ensure easy recall after consuming too many alcoholic beverages at the Fair. The plan was for us to return to Kathy's house where I would get my car then drop Maggie at her house in Bloomington on my way home to Chaska, which was about forty-five miles south of the Twin Cities metro.

Sloan led the way down the hallway to the race oval. An ambulance was on the track, lights flashing. "Is he still there?" I asked, faltering.

"Toby?" Maggie asked in a hushed voice. "Really?"

Sloan stepped in front of me, blocking my view. "They're just getting ready to remove him. You can claim the body in a day or so, after the autopsy is done."

I looked up at him. He was just four or five inches taller than me. This close I could see the stubble on his face, the creases around his mouth, and the fan-like creases around his eyes. His pupils were edged with darker blue, making them appear more intense. "Claim him?" I whispered. I closed my eyes. I think I swayed, because he put a hand on my arm, steadying me. "No, I can't claim Toby."

A golf cart-like vehicle was on the track. Maggie and Kathy got into the back while I took the passenger seat next to Marcus Sloan. As we drove away I glanced back, seeing a black body bag on a gurney.

Toby.

We didn't talk as Sloan drove us through the crowded streets of the fairground. Even at ten o'clock at night, the people were as thick as discarded French fries and equally unappealing. The fair had a completely different personality after dark. Now it was more of a honky-tonk than the family-friendly zany carnival of the daytime. I stared unseeing at revelers as we sped past, barely noting the garishly lit Log Roll, Tilt-O-Whirl, Land 'O Corn, or the Northwest Tool Barn.

Toby was dead. It was hard to believe. I hadn't even thought about him for years. I filed for the divorce after the requisite two years of non-co-habitation. I received the papers, which appeared legitimate, and I put the whole experience behind me. It wasn't until a Florida detective called me three months ago I discovered there might be problems. And I didn't get confirmation of those problems until a few weeks ago. I was, indeed, still married. That's when I hired my own detective to find Toby so I could rid myself of him once and for all.

"Over there," Kathy said suddenly.

I awoke from my trance, realizing we had arrived in the parking area. Sloan piloted us down the grassy rows of the meadow-turned-lot, the temporary lights making the place as garish as the midway. We stopped by Kathy's minivan. "Thank you." I turned to Marcus Sloan as the girls got out behind me. "You'll testify for me, won't you? I mean, you'll tell them—" I put my hand on his arm, leaning near him.

He put his hand over mine. A sudden jolt of energy shot through me, as though someone had touched off a spark near me. "Don't worry," he said. "I know cops. They're not stupid."

I was relieved. He held my gaze. Sympathy, understanding, and confidence seemed to radiate in his eyes. "Thank you." I meant it sincerely.

He pressed my hand then released it. I exited the cart, peering back at him as I entered the minivan behind Kathy. He waved then turned the cart and puttered away. I leaned back.

"Okay, somebody tell me what the hell just happened," Kathy said.

It took almost the entire thirty-minute drive to her house to summarize what I saw. When we pulled into her driveway next to my Benz, she turned to me. "This is bad shit. You can't tell them that you have ESP or whatever the hell it is. Nobody will believe you."

I nodded, exhausted. "I know. And nobody believes Toby and I have been separated for so long. It sounds suspicious even to me."

Maggie paused as she exited. "If they find out you tried to contact him..."

I ran my hand through my hair. "I know, I know." I yawned. "I'm too tired to think coherently right now. Maybe by tomorrow I can make sense of it."

Maggie and I got into the Benz, waving good-bye to Kathy, who still looked worried and who obviously wanted to talk. But I knew nothing productive would come out of further discussion tonight. Maggie was quiet as we drove until we were a few blocks from her house. "I know this is trivial in the face of what happened, but I'm still worried about that letter."

I'd forgotten all about it. "Don't worry," I said immediately. "As I said, I'll call Robbie. I need to inform him about Toby anyway. I'll get his advice."

Maggie stared out her window, lines of strain evident on her face. "I can't shake the feeling that Pat's behind this, Jane."

"He can't be. I didn't become Phire Foxe until after you two split up. There's no reason for him to associate us with that mailbox. And his father wouldn't—" I shut up. Actually, anything was possible with Pat The Bastard's horrid father.

"I don't know." Her voice was quiet. "It's just that...he gets out soon. I'm scared."

I mentally vowed to renew my matchmaking campaign. This was the first visit of Robbie's when he would have an opportunity to re-meet Maggie, whom he knew in our youth. Maggie deserved to have someone good in her life and I planned to nominate my brother Robbie for the position. "I know, I know. Let me see what I can do."

"You've already done so much."

I waved that away. "I have an idea on how I can get help for this whole Toby mess as well as that letter. You just let me handle it."

She laughed but I heard the tears behind the chuckle. I couldn't blame her. Pat Scarlotti was a psychotic monster. No restraining order or law would keep her safe from him.

But maybe Marcus Sloan could...

I left Maggie at her front door, relieved to see Ian come out to greet his mother when she exited the car. I waved to my godson then turned the Benz southward. My house was at the end of a country lane, which was at the end of two-lane county blacktop, which branched off the main highway. My little one-story abode had a miniscule front yard with the house nestled in a thick stand of woods. My back yard consisted of a small green verge lined with flowers then woods sloping down to the Minnesota River, one hundred yards below. My nearest neighbor was a quarter-mile down the road and the closest shopping was ten miles away. I loved the solitude, the quiet, and the isolation.

Tonight, though, it was eerie. I retrieved my mail from my clever elephant-shaped box at the end of my drive then parked the Benz in the garage before entering the house. William and Ezra, my two cats, glanced up from their cozy spot on the sofa in the sunroom, yawned, then returned to sleep. I had fed them earlier so I was of no immediate interest. I tossed the mail on the kitchen counter then went to the windows to view the river as it drifted past in the moonlight.

Toby was dead. Handsome, laughing Toby was dead. Over the years I considered he might have passed on, but I always had the unshakeable feeling that he would re-enter my life. I didn't guess he would re-enter it as a corpse. His death solved a great many problems for me. I suppose I should be grateful to whoever did him in, but to be honest, I was a bit stunned by the circumstances. I'd gone from being a divorcee to a widow. It was a role I hadn't anticipated ever playing in my life.

I gave up trying to analyze it, instead turning to the Home Depot bag. I dumped out the contents, spying the business cards and the odd letter. I examined Marcus Sloan's card. It had three phone numbers: one labeled 'messages', one with an extension noted, and one labeled 'Fax'. I examined the envelope Maggie had received then the business card again. I picked up my portable phone to leave Marcus Sloan a message when I glanced at the mail spilled on my kitchen counter.

An envelope without a stamp was on top, my name written on it in big red letters. I opened it, pulling out a piece of lined paper.

Janie: Surprise, surprise. Here I am, back in your life. I was sure surprised to hear from you after all this time. I thought the divorce was legal, too. What's the hurry, though? It's just a formality, right? So I started to wonder and I did some investigating of my own. What a shock to find out how well you're doing, and to find out about your little sideline. My, my, those books of yours are hot. It sounds like you've learned one hell of a lot since I knew you.

I won't waste your time. I know how busy you must be, getting ready for school, writing your steamy books, preparing for a new department chairman to come into your life. What I want is really simple. But it's always been simple. What have I always wanted?

Money. I'm going to contact you at the fair tonight so we can talk. I'm not greedy, Phire. I just want a cut of the profits, some of that inheritance your mother left you, and maybe a bit of a lump sum, to finance a trip overseas. It's negotiable. To a point.

See you soon, honey. I'm looking forward to it.

Toby

I dropped the paper on the floor. The one thought that kept running through my mind like a litany was, 'if the police see this, my goose is cooked.'

Chapter 3

I forced myself to reason logically. I didn't retrieve the mail every day. When had I last gathered it? How long did this sit, unnoticed, in the mailbox? At least a day, maybe two, I decided. Today was Thursday. I usually picked up my mail from my elephant mailbox at the end of the drive on Tuesday, Thursday, and Saturday.

How did Toby know I was going to the fair tonight? I'd planned to see ZZ Top, which in my humble opinion was the only musical act worth seeing during the fair's ten-day run. I was also planning to attend the *Prairie Home Companion* radio show on the last night, when Robbie would be in town. August was very quiet at TUSP. I barely saw my peers most of the month so they wouldn't know my intentions. Kathy and Maggie knew of my plans, but wouldn't advertise them. I paced the room, finally going to the cupboard to pour myself a healthy dose of Maker's Mark bourbon to facilitate my thought processes.

I stalked to the windows, tossing back a goodly portion of the MM and feeling the slow burn as it went down. I glanced at the clock. It was almost one in the morning. Robbie would be asleep in New York City. I longed to talk to him, but I needed a chance to mull my situation over more fully.

I gave the cats their nightly treats, locked up, put the letters into my underwear drawer then slipped between the sheets with two calico cats taking up most of the bed to keep me company. I fell asleep with dreams of Toby laughing at me as Marcus Sloan looked on.

I awoke at 5:30, my usual time, and went out for a brisk run. As I walked back in the door, the phone was ringing. I looked at the caller ID and rolled my eyes. I wasn't up to my little sister, Abby, at 6:30 in the morning.

"Jane, pick up, it's your sister, Abby." Her voice boomed out on my answering machine. "Come on, Jane, pick up. I know you're awake, nobody in our family sleeps past 6:00 a.m."

I picked up the phone. "You're my *only* sister, Abby." I tucked the phone between my chin and shoulder as I addressed the culinary needs of the two resident felines.

"Listen, it's about Dad."

"I'm fine, Abby, how are you? How are the kids?"

There was a suspicious silence. "I'll tell you about the kids later. First, about Dad."

Once Abby got the wind in her sails, it was hard to change her course. "What about Dad?"

"Did you know he's going to Branson with that woman?"

My widowed father, Walt, retired ten years ago to a senior community in Arkansas after almost forty years of teaching Physics at MIT. He had an extensive group of friends, some of whom were female. "Loretta? Yes, I knew. Several of them are going."

"Did you know they're sharing a room? Dad and that woman?"

I had a sudden vision of Abby, coffee mug in hand, glaring at the phone with her red and gold curls bobbing as she shook her head angrily. "No, I didn't know that. Good for him."

Abby made a rude noise. "Aren't you worried?"

"About what?"

"Him. You know, falling in love at his age."

I dished out dry cat kibble. It rattled merrily in the fish-shaped ceramic cat bowls I purchased at a pottery show. The cats watched my movements with an intentness that would have done a mesmerist proud. "No, I'm not concerned." There was a long pause. "Abby, what's really wrong? You didn't call to talk to me about Dad's love life."

There was a pause. "Something's come up." There was another long pause. "It's Tommi."

Tommi was Abby's oldest daughter. "I thought Laura was the one having problems," I commented. Laura, at twenty-one, was the baby of the family. She'd just married Carl, almost ten years her senior. Carl hadn't quite "found" himself yet. He was charming and I liked him, but I didn't understand someone who didn't work for a living. Then I remembered Toby. Maybe I had more experience in this area than I was giving myself credit for.

"No, it's not Carl," Abby said with some asperity. "It's Tommi."

"And what's up with Tommi?" I asked politely.

"She's moved in with this guy," Abby said all in a rush. "But I'm not supposed to know about it. And I haven't told Robbie, either, so don't talk to him or he'll get jealous I told you everything and I didn't tell him."

I doubted it. I dished up the cat food, wondering not for the first time why I had such an eccentric family. "Give me the whole story, Abby."

Apparently Tommi and her sister Laura had dined at a local establishment and the restaurant manager gave Tommi the eye. When they finished eating, Tommi went to the car while Laura said she had to use the restroom. But instead of going to the Ladies' Room, "Laura gave him Tommi's phone number and she got his, that is, this Joe guy's, email address. Well, to make a long story short, two weeks later Tommi moved in with him. And Tommi told Carl, who told Laura, who told me, that they, that is, she and Joe, have been arguing a lot and—"

"Then they'll break up and life gets back to normal." There was an ominous silence on the other end of the phone. "Abby?"

"Tommi sort of signed a lease with him."

"What does Richard say?" Richard was Abby's ex-husband, now living in Houston.

"Richard." Abby said it with disgust. "He says Tommi is a grown-up woman and it's out of our hands."

Well, he's right, I thought. "She is twenty-four," I pointed out.

"But she's very naïve in a lot of ways," Abby said hurriedly. There was a long pause and I braced myself for what was coming. "Jane?"

"Yes, Abby?"

"Do you think I should hire somebody to, you know, investigate this guy?"

I counted slowly to five, restraining myself from saying what I thought: It should have been done before Tommi signed the lease. "Yes, Abby." I thought about the letter Maggie received. "I know a person who does security work. Perhaps I can call him and ask him to do it."

"Would you?" The relief was obvious in Abby's voice. "I wouldn't know what to do."

"I can handle it. Give me what information you've got."

Abby rattled off a name, address, and general description of the young man in question. I said,

"You know she's financially liable for what she bought, regardless of why she did it?"

"Oh, I know," Abby said. "I don't know why she's doing this. She's usually so solid. Of course, Laura said—" Abby stopped abruptly.

"What did Laura say?"

"Oh, she said now that Tommi is getting sex on a regular basis she'd be willing to sign away her life. Honestly." Abby gave a shaky laugh.

Well, that was as good a reason as any. I wisely didn't say this out loud. "Okay, Abby, I'll check on it and get back to you."

"Thanks, Jane. I knew you'd know what to do. Don't tell Walt, he'll have heart failure."

I privately thought our father was made of sterner stuff, but I didn't disabuse Abby of her notions. It wasn't until I hung up I realized I hadn't told Abby about Toby. If I did tell her, she'd call Robbie. I wanted to talk to Robbie first. Satisfied with that convoluted logic, I went to shower.

As I toweled my hair I retrieved the business cards and letters out of my underwear drawer to examine them. It was Saturday so Sloan wouldn't be in his office, but perhaps he'd check his messages. Before I could consider my options, I dialed the message number.

"Hi, this is Jane Renard, we met yesterday at the fair. I have a bit of a security issue and I was hoping you could help me with it. I'd appreciate it if you'd call me at your earliest convenience so we can chat." I added my phone number then hung up. I was pleased with my message. I sounded suitably professional and unworried, almost casual. I wasn't sure how I'd introduce the letter Maggie received. That would take some thought if I wanted Marcus Sloan to investigate an infatuated literary fan writing letters to an erotica author.

And what about Toby's letter? I wouldn't dare

30

tell Sloan about that. His brother was investigating Toby's death. Surely my security guard would feel compelled to tell Sam Sloan about the letter.

My security guard? I shook my head. Where had that thought come from? I just met the man and here I was—

My phone rang. I picked up the extension in the bedroom. "Renard residence."

"This is Marcus Sloan. You just called?"

I looked at my bedside clock in surprise. It was only 7:00 a.m. "You're up early."

"So are you. How can I help you?"

"How did you know I called?"

"My message system automatically forwards voice mail to my cell phone. You said you had a security matter to discuss?"

I was impressed with his promptness. "Yes, I was wondering if I could rent you." Mortified, I stared at William, my fat calico cat, who was chasing a rainbow from my window-dangle, shining on the bedroom floor. "I mean, hire you to—"

I think he was chuckling. I wasn't sure. I heard a low sound then he said, "Our office is usually closed on Saturday but I could meet you there if this is urgent."

Office. I hadn't even thought about that. This might involve paperwork, forms to fill out, and an official record. "Um, well, I was hoping to chat with you...well, privately. Perhaps I don't even need a security consultant. Perhaps it's not serious. It concerns my niece. I'm worried about her, but perhaps I'm just being overly protective. And there's another matter, about a friend of mine. Her ex-husband is getting out of prison soon. I'd like to have his movements tracked. And of course there's this whole problem with Toby. I wonder if I need to discuss something with you before I go see your brother." There was a long silence. "Your brother on the police force," I added, in case he had multiple brothers.

"It sounds like you might need some security advice." I couldn't be sure, but I believe he was using dry humor on me. "I can meet you at the office in—"

"Oh, no, perhaps you could come here? Or we could meet somewhere?"

"I live in Hopkins. If you'd like to come here before you go to see Sam, that would work fine."

"I'm not certain I'll go to see your brother," I hastened to say, hoping he didn't think I was planning on confessing to a crime and turning myself in.

"If you're considering seeing him, you probably should see him. I live in south Hopkins." He dictated directions and a street address, which I hurriedly jotted down on the inside cover of my bedside reading material (*Bondage or Bandage—Pleasure or Pain?*). "I'll look forward to your visit." He hung up.

I had a busy day ahead. I would visit with Marcus Sloan then go to campus to begin my preparations for fall semester, which started the day after Labor Day. I doubted I would see Sam Sloan, no matter what Marcus Sloan said. But I'd reserve that as an option.

I had to dress correctly for this interview. My future, Tommi's future, and Maggie's future might all hinge on my appearance. I considered and eliminated shorts, pedal-pushers, slacks, and a skirt, settling on a denim skort that didn't make my thighs or rear look too disgustingly huge. I topped it with a lime green tank top covered by a pastel blouse. I tugged on my pastel Earth sandals, grabbed my Coach briefcase (a splurge when I sold my second book) and was out the door in fifteen minutes.

Fifteen minutes later I was pulling into Marcus Sloan's driveway. He lived in a quiet neighborhood, not far from Maggie's house in an older Twin Cities suburbs. The houses were all split-level ranch style on wide tree-lined streets with big back yards, also lined with trees. His house was gray with bright red trim. As I got out of the Benz I heard ZZ Top's "Sharp-Dressed Man" echoing behind the house. It wasn't annoyingly loud but was clearly recognizable. Curious, I followed the sound, almost fainting on the spot when I rounded a corner to find Marcus Sloan standing on a low deck, bare-chested and wearing skimpy shorts as he lifted weights.

My knees turned to unset jell-o. Sweat glistened on his chest and shoulders as he hefted what looked like massive dumbbells. His golden-brown chest was covered with a mat of gray and white hair, his belly was flat, and his shorts hung precariously on his hips. As he turned, I saw a marvelous bulge in those shorts that told me a great deal about his anatomy. I watched, fascinated, as his biceps danced while he curled up the big weight almost to his chin then slowly let it down. He looked as hard as a rock, sculpted, fit, and masculine.

As he lowered the weight to the deck floor, he turned. Our eyes met and held. It felt as though he was tugging me forward. I walked jerkily along the narrow path to the stairs leading up to the deck, smiling hesitantly. "I heard your stereo." I gestured to the boom box sitting on a chair nearby.

"I didn't think you'd get here so soon," he said, blushing.

"I'm sorry. I thought you meant I should come to see you immediately." His blush charmed me. Also charming was the way he fumbled on a sleeveless T-shirt to hide his nakedness. It was a pity to hide it, but it was also cute. "I admit, I tend to ignore speed limits so I'm not surprised I arrived faster than you anticipated. And I'm anxious to speak with you."

He picked up a towel, running it over his face. I heard it rasp on his cheeks and I shivered. What was it with unshaven men? I always had the heroes in my books doing exciting things with five o'clock shadows to certain portions of my heroine's anatomy. I walked slowly up the stairs. A breeze stirred my blouse and I knew my nipples were reacting in my tank top. His eyes flickered over my body then he looked at me. I saw appreciation in his gaze.

"Anxious?" he asked, draping the towel around his neck.

I nodded, suddenly remembering my purpose. "It's about my niece and her boyfriend. And Maggie and her ex. And..."

"And your late husband." He opened a sliding door. "Let's go inside and have a cup of coffee. You can tell me all about it."

I followed him into a small dining room opening into a living room ahead and a kitchen on one side. I took a seat while he got me a mug of coffee. He handed me the drink as he seated himself, then he looked expectantly at me. "So why are you so worried right now about this ex-husband of your friend? Did something happen to make you worried?"

I fidgeted with my coffee spoon. "Pat Scarlotti gets out of prison soon. I thought perhaps we should—" I made the mistake of meeting his gaze. I couldn't lie to this man. Something in his stare precluded it. "Oh, I suppose I should tell you the whole story. I'm so afraid Maggie's ex might be involved, although I don't know how. This is very confidential."

He nodded. I didn't think he understood the gravity of the situation.

"No, I mean, this is priest-in-the-confessional confidential. You're like a priest, right?"

He frowned. "Not really, but if you mean can I keep a secret, yes I can."

"This is really, really, cross your heart and hope

to die, secret." I sipped the scalding coffee, almost choking. "Very, very, ultra top secret."

He nodded slowly. "As long as you're not breaking the law, then I can keep a secret."

I took the plunge. "I have what you might call a secret life." He raised one eyebrow at me. "Oh, nothing like that. Well, okay, something like that. I write novels."

"What kind?"

"Not literary fiction." He just waited, watching me. "Not the type of fiction my department would approve of."

"And that is...?"

I sighed. "Romance novels. I write romance novels under a pen name."

"Oh, those Pink Books? That's a problem?"

I gave him an exasperated look. "Don't be fatuous. Romance novels aren't exactly considered an accepted literary genre in the English department at The University of Saint Paul."

"Fatuous? I'm being fatuous?"

"You know what I mean. What happened is this—I write romance fiction under a pseudonym." I saw his perplexed look. "A pen name. A letter came that was meant for me or, rather, my pseudonym, but it was addressed to Maggie and mailed to the mailbox I use for..." I stopped, searching for a reasonable use, "...correspondence that has to do with my novels. We want to know how this person got Maggie's name and my mail box number. I don't make this information widely known. My editors forward any fan letters to me."

"Can I see the letter? Was there something in it that bothered you?"

I felt my ears get hot. "Well, that is, I—"

He grinned. "What kind of books do you write, Dr. Renard?"

"They're...um...they're somewhat...explicit." I

hurried on. "Suffice it to say, we just need to find how this...fan discovered he or she could write to the author at this mail box number and why Maggie's name appeared on the envelope."

"What's your pen name?" He was suddenly briskly professional, pulling over a notepad and pencil preparatory to writing facts.

"Phire Foxe."

"F-i-r-"

"No, it's P-h-i-r-e F-o-x-e. It's a play on my name. Renard is French for fox and the other is a derivative of my middle name. P-h-y-r-e. It's Armenian for 'burning brightly.'"

His gaze shifted to my hair. "It's appropriate. I've never seen red hair quite that color."

"It's quite real, I assure you." I was very defensive about my hair color because people often assumed it was courtesy of a salon. My hair color was a red so dark it sometimes looked black. But in the light it looked red-blonde. It was unusual. "Everyone in my family has hair like this, curly and red. No, my middle name is derived from my genetic background. My maternal grandparents were Rom." I used the double-rr inflection. Then I grinned, remembering numerous family gatherings and the ensuing interactions. "My other grandparents were WASP."

"Rom?" He tried to duplicate my pronunciation but failed miserably.

"What you Gadja call gypsies."

"Gadja?"

I smiled apologetically. "Foreigner. Non-Rom."

"Ah. Okay, you write under the name Phire Foxe. Someone sent Maggie Carlson a letter, but addressed to you on the inside. And it came to a private mailbox only you know about?"

"Well, Maggie knows too, but yes, that's it."

"Mailbox address?"

I told him. He made more notes about Maggie's ex, the dates of Pat's arrest, and the accident that almost cost Maggie her life. "Okay, I'll get to work on this. Now what else did you want to see me about? You mentioned something you needed to see Sam about?"

This was going to be tricky. I hesitated, sipping the strong coffee. "Actually, my niece has me worried." I explained about Abby's phone call. Sloan took the sheet of paper I gave him covered with the Mysterious Joe information.

Then he looked at me again. I had the feeling he knew I was attempting to avoid revealing anything more. The man was too perceptive by half. "And your late husband? The thing you need to see Sam about?"

I hesitated. "I feel I need to try to explain about Toby."

He nodded. His white hair was standing up in little spikes from the sweat. He obviously hadn't shaved yet for the day because his cheeks were heavily stubbled. I had a hard time not staring at him as I talked.

"When Toby left me, I was so ashamed. I didn't want to tell anybody. My brother Robbie knew something was amiss, though. I was in Pittsburgh by then, teaching at Westmoreland. He'd taken a job in New York, but he came out to see me. I told him all about..."

I stopped myself in time. I almost revealed my Big Secret. How did Marcus Sloan do it? I barely knew him and I almost unveiled the biggest secret in my life. I backpedaled.

"After Toby was gone for two years, I could legally file for divorce in Pennsylvania, where I lived. I did so, receiving what appeared to be quite legal documents in return, which stated my divorce was final. I didn't...um... I handled it all myself. My

37

parents had warned me against marrying him in the first place and I wanted to show how independent I was by handling the mess I made of my life." I blew out a long sigh.

He smiled. I noticed for the first time he had a little scar running along the side of his face and onto his chin. It rippled when he smiled. "I know how that goes."

"Robbie tried to find Toby, but he'd vanished. It was Robbie who told the family what happened." I sipped my coffee. "I have a very large, extended family so everyone had to get involved. My uncle Phil, my cousin Petros, my uncle Vanya, my dad Walt—all the male relatives wanted to track down Toby and make him 'do the right thing'." I laughed shakily. "I wasn't sure I wanted Toby back, though. So I filed the papers."

I paused to order my thoughts and Sloan didn't pressure me. He just waited. It was very soothing. I struggled to make him understand without making it look as though I was hoping for a reassuring compliment. "I've always known I'm not the type of woman—" I stopped and started again. "I don't make men—" I stopped again. "I mean, I'm not terribly sexy. Toby was very sexy and sophisticated. When he paid attention to me, I was so flattered. And I was unsure about my future. I was starting a new job, but wasn't sure if it was the right career path for me. Toby lied to me. He told me he'd be deported unless I helped him. He told me he was here on a graduate student visa and..." I looked at Sloan, expecting to see pity at my stupidity.

Instead I saw compassion. It gave me the courage to continue. "Then, a few days after we got married I found he was sleeping around. Maggie—you met her? She saw him with another woman. I confronted Toby about it but he just laughed it off." I ran a hand through my hair, tugging at my curls in agitation. "It mattered a lot to me. I trusted him."

"I can understand how that must have made you feel," Sloan said quietly. "You trusted him and he threw it in your face."

I looked into his eyes but didn't see a hint of condescension or laughter at my naiveté. This was a man who understood trust and the converse of that—violated trust.

I believe it was at that moment that I decided to convince Marcus Sloan to introduce my virgin body to the joys of sex.

Chapter 4

I wasn't technically a virgin, of course. I tried sex once with Toby and once with a golf instructor when I taught in Pittsburgh. And there was an unfortunate experience in a nightclub in the 1990s that I preferred to forget.

But I've never had anything even remotely resembling the incendiary sex I wrote about. Before our marriage, Toby hadn't seemed interested, deflowering me with an almost perfunctory attitude. And within hours of getting married, he disappeared on what I later found out was a sex junket lasting nearly a week. When he returned, I refused to allow him near me because only God knew what kind of diseases he might have contracted. And after that, I was alone. Then I tried a romantic liaison again but it was disappointing. So I swore off men for a time, which turned into several years, which turned into...

Well, anyway. I'd never had an all-night romp with a real, live man. And Marcus Sloan definitely looked manly, lively, and viable. I wanted to have wild sex at least once or twice before I entered old age. He looked like the man to do it. I stored that thought for later consideration to focus on the issues at hand.

"Did you know he was in town?" Sloan asked.

"Well..." I looked around the room, wondering if there was an answer lurking behind the worn, comfortable-looking furniture.

"Dr. Renard? If you knew he was in town, you realize how that might look to the police. My brother's a smart man, but circumstantial evidence is hard to ignore."

My eyes snapped to his. I hadn't really thought it through to its obvious conclusion, but he was right. "I didn't know Toby was in town. But I knew he was alive. I hired a detective to find him."

"Why? Why contact him after all this time?"

"A detective from Florida contacted me. He said he represented a woman who was involved with Toby. He said my divorce wasn't legal." I stared down at the worn wood table, remembering the shock I felt when I received that news.

Once again, Sloan didn't press me. "I was stunned, of course. I haven't had many, well, relationships in my life so that wasn't an issue. But I thought he and I—" I cleared my throat, unclear what I was trying to express, stumbling to find words. "I thought it was over, but I began to realize perhaps I'd used the fiasco of my relationship with Toby as an excuse to avoid relationships altogether." I finally met Marcus Sloan's gaze and once again saw understanding and sympathy. The man was either a mind reader or amazing...or both.

"But I thought you wrote, um..." He flipped through his notes. "...explicit romance novels. Surely you've had several, well..." He paused. "I mean, it's been my experience people tend to stick with what they know."

"You see, that's why I have a pen name," I said, leveling my coffee spoon at him. "People assume because I write a certain kind of book, I'm a certain kind of person. People write murder mysteries all the time and they aren't killers."

"Yeah, but they've done research," he pointed out with a small smile.

"And so have I." I saw the look on his face and hastened to correct his misperception. "A certain kind of research that does not involve... One can read the literature. It's a very basic sort of fiction and quite easy to learn the tricks of the trade. And, anyway, I'm very imaginative." He nodded doubtfully. I plowed on. "I found out Toby was living in Florida so I contacted him and told him I wanted a divorce. A legal divorce this time."

"Did he reply?"

I felt my ears get hot again.

"Dr. Renard?"

"I didn't know he had, but he did." I fumbled in my briefcase, pulling out the letter from my mailbox. "I found that last night when I got home."

He held up a hand. "Please just remove the letter for me and open it on the table." He must have seen my bewildered look. "That way there's fewer fingerprints."

"Fingerprints? Who cares about fingerprints?" Then I remembered. Law enforcement personnel cared about fingerprints. "Oh." I took the letter out, opened it then put it on the table. He bent over to read it. I examined him as he did so. His hair was very thick and, although spiky, looked soft to the touch. He had impossibly long eyelashes, the sort a woman would kill for although perhaps in the light of current events that wasn't the best analogy. His body was solid, his shoulders thick in the T-shirt. All in all, he was very attractive in an older, virile, masculine sort of way.

"You found it last night?"

I explained how I don't always stop for my mail at the end of the lane. "You believe me, don't you?" I smiled weakly. "As my grandfather used to say: *Si khohaimo may pachivalo sar o chachimo.* 'Some lies are more believable than the truth'. This is the truth. I swear it."

Sloan nodded thoughtfully. "I believe you, but there's no postmark on this letter so it's hard to tell when it showed up." He made a note on the list at his elbow. "I'll check with your letter carrier to see if he or she noticed it when the mail was delivered."

The letter carrier... I hadn't even considered that. "Stan would notice it," I said confidently. "He's such a busybody. He knows all my business."

Sloan smiled quickly. "I'll check with Stan out in Chaska, then."

"Do I need to show this to your brother? And tell him I contacted Toby?"

He tapped the table with one slightly crooked finger. Perhaps it was broken at one time. "You need to tell Sam you contacted your husband. But this letter..." He looked at the wall clock. "Tell you what, let me make some calls and get showered. I want to verify things with the nosy Stan. Then we'll go to the station together."

"Oh, would you?" I hadn't realized until that moment how much I dreaded seeing the police. "Thank you so much. I have to tell you, Mr. Sloan, your brother was a bit intimidating. Granted, he isn't physically prepossessing, but he has an aura about him that's quite off-putting, even to the innocent."

He seemed to be puzzling over what I said. "He's scary," I clarified.

"Ah. Good. That helps him...as a cop. And you can call me Marcus. We'll be working together and it saves confusion when we're chatting with Sam."

"Marcus." I savored his name. It felt so good to have someone in the security business on my team, as it were. "Please. Call me Jane."

"Okay, Jane. You just relax for a few minutes while I get cleaned up." He stood up. I once again had a nice view of those skimpy, sweaty shorts and an equally nice view of his tight butt as he turned to put his coffee cup into the sink. He disappeared through a door on the opposite side of the kitchen while I remained behind at the table, basking in sunlight and the glow from such a warm-hearted, gentle man and an active imagination with hormones on overdrive.

Yep. He was the man for me. Fate, karma, an intersection of the stars, call it what you want. Marcus Sloan and I had a date with destiny.

I went into the kitchen, noticing the boomerang-design countertop, plain white appliances and the white enameled cabinets. It was all very simple and tidy. The living room was decorated in a similar fashion. It had restful pale green walls, maple floors, a green couch, two recliners which appeared well used, and several photographs in a bookcase housing a very large TV. I checked the photographs. Several were of Marcus and people who looked like family. I recognized Sam Sloan in one. One was of a man and woman in front of an immaculately restored older Mustang. She had red hair, too, although a lighter shade than mine. There was a 'Just Married' sign on the back of the car. The books in the case were mainly true crime with a sprinkling of fiction thrown in.

As I meandered toward the window looking out on the street, I heard Marcus speaking in the room next door. "I know it looks bad, Sam," he was saying.

I sidled closer to a closed door, which probably led to a bedroom. "She's got a blackmail letter from the husband, she contacted him and asked for a divorce and—"

I stiffened in outrage. How dare he tell all like that! I was getting ready to go inside and let him

44

know what I thought of such behavior when he said, "Would you let me finish? I talked to the postal carrier before he left for his deliveries today. He confirmed the letter was there on Wednesday when he dropped off the mail. So Considine put it in there sometime Wednesday night or Thursday. She got it Thursday night."

There was a long pause. I pressed anxiously against the door, straining to hear. "I'm her alibi, Sam. I saw Considine in the seats, talking to someone and it wasn't her." Another pause. "Yeah, I'm sure of it. No, I wasn't sure if it was a man or woman. I didn't pay attention until Jane came down and talked to me." Another pause. "Yes, you heard me, I said Jane. Don't get pissy about this. We'll be there in an hour or so."

Even from this distance I could hear a muted rumbling on the phone. Then Marcus said, "Sam, I know you're pissed off I retired, but don't take your job frustrations out on me. I'm going to help this woman and you can kiss my ass if you don't like it." The phone slammed down forcefully then footsteps headed my way.

Yikes. I scrambled away, tripping on the welcome mat at the front door. Then I heard a door open and immediately crash shut somewhere in the room behind the door where I'd been listening. Next I heard a shower start. Heavens. He was standing there, naked, talking on the phone. And I had almost walked in on him.

I had to sit down in a recliner to catch my breath. I positively *ached* to know what he looked like naked. I had a vivid imagination and I was a connoisseur of porn films, but I was dying to see the real thing in the flesh. I fanned myself for a few minutes then decided to put the time to good use. I dug my mobile phone from my briefcase and called my brother Robbie.

"Hey, sunshine," he said when he heard me.

"Robbie, Toby's dead." I didn't mean to utter it so impulsively but just hearing Robbie's deep, reassuring voice made me long to confide in him. He knew the whole story, of course, about the potentially not-legal divorce and had even assisted me in finding a detective in Florida to do some work for me.

"What?"

"Toby. He was murdered last night." In halting words, I told him what happened, interrupted by his many questions.

When I finished he said, "I'm flying out as soon as I can. Don't talk to any police until I get there." Then he paused. "Damn. My paralegal is out of town, on vacation. I was thinking Edward could take over on—Well, hell, the office will just have to manage. You can't talk to cops without your lawyer present."

"It's a bit late for that, Robbie. I talked to them yesterday and I have to see them today." I looked up as Marcus came into the room dressed again in the black jeans and white shirt with a 'Security' logo on it. He was probably going to work. I suddenly realized I was flopped back in his recliner, the footrest up, one sandal idly swinging off my foot and my skort somewhat high on my thighs. I must have looked like Goldilocks auditioning Papa Bear's favorite chair.

"What do you mean you have to see them today?"

I pulled the phone away. "It's my brother, Robbie. He's a lawyer."

"Who's there?" Robbie demanded. "Jane, who are you talking to?"

Marcus held out a hand. "May I?"

I gratefully relinquished the phone. "This is Marcus Sloan. I'm retired from the Hopkins Police

Department. I'm a security consultant with J A K Enterprises and we were on duty last night at the fair. I was with your sister when she discovered the body. I've talked to the detective in charge of the case and made a statement to that effect."

I could hear Robbie squawking on the phone. I winced. Marcus listened impassively as he walked into the kitchen. I heard the fridge opening and closing, then a liquid being poured. "I realize that, Mr. Renard, but your sister has hired me as her security advisor. I think I have the situation well in hand."

I struggled out of the overly comfortable chair, smoothing down my skort and stuffing my foot back into my sandal. Marcus came out, sipping orange juice. He held up the glass to me in question. I shook my head. "I realize that, but you can't get here until tomorrow at the earliest," he continued. "We do need to see Lt. Sloan today." Pause. "Yes, I said 'Sloan'. He's my brother." He listened some more then handed the phone to me.

"Jane, do you trust this guy?" Robbie demanded.

I could imagine Robbie's thunderous glare as he spoke on the phone from his tiny apartment in Manhattan with a view of the aftermath of the Twin Towers . I looked at Marcus, who was sipping orange juice and regarding me with calm scrutiny. "Yes, I do trust him," I said, returning Marcus' look with an unwavering gaze. I took a deep, calming breath. It was a long, long time since I'd extended trust to any man, but I just did it with no qualms whatsoever. I felt as if I'd cleared a large hurdle.

Marcus smiled very slowly. I swear his eyes became a deeper, darker blue. He nodded once then went back into the kitchen.

"I don't like this," Robbie said.

"I do."

There was a long pause. "Jane, what's going on?"

"Leave a message on my machine at home to tell me when I need to pick you up." I turned off the phone then joined Marcus in the kitchen. "Sorry about that. He's a protective older brother."

Marcus finished his juice then set the glass in the sink. "That's okay. I'm a protective older brother. I know how it feels. Ready to go face Sam?"

I took a deep breath. "Sure. Lead on."

We left through the garage, where Marcus pressed the opener to reveal an older model navy blue Honda Prelude. When he saw my gray Benz in the driveway, he said, "Nice wheels."

"Thanks. Should I just follow you?"

He nodded. "I have to report in at the fair after we see Sam. I'm working today." He followed me out to the Benz, holding the door for me as I got in. He glanced in at the charcoal gray leather interior. "Very nice. I'm surprised you can afford it on a teacher's salary."

"I'm frugal." I didn't bother to elaborate on the fact I bought it used, it was four years old, and I spent a bit of the money I inherited from Mom's estate plus the advance from two books, plus savings. As I started the car, Janis Joplin blared out of the speakers in full voice. I turned down the volume.

"I would have pegged you for Bach," he said. "You like rock and roll?"

"I have eclectic taste."

"You're eclectic, frugal, imaginative, and explicit. You're an interesting person, Dr. Jane Renard." He glanced down at the passenger seat. I followed his gaze. *Bondage or Bandage* was in plain sight where I tossed it to facilitate my quest for his house. "Research?"

I looked into his intense blue gaze. "Indeed."

Yep, I thought as I put the car into gear. *He's the man*. On the way to St. Paul I swapped Janis for The

Rolling Stones, ending at the police station with "Let's Spend The Night Together." I had hopes it would be prophetic.

Having an ex-cop as an escort got us through the gauntlet quickly. Marcus led the way down an antiseptic-looking hallway to a large room where several people were working at squat gray desks. A few looked up at our entrance and nodded to Marcus, who nodded in return. I saw his brother seated at an untidy desk on the other side of the room. As we approached, Sam Sloan looked up and frowned. "I told you that you didn't have to come," he said to Marcus in a low, angry voice.

"He's my security guard," I said, taking the chair near Lt. Sloan's desk then setting my briefcase on the floor.

The two brothers exchanged what I thought was an aggrieved look. "So how much are you charging?" Lt. Sloan asked. His voice seemed to crawl with innuendo.

I was taken aback. I hadn't even asked about a price. I opened my mouth to reply when Marcus said smoothly, "The usual rates. And I told you I'd be here, Sam. So let's get on with it." He pulled a chair over and sat next to me. "Jane has something you should see." He looked at me. "Show him the letter you found in your mailbox at home." He met my eyes steadily. I saw the message in them: *The blackmail letter, not the fan letter.*

"Oh, yes, of course." I dragged my briefcase onto my lap and began to rifle through it. The bag bulged with class syllabi, several scholarly articles on William Dean Howells and Henry James, Cliff Notes for Theodore Dreiser (whom I secretly detested), my netbook computer containing my latest manuscript, a copy of Ford Maddox Ford's *The Good Soldier,* a copy of Ambrose Bierce's *The Devil's Dictionary*, and a spiral notebook where I stored random ideas.

Luckily I left *Bondage* on the car seat in the parking ramp, so at least I didn't have to pull it out for the Lieutenant's inspection.

I finally found the letter tucked into a side pocket along with an advertisement for authoring software, ticket stubs to an Elton John concert, and a crumpled travel pack of tissues. I handed the letter to Lt. Sloan, who appeared to be peeved at the contents of my briefcase, which now adorned the edge of his desk. I hastily stuffed items back into the bag as he took the letter. He had put on a pair of those odd white gloves favored by doctors and, apparently, crime fighters. I watched anxiously as he pulled out the letter and read it.

I became aware of a silence around us. When I peeked over my shoulder, I surprised several people staring avidly at us. I smiled politely. They guiltily looked back at their computer monitors or paperwork. I wondered what had them so curious.

Lt. Sloan eventually looked up, not to me, but to his brother. "And you believe this?"

I sat up straighter in the chair, which was, of course, too tall for me so my feet barely touched the floor. "I believe you should be addressing your comments to me, Lieutenant," I said. "Although I have hired Mr. Sloan to act as my consultant, I am perfectly capable of—"

"Yes, I do," Marcus interrupted.

I turned to chastise him but he put a hand on my wrist, squeezing it very gently before releasing it. It was a surprisingly calming gesture. I subsided, deciding to let him handle the situation, at least for the moment.

"As I told you, I called—" and here Marcus pulled out his notepad from a back pocket and consulted it, "—Stan Wrakowski, who works at the Chaska Post Office. I talked to him at 7:34 this morning. He said the letter was in the box on

Thursday when he put the mail in. It wasn't there on Wednesday evening when he put the mail in. I also verified—"

"All right, all right." His brother sat back, tapping a pencil on the calendar blotter covered with doodles, phone numbers, and unappealing food stains. He directed his gaze to me. He looked very tired. I wondered if fatigue was a chronic problem with police people or if it was unique to him. "So you wrote to your husband and asked for a divorce? Another divorce? When was that?"

"Ah, I have that here." I tugged out my netbook, which unfortunately caused *The Devil's Dictionary* to begin a slide out of my bag. I rescued the book then opened the netbook, scrolling through various folders. "Here it is. I wrote the letter on July 24th." I checked the calendar on the netbook, which I kept synchronized with my Palm. "And I contacted Mr. Denton, the detective, prior to that, in order to talk with him about—"

"Never volunteer information, Jane," Marcus said quietly.

I looked up, startled. He was watching his brother, who was eyeing my little computer with obvious interest. I snapped it shut. "July 24th," I said, tucking the computer back in my briefcase.

"We may need a copy of that letter."

"And you may not get it," I said firmly. "It all depends on what my lawyer advises me to do. I will, of course, act on his counsel."

"Lawyer?"

"Her brother," Marcus said wryly. He looked at some benches on one side of the room. "Problems?"

I followed his gaze. A woman was seated there. She appeared young, perhaps in her thirties, with rather obviously blonde hair and a svelte, long-legged, country club appearance. Even her skirt, blouse, and lightweight sweater, all of which coordinated beautifully, bore out this high-society impression.

"Yeah, you might say that," Sam Sloan said. "That's the other wife."

"I beg your pardon?" This comment seemed to be directed at me.

"It's Mrs. Considine. Your husband's wife."

"Oh, dear. He remarried? That explains it. She must be the woman the detective who contacted me discussed." I shot the woman covert looks, trying not to be conspicuous. "Yikes. How long were they married? Or, rather, how long did she think they were married, depending on the status of my divorce?"

"Two years."

"Well, she has seniority," I said. "I was only married for four months. Rather, I was with Toby for four months. We were technically married for two years. Or possibly twenty-two years." I shook my head at the confusion of it all. "She has a vested interest in him, not I."

Sam Sloan looked at me thoughtfully for a long moment, but I just stared back, not at all unnerved by his scrutiny. He finally nodded. "I'll keep this note," he said, putting the letter on his desk into a plastic bag. "And now that my brother is acting as your security guard, I'm sure I'll know where to find you."

I inspected his words for a double meaning, but wasn't sure if I found one. I chose to be magnanimous. "Thank you." I stood up and slung my briefcase strap over my shoulder, nearly unbalancing myself as the weight settled. I really had to clean it out before fall semester started. "I appreciate you making time for me in what I'm sure is a very hectic schedule." I looked at the woman who was joined by a young man with dark blond hair and a tan as dark as the woman's. He was very physically fit, but not in a hard way like Marcus, more like a runner with a lithe, rangy appearance.

"That's the son," Sam Sloan said.

I stared openly. "Toby's son?" He didn't look at all like Toby. And he appeared to be in his thirties, which would make him too old to be the woman's child. This man was handsome in a Polo-ad sort of way, with wavy gold hair, craggy good looks, and a physique I associate with those who spend a great deal of time sailing and working out with personal trainers.

"It's more complicated than that. The guy is the woman's stepson. She married Money."

I could hear the capital 'M' as he spoke it. Marcus started to walk toward the door. I eyed the woman and man as we passed them.

Lt. Sloan didn't speak until we were several feet beyond the two people. "She was the second wife to Malcolm Fabersham, the shipping guy. When Fabersham died, she inherited."

"Well, that explains that," I said as Marcus and I walked toward the far door. "She's exactly the sort of woman Toby would find interesting."

"And how would you know?" a woman's voice asked.

Oh dear. I spoke too loud. The Other Woman leapt to her feet and glared at me. If looks could kill, I would have been eviscerated on the spot. I plastered on a placating smile and prepared to be pleasant, even if it killed me, as I turned to address my latter-day counterpart.

Chapter 5

"I'm sorry." I stopped so suddenly my bag swung, nearly overbalancing me. I decided to try to brazen it out. I extended my hand. "Jane Renard."

The woman now faced us. Her makeup was impeccable. She had smooth, soft-looking skin, artfully highlighted high cheekbones, beautifully crafted eyes, and lipstick I secretly envied. It appeared smooth, glossy, and natural, if a pink that color could be considered natural. I personally doubted it was a color found in nature, but it was pretty, nonetheless.

The woman put out a hand. It was smooth, well manicured, and slender. She shook my hand with a perfunctory, quick grasp. "Lisa..." She paused then raised her chin defiantly. "Lisa Considine. I want you to know, Miss Renard, I intend to fight you every step of the way for the right to call myself Mrs. Considine."

I held up my hands. "No fight. It's been years since I've seen Toby. You're welcome to him." Then I realized he was lying in a body bag somewhere and winced. "I mean, I hope you and Toby had a very happy life together."

Marcus put a hand on my arm, smiling politely at the lovely Lisa. "We need to go, Jane."

Sam Sloan was watching this little interchange with alert, interested blue eyes. I nodded briskly. "Yes, we do. I'm sorry for your loss, Mrs.—um—Mrs.—Lisa." I somehow just *couldn't* say 'Mrs. Considine.' It didn't feel right. "I know you and Toby were together for a long time, well, a relatively long time, comparatively speaking that is, and I hope—"

"Jane."

Marcus was speaking very softly into my ear. I shivered and looked up at him. His face was close to mine.

"We need to go," he murmured.

I nodded. "Of course." I turned back to the woman. For the first time I noticed the young man, who watched us from the bench near his stepmother. Something in his gaze was unsettling but I wasn't sure what it was. He had dark brown eyes, which contrasted with his boyish, blond good looks. But his eyes were assessing and very alert as he evaluated Marcus and me. "Well, I wish I could say it was a pleasure to meet you, but of course, under the circumstances—" Marcus was gently tugging on my arm. "I hope that things get resolved to your—" Marcus tugged harder. I was forced to keep step with him as he moved toward the exit. "I hope your stay is—"

We were out the door, standing in a small foyer near some vending machines. I turned to Marcus just out of hearing, not wanting to be rude in front of others. "You didn't need to rush me like that," I said, settling my briefcase strap more firmly on my shoulder. "I was simply trying to be polite to the poor woman and—"

"Why don't you wait here." It wasn't a question but a command. I saw his brother standing nearby, looking impatient. The man obviously had time management issues because he seemed perpetually harassed. I started to protest but Marcus didn't give me the opportunity. He joined his brother as they moved off to one side.

I wandered toward the vending machines to inspect the offerings. I usually bought organic vegetarian foods with the occasional foray into free-range carnivorous fare, so this was new territory for me, as had been the State Fair and its culinary oddities. There were a fascinating variety of options available, including some that sounded quite unpalatable, such as Pork Rinds. Why would someone want to eat something made of 'rinds' from a pig?

I switched my attention to the canned beverages. I was getting ready to purchase a 'Gatorade', which I believed was nutritionally useful, when I heard Marcus and his brother, talking in low voices around the corner from the beverage dispenser.

"I thought that bullet went in your shoulder, not your brain," Sam Sloan said angrily. "This woman isn't Mary Madison and—"

I peeked around the machine. Sam and Marcus were in a little cul-de-sac formed by some empty boxes, plastic cartons, and a wall. I sidled closer, careful to keep myself from being seen. Lurking was apparently becoming a deplorable habit with me. I stifled my misgivings and eavesdropped.

"This has nothing to do with Mary," Marcus said. From the glimpse I saw, I knew he was standing very tensely, his shoulders hunched. "I know you've got problems that I retired early, but it doesn't mean I got stupid. I got out when the time was right for me. I don't need to die on the job, like Dad did."

"It isn't about Dad and you know it, Marc." Sam Sloan's voice seemed to vibrate with suppressed energy. "You're letting yourself get involved with a client. That's what's stupid. You have a habit of letting women get you into situations that aren't the best for you."

Involved? Marcus was involved with me? I edged closer.

"I'm helping this woman, that's all. It's got nothing to do with my past."

Their voices were getting closer. I slid my bag to the floor to fumble for my coin purse, a clever little object made from a baby's sock and a snap closure. Mine happened to be red, gaily decorated with small grinning cats. I had just opened it and was peering inside it for the correct change when the brothers came around the corner, almost running me over. Marcus glared at me, his blue eyes snapping with anger. "We're leaving."

I looked from him to his brother. "I don't mean to be the cause of enmity between you," I said. "If it's a difficulty because you're assisting me, I can certainly—"

Marcus plucked the coin purse from my fingers, picked up my briefcase and stuffed the little coin purse into a side pocket. He put a hand on my bicep then firmly steered me out.

"Marcus, please, why don't we talk to your brother?" I looked back at Sam Sloan, who was walking back into the room-of-desks. Even viewing his back, I could tell he was terribly angry. "I'm sure we can come to some satisfactory compromise that would—"

"There is no compromise with Sam," Marcus said through clenched teeth. We got to the elevators where he punched the 'down' button.

"I'm so sorry," I said, reaching to take my briefcase from him. He didn't seem to notice, but just hefted it in one hand, jiggling it. "I didn't mean to cause problems with your family. That's okay, I can carry that."

He looked surprised. "It's heavy."

"I'm accustomed to it." I held out my hand.

He suddenly smiled. It was a real smile, too. His bad mood seemed to evaporate as suddenly as it had come. "Ah, come on, let me carry your books, teacher."

Oh, my. His warm smile and mischievous eyes seemed to envelop me. I followed him into the elevator where the people around us pressed us into tight quarters. "You know, you should make sure you and your brother resolve your differences." I shifted my position slightly, realizing he and I were almost thigh-to-thigh. It was rather exciting. "As my grandfather used to say, *O zalzaro khal peski piri*." I hurried to explain when I saw his confused look. "'Acid corrodes its own container.' You shouldn't let things come between you and your family. And I would feel terrible if I was the cause."

"Listen," he said, leaning down to talk quietly. "Sam has an idea of what I should be doing with my life but our ideas don't exactly mesh. And he's making assumptions about things he doesn't know about. It has nothing to do with you, Jane. Believe me." He touched my arm gently in reassurance.

The elevator chimed as the doors opened. We joined the others streaming toward the parking ramp. Marcus paused with me by my Benz. "I appreciate all the help you're giving me," I said as he stowed my briefcase on the seat next to *Bondage*. "And I do expect to receive a bill." I smiled at him. "I'm just so concerned about Maggie. Her husband is a real snake. We had so much trouble with him."

"In what way?"

I slid into the car, tugging my skort down so it covered me decently. "Pat's family is rich. They pulled a lot of strings to keep him out of jail. It wasn't until he almost killed Maggie the legal system finally acted." I jammed my key into the ignition. "I have to admit, I had a very poor opinion of the American way of justice until they finally threw that son of a bitch in jail."

He laughed out loud. "Jane, I didn't think you had a 'son of a bitch' in you."

I blushed. "I try to restrain my profanity, but Pat Scarlotti just brings out the worst in me. I apologize."

He bent over to look at me. "No apology needed. I'll be in touch. And try not to worry. I'll do everything I can to make sure the Minneapolis system of justice works better than the one in Pittsburgh."

I felt an immediate relief at hearing his words. He sounded like he truly meant it. I remembered how Maggie had struggled with red tape, bureaucracy, and indifference five years before. I now knew it wouldn't happen again. I wanted to throw my arms around Marcus Sloan and hug him. "Thank you," I said, touching his hand where it rested on the door. "I mean that."

He smiled then stepped back. "I'll call."

Oh, I hoped he would. The warm, happy glow lasted all the way to TUSP, on the other side of town, near the juncture of Interstates 94 and 35. As always, when I ventured onto campus the gentle peace of the old place enfolded me. TUSP was one of the oldest schools in Minnesota and managed to hold on to the grassy spaces, big trees, and old limestone buildings that characterized campuses a century earlier. I parked in the faculty parking lot, stuffed *Bondage* into my briefcase lest it be seen by a passerby, and hurried inside.

Our department was housed temporarily in nearby Webster Hall. The 'temporary' lasted a year while our quarters were being updated. Only this summer had we been allowed to return to our real offices. The directional signs still ushered those interested in the English Department to Webster Hall instead of Merrill Hall, our true home. This resulted in considerably less student traffic at our offices in the summer, causing some of us to jokingly suggest the signs not be corrected. I noticed as I crossed campus the signs were still incorrect. With only a week to go until classes started, I suspected our reprieve wouldn't last much longer.

I entered Merrill via a side door. The building was at least one hundred years old but had been extensively renovated. Luckily the re-design team had not eliminated the graceful wide hallways, large windows, high ceilings or wood floors. But thanks to a grant from a long-dead alumnus, the building had improved lighting and full air conditioning now. I breathed a sigh of relief as I entered the main office of the English Department, escaping the August heat.

Kathy Sylvester was on guard in her place behind the big oak desk in the middle of our department lobby. Behind her was the Department Chair's office. I eyed my new boss' domain but the shades were drawn in the glass-walled room. "Is he here?" I whispered.

She peered at me over her half-glasses. "Yep. Prowling the halls. Crowndorf is here, too, somewhere. I saw him come in earlier. He probably came to suck up."

"Yikes." I had met our new department chairman, Dr. Hamilton Cross, but had not had a great deal of social interaction with him. He was a short, dynamic, bustling sort of man with impressive academic degrees and a 'plan for the department to make our work more visible.'

I was already missing Dr. Hilary Backus, who retired at the beginning of summer. Her idea of 'visibility' was an occasional faculty picnic or bowling outing with our picture in the local school newspaper. She encouraged us to publish but hadn't been overly concerned about it, focusing instead on student feedback about her faculty's performance.

I was comfortable with that because my student evaluation scores were always high. But my publishing, at least in scholarly areas, suffered in the last few years. I suspected Dr. Cross would expect more from his faculty than Hilary had. "Listen, I talked to my security guard this morning."

"Your guard?" Kathy continued to sort mailing labels and stuff envelopes as I filled her in on my morning's activities. Her black hair, liberally streaked with gray, was bundled into a clip, loose strands reflecting her bustling energy.

"So you see, hopefully we'll have a lead on Pat and his activities long before they occur," I finished. I pulled my mail out of my mail slot and jammed it into my overflowing briefcase. "And Marcus said he would look into Tommi's boyfriend and how that fan letter got into the mail box." I sighed happily. "It's so nice to have someone competent helping me."

"Marcus, hmm? It seems to me you're getting awfully close awfully fast."

I waved that away. "Nonsense, it's client-detective privilege or whatever it's called when one is talking to a security guard. Anyway, I'm just glad someone is keeping an eye on Pat The Bastard."

Kathy pummeled her stapler unduly harshly. "No kidding. The earth would be a better place if that asshole was six feet under it." She eyed my briefcase, which I was futilely trying to manage. "Getting ready for the semester? Want to grab some lunch later?"

"I'm not sure, give me a call when you're ready to go out." I swung by the coffee pot and filled my John Prine Bruised Orange mug then headed for the door. "And try to give me some warning if the new guy is prowling in my direction."

"Will do, but no guarantees."

I hurried down the hall, up one flight of stairs then down the upstairs hallway to my office at the end. It was a bright, sunlit space crammed full of books, a couch, two chairs and the old wooden desk I inherited from some unknown professor. Toulouse Lautrec prints adorned my walls and one bookcase shelf held family pictures. Even though it was freshly painted during the renovation, it still had the feel of my old, comfortable space. I set down my coffee, dropped my briefcase into one of the chairs then sank into my old wooden office chair, swinging around dizzily. I was giddy with excitement. The end of several problems was well in sight and all because of one man.

Marcus Sloan.

I was positive my confidence was not misplaced. Marcus Sloan was competent, capable, and comfortable, three endearing qualities in a man. I rubbed my hands together, plotting my strategy. We would need more time together alone, that was certain. And perhaps I should go shopping for some more alluring clothing. I looked down at my serviceable denim skort and frowned, remembering the stylish Lisa from the police station. I should probably look for something more feminine. Then I discarded the idea. If I had my way, I'd be out of my clothes very quickly. Besides, Marcus didn't look like the kind of man who was swayed by superficial appearances.

Pleased with my reasoning, I loaded up my CD player, pulled papers out of my briefcase then opened my laptop. Time to get started on Fall Semester.

I wasn't sure how much time passed, but I eventually became aware something in my environment was amiss. I looked around the office, trying to put my finger on it. Then I realized my CD player was silent. It was a while since Eric Clapton sang to me about bell bottom blues. I pressed the remote control but nothing happened. I got up to check and saw the power light was off. That was odd. I looked around the room, noticing for the first time that one of the lights near the couch, which I'd switched on, was off. I tried the wall switch, flicking it, but nothing happened. The power was off. I checked my laptop and saw the 'battery' icon showing in the taskbar.

I peeked into the hallway but it was lightless. My office, which faced south, was bright, but the hallway was in murky dark, broken only by bands of light from the transoms over doorways. It was also amazingly quiet now the air conditioning was off. I returned to my office and considered opening a window, but the phone rang before I could implement my plan. I picked it up.

Nothing. There was just a vague, throaty sound, as though someone was...breathing?

I slammed the phone down, suddenly panicked. Who would be calling me here, at the office? No one knew I was here. I hadn't told Marcus where I was going and no one else knew.

The phone rang again. I picked it up. Again, all I heard was that heavy, wheezing sound, as though someone had just run a mile and was trying to catch his breath, or had just... Oh, no. Perhaps he'd just...? Oh, heavens, no, that couldn't be it, could it? I've heard about such things, of course, but with the advent of advanced technology, I was under the impression such indecencies didn't happen any more.

"Touch me."

Oh. My. God. The voice was guttural and excited. Granted, I didn't have much experience in such matters, but I was sure it was a man who was in the throes of... Oh, it was nasty. I slammed the phone down again, my hands trembling. I was sweating and it wasn't just from lack of air conditioning. I felt trapped, disgusted, and soiled. I backed away from the desk as the phone rang again, sounding abnormally loud in the hot, close air of my office.

I picked up the phone, my hands sweating so badly I almost dropped it. I took a deep breath, prepared to shout at whoever was there and give them a real piece of my mind, preferably in several different languages. As I did, I heard footsteps outside my door.

They were very quiet. I probably wouldn't have heard a sound but the carpet runners were bundled up and taken away for cleaning. The footsteps echoed on the creaky old wooden floors of the hallway. I listened tensely, straining to hear. The footsteps walked down the hall. I started to breathe a sigh of relief. They were going past my door.

They stopped.

I stared, my stomach churning, as the doorknob started to turn. No one knew I was here. Kathy knew, but she was far away, on another floor at the other end of the building.

I was alone.

I put the phone to my ear, again hearing that throaty breathing.

"I love it when you touch me like that."

I thought I might vomit. The words were so filthy. Well, not the words, but the way they were said was. It was horrible. I stared at the door. What if the person on the phone was the person at the door? What if the person on the phone was using a cell phone? I didn't have caller ID on this ancient black telephone, hard-wired into the wall. I barely had a dial tone, much less any 21st century amenities. I could be on the phone with a rapist or a murderer as said rapist or murderer was entering my office.

My hands trembled so badly I could barely hold the phone.

The doorknob turned.

I watched in horrified fascination as the white enamel knob inched around, like the second hand on a clock ticking my life away. I slowly replaced the phone receiver, trying several times to find the proper niche for it. My eyes were riveted on the door as it slowly, slowly, slowly opened.

Dr. Hamilton Cross peered around the edge of the door, his long face, dark black beard, and bright, dark eyes appearing disembodied. He looked rather like Freud, albeit slightly less hairy than the hirsute doctor. "Dr. Renard, there you are. Kathy mentioned you might be here. I knocked but I don't think you heard me."

No, I probably hadn't because my heart was pounding so loud I wouldn't have heard a rhinoceros if he thundered in and sat down for a bit of gossip and a cup of tea. "Dr. Cross." I sounded like a warbling bird, my voice cracked so badly. I cleared my throat. "Fancy seeing you here. Kathy mentioned you were out prowling the halls." I stopped, horrified at the words issuing from my mouth. "I mean, she mentioned you were getting acclimated to the new surroundings." I smiled weakly. "Come in, please. Have a seat." I gestured expansively, nearly toppling my laptop in the process. I grabbed for it, causing piles of paper to go fluttering around my desk like souls released from stasis.

He entered. As he did, I saw the lights had come back on in the hallway. My CD player chose that moment to come to life, clicking onto Meatloaf's "Paradise by the Dashboard Light" at the exact point where the male and female singers were producing remarkably lifelike sounds of orgasm (again, I have little first-hand experience, but I think I recognize *some* vocal innuendos). I pounced on my remote control, again stirring papers and books, to turn off the gasps and moans as Dr. Cross took one of the ancient visitor chairs in front of my desk.

As I resumed my seat in my office chair, I checked my seat surreptitiously to make sure I hadn't left a stain. I was almost sure I'd peed myself from fright. To my relief, I saw no visible sign. That was good. Peeing oneself was not the way to make a lasting first impression on the new boss.

The phone rang again. I glared at in exasperation. Heavy breathing no longer frightened me. I'd been scared witless by a stranger at my door. Orgasmic strangers jerking off as they talked to me on the phone held no fear for me now. I picked it up. "Yes?" I know I sounded cool, in charge, and confident.

"Jane?"

I barely recognized the frightened voice as Maggie's. "Hello?" I smiled apologetically at Dr. Cross, who was peering idly at my desk. I followed his gaze. *Bondage* was barely visible under a stack of papers. I casually leaned forward, sliding the papers further with my elbow. The book disappeared from sight.

"Pat's out."

"What?" I straightened up, the papers slid further, and *Bondage* began a precarious shift toward the edge of my desk. I grabbed it, nearly dislodging my phone in the process. I pushed the whole mass back into a giant pile. "What do you mean?"

"He's out. Pat's been released."

Chapter 6

"That's impossible!" I leapt to my feet. That proved to be the undoing for the mass of papers on my desk. Several slid to the floor with a muted thump. I ignored them and Dr. Cross, who bent down to pick them up. "Maggie, that's not fair. How did that happen?"

"I don't know." I could hear her tears. I began to sniffle, too, in sympathy. "But the D.A. who prosecuted my case called me just now to tell me."

I sagged back into my chair and grabbed a pen. I pulled over a copy of Masterson's critique of Howells' *A Modern Instance,* a book that has always struck a discordant note with me given its theme, to jot down information. "I'll call Marcus right away. I talked to him this morning. We discussed your problem." I looked up, belatedly realizing my boss was sitting there, regarding me politely. "I'll leave a message for him to make sure he knows. Try not to worry. We'll make sure there's no...ramifications from this." I murmured a few more placating words then hung up the phone, taking a tissue from the box in the top drawer of my desk then dabbing at my nose. "Hay fever," I said to Dr. Cross.

"Of course." He looked pointedly at my desk, which was now in complete disarray. "I don't want to keep you from your work. I just wanted to drop by while I was pro—in the area and say hello."

My face heated. I again mentally berated myself for my slip of the tongue. "I hope you'll let me know if there's anything I can do to help as you become accustomed to our department. I've only been here eight years so I remember quite well what it's like to come to a new town and get settled in." I frantically tried to remember his marital status, but the various curriculum vitae of the candidates we'd interviewed all blurred in my brain.

Perhaps he saw my confusion because he said, "My wife is adept at getting our family set up. This is our third move in fifteen years. We're hoping to be here for quite some time."

I smiled politely then glanced down at the note I scribbled on *Instance*. Thankfully he saw it because he stood. "I'm looking forward to our faculty meeting next Thursday."

"Meeting?" I dabbed at my nose again.

He gently tapped one of the papers on my desk, this one a florescent pink, indicative of one of Kathy's *Must Read* memos.

"Oh." I dug it out and skimmed it. *Faculty Meeting, Thursday, Sept. 1, 10:00 a.m.* "We're meeting before Labor Day? Usually we have the first faculty meeting after Labor Day because so many people go out of town." Then I realized I probably sounded critical. I shut my mouth, lest I insert my foot any further and choke.

"Kathy assured me most faculty would be in town. I thought it might be nice to kick off the school year with a meeting." He smiled, looking rather like a benign dachshund with his long pointed nose. He put several papers on the desk. "It was good to chat with you."

"Yes, thanks for stopping by." I watched him leave, dropping something into the chair as he exited. When he was gone I peered over the edge of my desk to see what it was.

My copy of *Bondage*.

I groaned and put my face down on the desk.

****

I was a good little soldier and put in a full afternoon at my desk, sorting, clearing, and preparing for the upcoming semester. I told Kathy about Maggie's call. She promised she and her husband Mike were available if needed. "Mike's not good for much, but he looks tough," Kathy said cheerfully. "But I think your security guard would be a better bet to help."

I was secretly pleased she thought of Marcus as "my guard". It gave me a little proprietary thrill to think of it. I called Marcus, leaving him a message. I was disappointed when he didn't immediately return the call as he had earlier. By five in the afternoon I was speeding home, pausing long enough at the grocer's for some shopping to prepare for Robbie' impending visit. Then I was home to my little house on the river and my two annoyed feline companions.

Ezra Pound Cat greeted me the loudest. It was time for his thyroid medication, followed by his Tuna Treat. I quickly stuffed the pill down his throat then dolloped a healthy hunk of Tuna Taste Treat onto a saucer. William Dean Howls, his companion, ignored the tuna as beneath his notice, instead stropping me with his fat calico tail and steering me to the kibble dishes. I served up his Fancy Feast then turned to my answering machine.

Marcus had called twice. His first message was short and to the point: *Jane, I don't have your office or your cell phone number, so call me as soon as you can. I'm working at the fair, and don't have access to a computer, but I'll get back to you.* His second one, left just an hour previously, was reassuring. *I contacted some friends of mine on the Pittsburgh PD. They'll keep me posted on Pat Scarlotti's whereabouts. Give me a call and we'll talk.*

I called the message number I had for him. Within minutes he returned my call. "Thank you so much for taking Maggie's problem seriously," I told him in a rush. "Pat was just so awful to her and—"

"I got a copy of the police report," Marcus said. I thought I could hear the burning anger in his voice. "And like I told you, I've got some buddies on the PPD. They'll keep me in the loop on what this—" I heard him take a deep breath, "—guy is doing."

"Thank you. Kathy and I will take turns staying with Maggie when the boys go away to school. I don't want her left alone until we're sure where Pat is."

"Boys? I thought they were college age."

"It's a figure of speech. I've watched them grow up, it's hard to get out of the habit."

He chuckled. "Yeah, I'm that way with my nieces and nephews. Speaking of which..." I heard papers rustling. "I got some information on Joe Robinson. I can fax it to you."

"Would you?" I gave him the number for my printer/fax in the den after ascertaining the machine was turned on. I watched as the pages spit out, some of them typed with others handwritten in a small, scrawling hand. I wondered if it was Marcus's writing. I skimmed through the information, settling back in my comfy chair at my desk overlooking the river. "I appreciate this so much, my sister will be so relieved."

"Yeah, the kid looks legit. Now, about that other thing, the fan letter you got in that mailbox. I plan to go there tomorrow to talk to the clerk. I want to know who they've been talking to."

"Exactly. That's supposed to be a confidential service. I'd like to know if my business is being shared with every Tom, Dick, and Harry on the street."

"What business?"

His voice was deceptively mild but I heard the laughter in it. "Private business," I said in a teasing tone.

"Ah, come on. You can share with me. I'm your security guard, remember?"

My security guard. I sighed, just thinking of it. "A woman needs to have a few secrets, Mr. Sloan."

He laughed softly. "You've got more than a few, Jane Renard. I'll call you tomorrow to let you know what I find out. If you stay with Maggie I'd appreciate it if you'd let me know. I want to be able to reach you at all times. And I want you to call me if you're worried about anything—anything at all."

Like my sex life? I smiled, thinking of it. "Let me give you my mobile number. And why don't you give me yours? That way I can easily stay in touch."

We exchanged numbers. I kicked off my sandals then swung my legs up on the desk. "Marcus?"

"Hmm?"

"Thank you. I appreciate all this...attention." I wondered if he would hear the innuendo in my voice.

I think he did. His voice was husky as he said, "It's my pleasure, Jane. Oh, by the way."

"Hmm?" I stared dreamily at the darkness beyond my window.

"I bought and downloaded a couple of your books. I'm looking forward to reading them. Good night." Then I heard a dial tone.

I tipped backward, almost crashing into the potted palm in the corner. I had barely picked myself up when the phone rang again.

"Why the hell didn't you tell me Toby was dead? Robbie told me all about it. Good heavens, Jane, I can't believe you found him like that!"

Oh, dear. It was Abby and she was on the

rampage. I rubbed my thigh, where I was certain a bruise would form in the morning. "Sorry, I was so worried about Tommi I forgot. I got that report back on Joe Robinson."

"Ooh, what did you find out?" Abby immediately put my personal life on hold for more interesting things.

"Hold on, I'll get the file. Joe looks legit, Abby. He graduated from the University of Colorado, B.A. in business, has a moderate debt load, probably more than he should have at this point in his life." I peered at the words on the screen. "Oh, oh."

"What oh-oh?" Abby demanded.

"He's been engaged. They broke it off before it got too far."

"How far was too far?"

"Looks like they announced it but that's as far as it got." I puzzled over some of the information, making a note to check with Marcus and have him explain it further. "It looks like he might be playing the market. So far he seems to be doing fine, so I wouldn't worry too much. That's it, Abby. He looks legitimate. I don't know that it's smart that Tommi is involved with him, but he's not a scam artist that I can see."

"Well, at least he's not a murderer or a rapist," Abby said. "That's something."

"That reminds me," I said, once again engaging my mouth before my brain. "Pat Scarlotti's out of prison."

"What!!"

I pulled the phone away from my ear. "You heard me."

Abby swore long and fluently in Italian, which was her profanity language of choice. "He'll come after Maggie, you know he will, Jane. I've seen movies about that, there was one with what's-her-name, the girl with the big smile and all the hair, you know—Julia Roberts, that's the one. The ex-husband chased her and she had to kill him. If she had a good security guard it would never have happened. I hope you're doing something to make sure she doesn't have to kill anybody!"

"Julia Roberts?"

Abby swore in Spanish, her profanity language of second choice. "I'm talking about Maggie, you big idiot. Although if she wanted to kill the bastard, I for one wouldn't begrudge her, because what right does an ex-husband have to terrorize a woman, for cryin' out loud. Richard and I manage to get along. Granted, there were times when I wanted to shoot the son of a bitch but I was never afraid of him. Do you need any help out there with this?"

I had a sudden vision of Abby and the girls, all descending on Minneapolis armed with Julia Roberts videotapes and DVDs. "No, Abby, I think we've got it handled. We're doing the best we can."

"I just wish there was something we could do to—"

"Don't you dare tell anybody about this, Abby," I warned. Knowing her, she'd tell all the uncles and aunts. Before I knew it, I'd be overrun with helpers.

"We're family, Jane. What's family for if not to help and to care? Honestly! Oh, there's Laura. Okay, I have to go now. I'll talk to you later."

I looked down at Ezra, who'd joined me. "I give it five minutes." I glanced through the file Marcus faxed me. Two minutes later the phone rang. I checked my watch. "A record, even for her." I picked up the phone. "Which family member is it now?"

"Jane, what the hell is going on? First Toby, now Maggie's in trouble again?"

"Good to hear from you, Robbie. I presume you've spoken with Abby?" I gasped when Ezra landed with a thud on my lap. He was a portly monster, no longer the svelte kitten he used to be.

However, he was only using me as a steppingstone on his ascent to the desktop. "Yes, Maggie's ex is giving her trouble again. You remember Maggie, right? She and I were best friends in Boston? She stayed overnight at our house quite often. Her brother and you used to be great friends and made a big show of ignoring us?"

"Of course I remember her and I remember the trouble she had before. Does it have anything to do with Toby?"

"How would I know, Robbie?" I rubbed at my head, which had sustained a mild blow when I toppled over at Marcus Sloan's surprising words. "I don't think so, but I'm not sure. Marcus is looking into it."

There was a long, ominous pause. "Marcus?"

"My security guard."

"Okay, listen, Jane. I think you need to take a step back from this to consider the legal implications of this. The man you've hired is related to the detective in charge of the case. That's not a good thing. You've just met this man and you're..."

I tuned out Robbie's well-intentioned words and watched Ezra prowl around my desk, my mind miles away. What would Marcus think when he read my books? Tilda Marlane, the main character in most of my books, had the most exciting adventures whenever she traveled as a paid assassin for a hush-hush government agency. Of course, Tilda was tall, long-legged, big-chested, and blonde. All the things I wasn't. She also had an audacious personality, an experimental nature, and a willingness to engage in sexual athletics with men she barely knew.

Would Marcus think I was like Tilda? Would he think I'd patterned Tilda on my life? Tilda never settled down with any one man, and, to be fair, most of the men she met were the kind who weren't interested in long-term relationships or love. Since those were the only kind of men I'd really had much contact with, sexually speaking, I had no other basis on which to build a hero.

"...Jane?"

"Of course, Robbie," I said automatically.

"Jane, this is important. You need to pay attention."

"What time are you arriving?"

My pragmatic question had the desired effect. "You're right, we'll discuss it all tomorrow. My flight arrives at eight in the morning. I'm going to call some friends of mine. I think we need to discuss this, maybe on Sunday."

"Oh, fine. I'll call Marcus and see if he can attend."

"I don't think that would be wise."

"I do."

"We'll discuss it tomorrow."

"I'm sure we will." Tomorrow I'd let Robbie fuss and talk. In the end, Marcus would attend any 'discussions' Robbie set up. I knew my big brother very, very well. We decided on a meeting place at the airport then I hung up and prepared for bed.

Having Robbie in town might put a damper on my campaign to have Marcus Sloan initiate me into wild sexual escapades. I would have to renew my efforts to get Robbie and Maggie together, not just for Maggie's well-being, but mine, as well. I fell asleep plotting strategies to throw them together, determined to begin my campaign the very next day.

I went to the gym early in the morning for a quick workout then met Robbie as planned at the airport. He is as unlike me as a person can be, except for the hair and eye color. Robbie is tall and big-boned, his hair a dark red with just a touch of gray and he has dark, amber eyes. "You're looking well," he said, sweeping me into a big hug.

"Minnesota agrees with me." I looked at him

with concern. He seemed paler than I remembered and thinner. "New York doesn't seem to agree with you." He lost many friends in the WTC disaster, barely escaping death himself due to an auspiciously scheduled meeting that took him out of his office that day.

"It's hard," he said as we walked to the car. "It just doesn't seem the same. It's not just the building and the reminder. Somehow a high-powered career isn't that important to me anymore, Jane."

The children of our generation in the family were all over-achievers. My cousins were physicists, researchers, scholars, doctors, and academicians. Robbie's position with a Wall Street law firm was par for the course in our immediate family. To hear him say his career wasn't important anymore was tantamount to hearing one of my cousins say they thought they might run away to become a politician, the kiss of death to a Rom. If they said they were joining the circus, that would be acceptable because several great-aunts and uncles had performed under the Big Top. "Perhaps this vacation is what you need, then," I said. "Perhaps you need the chance for reflection. There's more to life than a career, Robbie."

He didn't agree or disagree, just changed the subject to talk about Abby, our father, and other family members. It wasn't until we were in the car and driving toward Maggie's house he turned the conversation to Toby. "How do you feel about him?" Robbie asked, turned toward me in the passenger seat.

I tried to sort through how I felt. "Relieved, I guess," I said honestly. "I was so upset when I found out about the divorce thing. Now I don't have to worry about it."

He rolled his eyes. "For heaven's sake, Jane, never say anything like that when you're around a stranger." He paused for effect. "Like your security guard."

"You're completely wrong about Marcus," I insisted as we entered Maggie's neighborhood. "I've seen his interactions with his brother. I don't believe family loyalty would sway him or prevent him from helping me." I glanced at Robbie and grinned. "He doesn't appear to have quite the same kind of family we have."

"No one has the same kind of family we have. Speaking of which, Uncle Vanya called me yesterday. He remembered I was coming for my annual visit. He heard about your problems and Maggie's problems, probably from Abby, who probably told one of the cousins. He and the boys want to join us tomorrow."

"Oh, no." Vanya Petrovitch was my mother's father's brother's son and his 'boys' were all in their forties, huge, and prone to fighting. They lived west of the Twin Cities and owned a chain of restaurants and bars. They were a force to be reckoned with.

"And Aunt Sophie will bring the food."

I brightened. That was a consolation. We pulled into Maggie's driveway. She was by the side of the house, inspecting a flowerbed and holding a loose bouquet of daisies. She wore denim shorts, a pale blue golf shirt tucked in, and the breeze had mussed her brown/blonde hair. As I stopped the car she turned and waved. I glanced at Robbie and noted his google-eyed amazement.

"That's Maggie? Little Maggie Carlson?"

I smiled smugly. "Yep."

"You might have warned me."

"About what?" I asked innocently. I looked at Maggie as Robbie unfolded himself from the car and stood. Her blue eyes were wide with surprise when she saw what a difference thirty years had made to a person. The gawky college freshman was gone, replaced by a handsome, confident businessman.

Then I looked at Robbie as he looked at Maggie. I could almost read his mind: *what happened to that funny little high school girl who used to giggle with my sister?*

Yep. I knew my big brother very, very well.

Chapter 7

I smiled at Maggie as we joined her near the flowerbed. "You remember my brother Robbie, don't you? He and Brian always used to ignore us when we were kids."

Maggie looked stunned. "Robbie?" she asked weakly.

He strode forward. "It's me, Maggie. Rob Renard."

"Oh, of course I remember you." She tried to laugh casually but I heard the strain. I secretly smiled to myself. Things were working exactly as planned. "I had such a crush on you in high school." Then her cheeks flushed a dark red.

And you do again, I thought gleefully.

Robbie glanced once at Peg the Leg then resumed staring at Maggie. "I'm sorry for what happened to you. I'll make sure nothing like that happens again."

I almost rubbed my hands together at the protective sound of his statement. I believe I just witnessed love at first sight. Oh, all right, it wasn't technically 'first sight' because Maggie and Robbie knew each other so many decades ago. But as my father used to say, it was close enough for government work.

Maggie put a hand to her hair. "I didn't realize you'd be stopping by so early." She shot me a dagger-filled look.

"Oh, you're somewhat on our way home," I said. "Robbie's concerned about Pat the Bastard. He said he wanted to have a discussion tomorrow." I turned to Robbie. "To talk about Toby and about Pat, right?"

"Yes." Robbie wasn't looking at me. He was looking at Maggie. The expression 'love-sick cow' flashed through my mind, uncharitable though it was. "Jane, I think you should have that security guy come over, too. The more people we have working on this, the better."

"Oh, you really shouldn't..."

Maggie's voice faded as Robbie moved to stand near her. I smiled at the discrepancy in their heights. He was very large, masculine, and protective. "Let me help, Maggie. Please."

She took a hesitant step back and Peg twisted awkwardly. Maggie almost stumbled but Robbie put a hand on her arm, steadying her.

"Thank you, Robbie."

They moved ahead of me into the house. I followed behind, barely restraining myself from patting myself on the back. We went to the kitchen, where Maggie poured us all coffee from the big pot already brewed. We were just sitting down at the small kitchen table when Perry and Ian came in, talking. They stopped when they saw the Strange Man sitting with their mother.

"How was the film last night?" Maggie asked. "You guys got in late."

"Cool," Ian said. "It was a four-ax flick."

Maggie raised an eyebrow. "I beg your pardon?"

"Four ax, Mom. Not four ex."

I saw the astonishment on Robbie's face as he

evaluated the two big boys-almost-men. Perry was six feet tall and Ian not far behind. They both had their father's dark good looks but luckily neither had inherited Pat Scarlotti's appalling personality.

I know the boys tried to defend their mother from their father. They had initially felt guilty they hadn't succeeded. We had many a long talk while Maggie was recovering in the hospital. I flew out to Pittsburgh, staying with the boys at their house, helping as best I could, assisted by a shirttail cousin who lived there and who was invaluable in helping me navigate the city and the justice system. I would never forget the terror of those first days after the accident, when I finally realized what a monster Pat had become.

"I don't think you've ever met the boys," I said smoothly, hoping to cover Robbie's gaping amazement. "These are Maggie's sons. That's Perry and that's Ian. Boys, this is Robbie."

"Hey." The two boys leaned against the counter, regarding Robbie with cool curiosity.

"So, you're Jane's brother, huh?" Ian poured himself a glass of milk, tossing the question over his shoulder.

"Yep." Robbie sipped his coffee, his glance flickering between the two other males in the room who were interested in Maggie, albeit in a far different way.

"Hmm. So what do you do?" It was Perry, grilling him. I could tell Robbie would be a tough sell. Perry was very protective of Maggie.

"I'm a lawyer in New York," Robbie said, making a face.

"What? You don't like New York?"

Robbie shrugged. "Since 9-11 it's been..." He shook his head. "Weird."

"Wow. Were you there that day?" Ian asked.

"I missed the attacks because of a meeting,"

Robbie said, staring at his coffee mug. "I went to a meeting first thing in the morning. If I hadn't, I wouldn't be sitting here today. My office was on the 105th floor."

"Robbie." Maggie whispered his name. Her hand went to his arm and she gave him a reassuring touch. "That's awful. You lost all those friends and people you knew."

"Man, that's tough," Ian said. "Why don't you move?"

Robbie shrugged again. "I guess I haven't been motivated." He looked at Maggie. I know he saw the understanding in her eyes. She knew what it felt like to be trapped in one place, regardless of the reason. "I've been waiting to move on."

Her hand was still on his arm. I watched Perry as he watched Robbie, holding my breath. Perry finally nodded and said, "I guess it's hard to make big changes like that." He said it grudgingly but with a certain amount of understanding that surprised me. His next words surprised me even more. "Jane always says how it's important to try things, even if you're not quite sure it's the right thing to do. Sometimes if you just try, some other new opportunity will open up." Perry's admiration was obvious in his voice.

Robbie smiled. "Yeah, that sounds like Jane."

"Well, heavens, I didn't know I made such an impression," I said, flustered. "Had I known you were listening, I would have said something more important like 'eat your vegetables' or 'never kiss on the first date.'"

Everyone laughed and the subtle tension in the room lessened. I exhaled a sigh of relief. Robbie had passed a Big Test with the kids, coming through with colors flying. I knew he would, but still, it was nice to have confirmation. "Boys, Robbie has suggested we have a meeting tomorrow to discuss what to do about your father." I glanced at Maggie, who nodded agreement. "You know he's out of prison?"

My matter-of-fact approach was the correct tactic. Perry and Ian both appeared angry, not embarrassed. Perry nodded. "We were talking about it last night," he said, pouring a cup of coffee. "We're afraid Pat might come after you, Jane." They never called Pat 'Dad' anymore. I couldn't blame them. I'm sure it was hard to even acknowledge he was related to them, much less to show that monster any paternal affection.

Now I was the one to be startled. "Me?"

"Yes." Maggie seemed so worried I wished I could hug her. No one deserved to have such anxiety in her life. "Pat blames you for so much, Jane. You sheltered us when we ran away, you hired the detective to follow Pat, you even faced down Vito." She turned to Robbie. "Vito Scarlotti is Pat's father. He's one of the nastiest people you'd ever want to meet. When Pat broke my arm that one time, Jane stomped into Vito's mansion to read him the riot act for raising such a bully."

Robbie's face underwent an amazing transformation. The gentle, concerned older brother was gone, replaced by an angry, iron-willed stranger. I suddenly realized he hadn't known the details about Pat's history of abuse.

"Maggie tried to run away twice, with the boys," I told him. "The first time she didn't get far. Pat found her and beat her. He was sentenced to family counseling and probation. The second time they got to me, here in Minnesota." I smiled at the boys who shared Robbie's expression: grim, appalled, and determined. "They were safe for almost a month but Vito hired a high-priced lawyer to dispute custody of the boys. Maggie was forced to go back." I glanced at the boys. "It wasn't your fault." I had repeated that statement many times before, but I know the boys still felt guilty.

Robbie took a long, steadying breath. He and the two boys exchanged a look. I felt immensely relieved at the solidarity and understanding that passed between them all.

"Okay, here's what we need to do," Robbie said. "I need to rent a car because I have to run some errands today. And I want to talk to Billy Armstrong. He's a friend of mine who practices criminal law out here."

"Billy Armstrong? Didn't he used to play football?" Ian asked, brightening at the thought of meeting a professional athlete, or so I presumed.

"Yeah, he played for the Vikings. I want to chat with him. I want your security guard in on this, too," Robbie said, obviously unimpressed by Mr. Armstrong's previous athletic accomplishments. "This guard has an in with the police. We need all the help we can get."

"Jane has a security guard?" Perry asked. Ian said something in a low voice and Perry broke into a grin. "Oh, right."

I didn't have the opportunity to pursue whatever innuendos Ian was casting, because Maggie sagged back in her chair, a tear wending down her cheek. "Maggie, what's wrong?" I leaned over to my friend anxiously.

"It just feels so good to have people to help us," she whispered. When she smiled at her boys, they immediately crossed the room to stand near her.

I recognized the look in Robbie's eyes. Pat Scarlotti had just met his match. He glanced at his watch. "If I know Billy, he's out golfing. Excuse me." Robbie went to the opposite side of the kitchen. I followed him, watching as he pulled out his Palm Pilot, found a phone number and dialed it on his cell phone. When someone answered, Robbie listened then said, "It's Rob Renard. I'm in town and I need some help. Sink the damn putt." He waited patiently, his glance flickering from me to Maggie, who was talking in a low voice to the boys. "Why didn't you tell me how bad it was, Jane?"

"What could you do to help?" I asked with a shrug. "It all happened in Pittsburgh, when I lived there. Then the accident happened after I moved. That's when we were finally able to get Maggie here and—"

He held up a hand. Obviously Mr. Armstrong had wrapped up his golf game because Robbie resumed his conversation. I listened to him speak, one-sided though it was.

"Yes, I'm visiting my sister. Listen, something's come up. I may need a consultation here in town. Do you have your Palm with you?" Robbie laughed at whatever Armstrong said then continued. "Here're the basics. A friend of mine—of my family—had trouble three—" I held up five fingers, "—five years ago with one Pat Scarlotti, in Pittsburgh. She was married to the bastard, he tried to kill her, he was put in prison, and now he's out. And we're afraid he may be coming after Jane, my sister."

There was a long pause as Mr. Armstrong apparently was remonstrating with Robbie, who paced and frowned. "I appreciate that, Billy, but we need to be as prepared as possible. I happen to care about Jane, annoying though she is at times."

I gave him an outraged look but he just grinned.

"I need you to meet with me and some other people at my sister's house, tomorrow at eleven." He looked a question at me.

I nodded in affirmation. I'd make sure Marcus was available.

"We're going to have a strategy meeting." He listened to Mr. Armstrong then said evenly, "Maggie Carlson is my friend. She was hurt badly and I want to see to it that it doesn't happen again." He nodded at whatever Mr. Armstrong replied. "Good." He gave directions to my house then said, "I appreciate this, Billy. If I can return the favor..." He grinned at something his friend said. "That's a deal." He closed the phone, turning to me. "You need to autograph a book for Billy's wife. She's your biggest fan."

I considered then discarded several replies, settling for, "It's the least I can do." I lowered my voice. "Do you foresee any consequences with my Toby problem?"

Robbie rolled his eyes. "Gee, I can't believe I forgot about that."

"There's probably nothing to worry about," I said hopefully. "Especially since Toby had remarried. Surely his current wife would have more concerns about his death than I do."

"What?" When I started to explain myself, he held up a hand. "Explain on the way to the rental car place."

"Are you sure you need a car? I can drive you anywhere you need to go."

Robbie's gaze went to Maggie. I could almost read the thoughts going through his mind. He needed the flexibility a car would give him. I smiled when he said, "I need to get a car. Then I'm going to visit the police station to see what I can find out about Scarlotti and Toby."

I considered telling him about the odd letter Maggie received but decided he had enough worries at the moment. I'd tell him when we got home. I nodded. "Excellent. And I'll verify with Marcus that he can meet us. I'm so glad you're here, Robbie. I'm sure between you and Marcus, we can alleviate Maggie's worries."

"I'm as worried about you as I am about her," he said as we rejoined Maggie and the boys. We all walked to the car, Maggie going outside with Robbie and I, watching anxiously as we drove away.

The nearest rental car office was in Bloomington, just a mile or two from Maggie's house. I told Robbie about my visit to the police station the day before and the latest Mrs. Considine. I also alluded to possible problems between Marcus and his brother.

Robbie got a very thoughtful expression at that. "I'll look into it. The more I know about this guy, the better."

"Well, for heaven's sake, it's not like I'm going to marry him," I said dismissively as we entered the rental car lot. "I don't need a dossier on him. He's just doing a bit of work for me."

"What's he charging?"

"What kind of car do you want?" I asked briskly. "It appears you have quite a wide variety to choose from."

"Jane."

I recognized that cautionary tone of voice. "We haven't exactly settled on a fee," I said evasively. "Oh, look, a sports car. You like sports cars."

"I'll discuss this with Mr. Sloan tomorrow," Robbie said.

I made a mental note to call Marcus to make sure we got the fee business straightened out before Robbie had an opportunity to get involved. Robbie rented a Mustang and we finalized arrangements to meet later at my house, for dinner. As I drove away, he was talking on his cell phone again. I wondered what reinforcements he was calling in now.

I merged onto busy Interstate 494, heading west toward home. I immediately entered a construction zone, a maze of big concrete barriers, lane changes, and a bewildering assortment of traffic, all jammed together. As I negotiated the zigzag construction, a car pulled up beside me, bigger and heavier than my Benz. It was all black with darkened windows. Even in the bright August morning light the inky darkness of the tint gave no hint as to its occupants. It was on my left as we entered a particularly tricky part of the maze where two lanes of traffic had to zig very hard to the left then almost immediately zag to the right.

As we entered the zig, the big car must have hit a bump because it swerved toward me. I had nowhere to go. A large concrete barrier was on my right, perched at a sharp angle to keep traffic moving in something like the correct direction. As the nose of the black car edged toward me, I inched the Benz away, thankful I hadn't paid attention to my immediate instinct to jerk the wheel. I glanced at the black car and that's when I almost lost control.

Vito Scarlotti stared back at me from the passenger seat.

I had no time to process the amazing information. We were entering a part of the road that appeared to narrow to a point. The zig was becoming the zag. The center dividing lines on the road were no help. The temporary lane designations had long since worn away, leaving only a vague trace of their passing. I focused on the concrete barrier on my right and keeping the Benz out of danger.

The big car wasn't going to let me have the room I needed. It inched closer to me. I gritted my teeth, clutching the wheel and holding my ground. If I moved to the right, I would scrape the barrier for sure. Our two cars went into the zag only inches apart. I clung to the wheel and stared ahead, looking for any room, any space, any help.

I found it. The concrete barriers disappeared and an exit lane materialized on my right hand side. I jerked the Benz out of danger, into the lane.

The black car paced me, staying with me like a shadow, to the blare of horns from cars behind us. The exit lane was long but I could see the ramp ahead. I glanced at the black car, catching a glimpse of Scarlotti's darkly handsome face. As the ramp came into view I gunned the Benz.

The black car swerved toward me but I scooted past and ahead of it, leaving the sound of squealing tires and horns behind me. I emerged onto the shoulder, glanced in my rear view mirror then re-merged with the westbound traffic. The black car was on the exit ramp, stopped, cars swerving to avoid it.

I took the next exit, trembling so badly I could barely steer. I was in Hopkins. I frantically tried to remember the layout of the streets. Like a homing pigeon, I made for Marcus' house. When I finally pulled into the driveway, I was crying. I staggered out of the car and pounded on Marcus' front door. When it opened, I fell into his arms.

He made some murmuring sound of concern that didn't penetrate my fear. It wasn't until he hugged me so strongly my breath left me I realized what I was doing. I pulled away to peer up at his shocked, concerned face. "It was Vito Scarlotti," I stammered. "I saw him. He tried to run me off the road. I saw him."

Marcus led me into the living room, keeping an arm around me as I choked out the story of what happened. He got me situated on the couch then left, bringing back a glass of water, which he pressed into my hand. "You're sure?" he asked, sitting next to me.

I sipped the refreshing liquid. It tasted like the finest wine. My mouth was full of a terrible bile taste. Fear, I realized. I had choked on fear. I set the glass down with a trembling hand. "I'm sure. I'll never forget Vito Scarlotti as long as I live."

"Where were you right before this happened?"

Understanding dawned on me. "Oh my God. Robbie! Maggie!" I jumped up but Marcus was ahead of me. He prevented me from racing out of the room by simply putting his arms around me.

"Jane, tell me where you were."

I babbled out the news that I picked up Robbie at the airport then we went to Maggie's house before getting Robbie a car. As I talked, he nodded calmly.

"That means you were followed," he said when I finished. "It was an unplanned trip. They probably just followed you." He still had his arms around me. He stared down at me then suddenly bent his head to kiss me quickly. "I've been wanting to do that for a while," he said with a little smile. "Now call your brother and I'll call Maggie, just to make sure things are okay."

He released me. I dropped back on the couch like a limp sack of potatoes. Had I been less flustered, I would have taken advantage of the fact that I was (a) just in his arms and (b) kissed. As it was, though, I was too bemused. "How do you know Maggie's phone—?"

He already had his phone in hand. "I'm keeping a file," he said as he dialed.

"Oh." I fumbled open my mobile phone to dial Robbie's mobile. I almost cried with relief when he answered. I made an inane excuse for calling by asking him what he wanted for dinner that night. I knew if I told him the real reason for my call, he'd insist on meeting me.

"Are things okay there?" he asked. "You sound upset."

Marcus finished his conversation with Maggie and was watching me. "Can't talk, I'm busy," I told Robbie then I hung up. "He's fine." As I got up to get a refill of water, the familiar yellow and black markings of Cliff Notes on the end table near the recliner caught my attention. I eyed it as I walked past, surprised to see *The Rise of Silas Lapham* on the cover.

I glanced away quickly. What a sweet man, I

thought. He's doing research on a client's interests. "Robbie was hoping you could attend a meeting tomorrow at my house," I said from the kitchen. "He'd like to discuss the whole Toby situation, as well as what's happening with Maggie."

I leaned against the sink, my heart rate finally returning to normal. The whole incident with Vito seemed like a bad dream. I don't know if it was the proximity of Marcus and his reassuring presence or my own innate optimism. But regardless, I felt almost jaunty as I winked at Marcus, who'd followed me and now stood in the doorway. "Do you believe in love at first sight? I think Robbie's fallen for Maggie."

He smiled slowly at me, his hands jammed deep in his jeans pockets. "Oh, yes," he said softly. "I believe in love at first sight."

I almost dropped the glass at the look in his startling blue eyes.

Chapter 8

I reacted like a tongue-tied idiot while Marcus gently steered me out of his house and back to my car. I was literally unable to say a word, so stunned by the kiss, the sight of Vito Scarlotti, and my relief my brother was safe. Marcus firmly positioned me in the driver's seat, promising to follow me home to make sure I got there without incident. I barely noticed the drive to my house. My mind was awhirl with speculation about Marcus' comment.

Could he really be falling in love?

Nonsense, I finally decided. He was just being flirty. Marcus Sloan struck me as the sort of man who would enjoy easy-going flirtations. He was obviously worldlier than I. He'd been a policeman. Heaven knew what he saw and did as a cop. And the Cliff Notes were probably just his attempt to understand the woman who hired him. I once again made a mental note to ask him about a fee as we pulled into my driveway.

"You're isolated out here," he commented as we went into the house.

"Oh, somewhat," I said, dropping my purse and car keys on the kitchen table. "It used to be someone's weekend getaway. Now urban sprawl is creeping up on us. Chaska is considered a suburb now, although a far one." My two cats ambled out to inspect the newcomer. "That's Ezra Pound Cat and William Dean Howls." I smiled apologetically. "That's my attempt at English major humor."

"A pretty good attempt, I'd say." Marcus let them sniff his fingers then turned to me. "I'm working at the fair again today, but I'll make sure to be here for the meeting tomorrow." He took a step closer. "It's becoming a full time job to keep you safe." His arms went around me. It seemed like the most natural thing in the world for me to slip mine around him.

He was so big and solid. All I could feel was hard muscle and the solid thump of his heart. I looked up into his eyes. "Thank you for taking on the job."

Marcus lowered his face to mine. "My pleasure."

His lips were firm and felt very warm. I'm no connoisseur of kisses or kissers, but it seemed he knew just what he was doing. It started off rather tame, just a pressing together of lips. Then he moved his body somehow and it felt insistent, as though he was anxiously straining against me. That was when I realized *I* was straining against *him* even as I was inching upward on my tiptoes, anxious for more.

Oh, and I got more. It seemed to go on forever as we explored each other with our mouths. He nibbled and teased me. I moaned when one of his hands moved down to cup my bottom, pulling me against the delicious hardness I felt rubbing against me. Warmth seemed to flow through me, starting at my toes then moving upward until I was enveloped in a hazy, sensual fog. You've had kisses before that made your knees watery, your stomach do flip flops, and your eyes cross, right? So you know what it's like.

I retained some semblance of hearing because

when my phone rang, I was able to pull away from Marcus to pick up the receiver. "Jane here," I mumbled. Marcus ran his hands down my back, his eyes intent on my face.

"Hey, Auntie J, it's Tommi."

I dearly loved my niece, but she had appalling timing.

"Hello, T. How's it going?"

Marcus started to move away from me after kissing the tip of my nose.

"Two reasons I called," Tommi said. "One, don't forget to update your website registration, it's due soon."

I'd completely forgotten about it. Tommi helped set up Phire Foxe's web site a few years ago and we registered the domain for three years. It would be up for renewal soon. "Thanks, honey, I forgot. What's the other thing?" I reluctantly released Marcus, who pointed to his watch, mouthing *I have to go soon.* I nodded.

Tommi sighed. I could imagine her with her blunt cut red-blonde hair and angular body, glaring into the telephone as she talked. Tommi was an energetic, feisty, volatile soul with a heart of gold. "I'm in a bit of a pickle and I don't know what to do."

"What's the problem?"

"I'm sort of involved with this guy," Tommi began. "And I care for him a lot. But I don't know much about him. I was wondering...do you think it would show a lack of trust if I, like, had somebody look into his background?"

I grinned at Marcus. "I think that's a very intelligent idea. I know of someone who might be able to help. He's an ex-cop who does security work." Marcus touched his chest and I nodded. "I could call him and arrange it."

"No, I want to do this myself and have the information come to me."

I thought quickly. "I'll make some calls and have somebody contact you, how's that?"

"That would be great. You know why I have to do this for myself, right?"

"Sure, I do," I said softly, recognizing a kindred independent spirit.

"Oh, and don't tell Mom about this, okay? She doesn't like Joe already. If she knew I was doing this kind of thing, she'd freak."

"No problem." I was getting a headache trying to remember who knew what and who not to tell what to. "I'll have somebody call you on your cell later on today."

"Thanks. Love you."

"Love you, too, sweetie."

When she hung up I turned to Marcus. "Remember that Joe Robinson I had you check for me? Well, my niece wants me to find her somebody to do a background check on him. I figured because you've already done it, I'll have you call her. You pretend you've never heard of the guy. You can pretend to gather the info then just give her what we already have."

Marcus was puzzled. "So you want her to pay me to do what I've already done for you and what you're paying me to do?"

"What are you charging?" I asked, suddenly remembering my several mental memos.

He smiled. "The usual fee. If I did this supposed work for her, that would be double billing."

"Donate the money to a charity. Or charge her half your usual fees. Just don't let her know I've had you do a search on him. She wants to handle this herself."

"This is odd, but the scary thing is, I think I understand it. Is she going to call me?"

"No, you call her on her cell." I jotted the number on a scrap of paper. "Wait another hour and give her a call. Her name's Tommi."

"Like the rock opera? Cool."

"Like Thomasina," I said dryly. "She hates her name."

"Can't say I blame her," Marcus agreed. He pocketed the number then took me in his arms again. "I hate to leave you like this, but I'm due at work."

"Robbie will be home soon, so don't worry." I remembered my earlier scare, with the car on the interstate. "Vito was just trying to frighten me, wasn't he?"

Marcus nodded. "There were too many witnesses around. You're right to be scared, Jane. The Scarlotti family is bad news."

"I know. I'll be careful."

"Don't leave unless you're with your brother." He kissed me gently. "We'll continue this at a later time."

I returned the hug, anxious to have that hard length of man against me. "I'm looking forward to it."

As I watched him go, I almost twitched with excitement. Marcus Sloan was interested in me. Definitely. Everything was working out just like I planned: Maggie and Robbie were interested in each other, Marcus Sloan was interested in me, and would more than likely be anxious to have sex, and I had several people working on the Pat The Bastard problem. That just left Toby to worry about.

And the damn letter Maggie had received. I considered that as I made coffee then sat on the couch in the sun porch, the warm breeze off the river stirring the papers on my battered wooden coffee table. Marcus said he was going to talk to the clerk at the mailbox store. I wondered if he found out anything. I pulled over a notepad to begin jotting down questions but hadn't proceeded too far when the phone rang.

"This is Declan Fabersham."

The man said it as though the name had meaning and I should exclaim in wonder that he was calling me. Instead I said politely, "I'm sorry, I believe you have a wrong number."

"You talked to my stepmother yesterday at the police station."

Stepmother... Ah. "Oh, of course. Toby's wife. I mean, Toby's other wife." I had almost forgotten about her. "How can I help you, Mr. Fabersham?"

"Lisa is anxious to take her husband's body home for burial. I was hoping you could talk to the police to see why there's a delay."

"Delay?"

"Well, how long does it take to do an autopsy?"

He asked the question as though I would know the answer. "I really have no idea."

"The man was knifed to death. It's pretty straightforward."

Knifed? This was news to me. I decided to do some investigating on my own. "I'm sure it's just a formality because foul play was involved. What else did the police tell you?"

"They didn't tell us anything, they just asked a lot of questions about Toby, the estate, their marriage. The usual stuff."

He spoke as though he was accustomed to police investigations. I jotted a note to myself to research the Fabersham family. "Did you know Toby was coming to St. Paul?"

There was a pause. "Not until he left Florida."

"Really? When was that?" There was another pause and I filled the conversational vacuum quickly. "I only ask because I had no idea Toby was coming for a visit. Do you know when he arrived? Perhaps he tried to contact me and I wasn't available."

"No, we don't. I have to go now, Miss Renard. I'd appreciate it if you could do whatever you can to expedite the release of the body. Lisa is very distraught. The sooner we can put this behind us, the better."

"I'll do what I can, of course, but—"

"Thank you." He hung up before I could tell him I really had no influence at all.

Curious, I logged on to my laptop to begin ferreting out what I could about the Malcolm Fabersham family. I was deeply immersed in research when Robbie came in.

"Did you know Lisa Fabersham inherited almost ten million dollars?" I asked him as he joined me on the sun porch.

"Who's Lisa Fabersham?"

"Toby's wife. His other wife. Remember? I told you about her."

"She did?"

I nodded, pointing to the obituary report from eight years previously now displayed on my laptop. Malcolm Fabersham was a shipping tycoon in Ft. Lauderdale whose first wife died of cancer. He married the lithesome Lisa, only to die three years after their nuptials. Two years after Malcolm Fabersham's death, Lisa met Toby. They were married within a few months.

"I wonder who inherits now?" Robbie asked, tugging the laptop out of my hands.

"What do you mean?" I watched as he accessed several web sites in rapid succession.

"It's typical when a woman marries to make her husband the beneficiary," Robbie said, his face thoughtful as he stared at the information on the screen. "So if Toby was the beneficiary, who's next in line?"

"Her stepson?"

Robbie shook his head. "Declan inherited from

his father. I doubt if she'd—" He broke off, then whistled softly. "Damn, this is crazy."

"What?" I crowded close to him, peering over his arm.

"This isn't an official legal document, but she's an avid supporter of Save The Manatee as well as the Humane Society."

"Worthy causes to support," I said, glancing at Ezra and William. The two former residents of the South Metro Humane Society's no-kill shelter were curled up in their well-furred wicker chairs.

"She was quoted at a benefit where she was the keynote speaker. She advocated that people consider donating a substantial part of their estates, in their wills, to causes such as the Humane Society."

I sat back, frustrated. "Again, a laudable notion. What does that have to do with this?"

"Think about it, Jane. The police always consider the spouse first whenever there's a murder. That's one reason I'm so concerned about your role in all of this."

"I'm hardly a spouse, Robbie. I haven't seen Toby for—"

"I know, I know. And Lt. Sloan verified you and Toby have had no contact lately, despite that letter you got, which, I have to admit, is very damning."

"You spoke with him? With Sam Sloan?"

"Sloan and I had a nice long chat about Toby and other things." He held up a hand when I would ask a question. "Let me finish this line of thought. Toby was Lisa Fabersham's beneficiary, but he's dead. If she dies now, the money goes to a charitable group or so we can assume."

"If you're suggesting an animal assistance group is gunning for Lisa Fabersham in order to get their hands on her cash, I seriously doubt it."

"The money she's talking about donating is also part of her stepson's inheritance. It's all tied up in a trust fund. Lt. Sloan told me that Toby and Declan Fabersham had a legal arrangement worked out. If Toby inherited, he'd split the trust fund with the stepson. But if Toby's not around to inherit..."

"The money goes to animal rights groups and Declan Fabersham's inheritance is tied up in court while he's protesting his stepmother's will," I mused.

"Exactly." He set the laptop aside and went into the kitchen. I followed.

"But this is all speculation," I said. "As long as Lisa Fabersham is alive, she may remarry. Presumably another man may inherit the estate."

"When's dinner?" he asked, peeking into my refrigerator then emerging with a beer. "Smells good. Tuna casserole?"

I checked the timer on the stove. I'd made Robbie's favorite dish in anticipation of his visit. "Half an hour." I busied myself with slicing bread, making a salad, and setting the table while Robbie watched. "So how does all that speculation help us figure out who killed Toby?"

"It helps eliminate people," Robbie said. "Declan Fabersham for one. He had nothing to benefit from Toby's death. And it eliminates you. Lt. Sloan agreed with me that Toby's demand for money had to be a front for something else because, let's face it, you don't make money in the same league as Lisa Fabersham."

"True," I admitted. "And it's also true I haven't told my new department chairman about my secret life as Phire Foxe. But I will, if necessary, and I'll do it as soon as I feel the time is appropriate. I'm sure Dr. Cross will have no problem with it."

Robbie didn't appear convinced at my words. I privately agreed with his lack of confidence. I had no idea how Dr. Cross would react. Revealing my secret life was a discussion I wasn't ready to face yet.

"Let's just say Lt. Sloan isn't convinced you have

the stuff it takes to knife a man to death in front of several thousand people. Not to mention the fact his brother is your best alibi, as well as several dozen people who sat near you in the stands and will swear you didn't leave your seat until the moments before Toby was discovered."

"Well, that's a relief, at least." The stove chimed. I plucked the casserole from the oven, placing it on the lopsided cat-face trivet Tommi made me in her junior high pottery class. "You implied you and Lt. Sloan discussed other topics, too."

Robbie sampled his helping of tuna casserole, assisted by Ezra who took a seat at the table next to my brother, watching every fork movement in hopes of an accident. "Sam Sloan told me his older brother just retired from the Hopkins Police Department after he was wounded in the line of duty."

Something in the neutral tone of Robbie's voice alerted me to the fact more was at work here than met the eye. "And?" I prompted.

"Apparently he was trying to rescue a woman." Robbie glanced at me then fed Ezra a tiny bit of tuna, a ploy I recognized from our youth when Robbie would slip food to the family pet in order to avoid my father's interrogations about Robbie's dating shenanigans. "The woman's name was Mary Madison. She's short, petite, red-haired, and fluent in several languages. In fact, Lt. Sloan mentioned you reminded him a great deal of Miss Madison."

I considered this fact as I buttered a slice of crusty bread. "And your point is?" I finally asked. "Are you saying Marcus is helping me because I remind him of someone from his past?"

"Sam Sloan all but said Marcus had fallen in love with this woman," Robbie said, abandoning subterfuge to speak bluntly. "He's afraid Sloan is helping you out of some misguided notion of..." He stopped talking and Ezra was the recipient of

Robbie's futile attempts to disguise his agitation.

"Of what, Robbie? A misguided notion that I'm his long lost love?" I strove to keep my voice light and even. Could Marcus view me as a substitute for a woman he couldn't have? "What happened to Miss Madison? Was she injured? You said he was trying to rescue her. That implies that he failed."

Robbie shook his head. "The woman is fine but Sloan was injured. It took several months for him to recover. During that time the woman married someone else, another man who was involved in her rescue. Lt. Sloan said shortly after she got married, his brother decided to take early retirement, which the Lieutenant views as a waste of talent. His family apparently has a long history of police involvement. Sloan was a good police officer with a chance at a high-profile job. He turned all that down, walked away, and took a job doing part-time security consultations for a local firm in town."

Robbie shrugged, diverting another chunk of tuna to Ezra, ensuring the chubby feline's undying gratitude. "His brother is bitter about how it all played out. The family tried to talk Sloan out of retiring. Apparently they didn't think it was the best thing for him. They think he's been sort of drifting since then."

"Oh, for heaven's sake," I snapped, finally allowing my temper to be seen. "That's a lot of innuendo and supposition and very few facts."

"The *fact* is, you're a dead ringer for this woman," Robbie shot back. "And Lt. Sloan is convinced his brother is allowing his feelings for Mary Madison to affect his judgment about you and what's going on." He held up a hand when I would have spoken. "The lieutenant told me we shouldn't rely on Sloan's so-called expertise because his feelings are all fucked up. The lieutenant's phrase, not mine."

I sat back, not sure how I felt. Disappointed, certainly. No woman wants to think she's a substitute for another. And I was bewildered. I could have sworn Marcus was interested in me, not some ghost from his past. Could I really be so wrong?

Then I thought about Toby. My track record with men was obviously abysmal. Look at how I misjudged him and the few other attempts at romance in my life.

Yes, I could be wrong. In fact, I probably was. Robbie must have seen my depression. "Cheer up, Phire," he said softly. "You've still got the family."

I sighed. Family was all fine and good, but I wanted hot sex with a willing man. I wanted someone who wanted to...I brightened. Maybe it could work out. I wasn't asking Marcus to fall in love with me. Who cared what his motivation was? Who cared if, when he saw me, he saw, instead, another woman? If I had to take second-hand affection, I would. I wasn't asking for a lifetime commitment, after all. All I wanted was raw sex and a good time.

I smiled at Robbie. "I'm not upset at all," I said. "Don't worry."

His doubtful expression told me my words were in vain.

Chapter 9

On Sunday morning, Maggie and the boys arrived at my house first. I had rearranged the furniture in the sunroom to accommodate the influx of people, so I set Maggie to work positioning coasters, napkins, and the other accoutrements that would be needed.

The boys joined Robbie in the garage at the impromptu bar he set up, composed of two plastic laundry baskets filled with ice and cold alcoholic beverages, mainly beer. A battered wheelbarrow with two pieces of wood on the top was pressed into service as his countertop.

Next to arrive was Aunt Sophie and Uncle Vanya, driven by their oldest 'boy' Aaron in one of the world's biggest SUVs. Robbie directed them into the kitchen, where I was inventorying my glassware and liquor supply.

"Ah, sweetie, there you are," Aunt Sophie said, bustling in like a small, energetic garden gnome, complete with flowered dress, white hat and sturdy Birkenstocks.

I gestured her into the room as Cousin Aaron hefted in several boxes. "What did you bring, Aunt

Soph?" I asked. She started opening my white bead board cupboards, peering inside.

"You know, just a few things for us to nosh on. Some broasted chicken and a bit of kielbasa. Oh, and some of those pierogies you love so much."

I started to salivate. Aunt Sophie's pierogies were to die for.

"Some creamed onions, a couple loaves of crusty bread and some of the sweet butter that Della down the street churns. Marveen made a few pies, the blueberries are so good now, so I brought those. And I got some chipped ham, some of that spicy mustard Robbie loves, a bit of that caraway cheese your Uncle Vanya favors, those scalloped potatoes your mother, God rest her soul, used to make..."

As she spoke she directed traffic, gesturing, pointing, unpacking boxes, examining my stove, opening the fridge, checking my cupboards. She saw me watching her. "Go, go. You have things to discuss with the men about that monster who's chasing the sweet girl your brother fell in love with."

I stared incredulously at her. "Robbie? He's in love with Maggie?"

Sophie gave a nonchalant shrug. "Trust me, I know these things. Go, you have to make plans to get that maniac, *te malavel les i menkiva.*"

I grinned. This had been a favorite curse of my mother's. 'May a malignant disease waste him.' It was apropos for Pat, I thought.

"And when you get a minute send that man of yours in here," she said as I started to leave the room.

"What?"

She tapped her heart. "A mother knows these things. Send him in. I need to talk to him, make sure he's good enough for our Janie."

I mentally vowed to make sure Marcus stayed far away from the kitchen. I rejoined Robbie in the sunroom, discovering that Marcus and the legendary Mr. Armstrong had arrived. Perry introduced me to the man, telling me in an aside that Mr. Armstrong had been a lineman for the Viking football team, whatever that meant. Given his size, I surmised he'd been involved in something that required hitting other large men and tackling them to the ground.

Today he appeared quite civilized in a pale brown golf shirt that strained across his massive chest, and khaki pants. The outfit suited his dark-brown African appearance. Marcus was in a pale blue shirt with the sleeves rolled up and blue jeans. In his own way, he was as impressive physically as the redoubtable Mr. Armstrong. He and Robbie were talking in low voices in a corner, obviously seeking privacy.

I hastened to join them, but I was diverted by the need to introduce Mr. Armstrong to Maggie, who seemed alarmed at all of the testosterone-fueled firepower assembled to assist her.

"I'm Maggie Carlson. I'm the reason Robbie asked you to give up your Sunday golf and come here." Maggie stuck out her hand nervously.

Billy Armstrong laughed, taking her hand. His glance took in Peg the Leg then he raised his eyes to Maggie's face. "I probably would help him anyway. What was done to you is wrong." Then he raised her hand to his lips and kissed it.

Maggie blushed. Her damp eyes widened. Robbie appeared at that moment, thankfully preventing a full flood of tears. "Does that mean I don't have to write you a check?"

Billy's alert pale gray eyes, such a contrast in his brown face, gleamed with laughter. "I told you my fee." He turned to me and winked. "My wife, Jodie, will be so excited I had a chance to help one of her favorite authors." He leaned close to me. "And I have to thank you, too. Your books have added quite a bit of zest to our evenings."

Now it was my turn to blush as Marcus watched this exchange. I wondered which books he downloaded or if he had an opportunity for any reading.

Uncle Vanya and Aaron joined us, settling into the chairs on the sunroom, while Sophie manned the kitchen. We could hear her cheerfully conversing with William, who had designated her a woman to watch. Ezra was sticking close to Robbie, in case more tuna materialized.

According to Rom tradition, it is necessary to have a minimum of a dozen participants in order to assure a successful outcome. I was counting on my nosy sister and nieces to join us and provide the necessary numbers and I wasn't disappointed. When the phone rang, my family all breathed a sigh of relief.

"Okay," Abby said from the phone. "Let's get this started."

I pushed the 'conference' button on my landline. "Hello, Abby," I said.

"Hey there, kids," my father's voice rumbled.

"I've got Laura and Tommi here with me," Abby said. "Now, where were we?"

"We were just getting started," Robbie said, glancing at Maggie who was next to him on the love seat.

I was proud of the way I managed that, adroitly maneuvering the two of them so they had to sit together. The rest of us were in various spots on the floor, in chairs (de-furred for the occasion) and in the lawn chairs I brought in to accommodate the crush. Marcus sat across from me, sipping a beer and watching as Robbie pulled out a notebook then began to talk.

"There are three things we need to talk about today."

Three? I frowned. We had to discuss Pat the Bastard and Toby. There were only two items on the agenda.

Robbie correctly interpreted my expression. "Maggie has concerns about her ex-husband, Pat Scarlotti. Toby Considine was murdered three days ago. And Jane is receiving some disturbing mail, mistakenly addressed to Maggie." He glanced at Perry and Ian, and I knew what wasn't being said in front of the boys. I was getting more erotic fan mail.

"What?" I sat up straighter, looking from Maggie to Robbie.

Maggie handed me two envelopes. "I got those yesterday. They were forwarded on to me, just like the first one."

I opened the first letter.

Dear Phire: I have decided I need to see you, in person. I know, I know, it's so impulsive. But I can't tell you how much I want to meet you. I know your friend got this mailbox for you, in order to help protect your identity. Believe me, your secret is safe with me. In my position, it's second nature to be protective of a client's identity. And I'll protect your identity, if for no other reason than to have you all to myself.

I'll be in the Twin Cities soon, and you can expect to hear from me. I'm looking forward to it. I hope you are, too.

"Oh, dear," I murmured. I automatically handed the letter to Marcus when he came to stand next to me. I read the next one.

My darling Phire: I hope my last letter didn't frighten you. I promise I won't intrude on your life— your 'other' life. I only want to meet you, talk with you. I feel such a connection to you and I'd love to see if that connection is real or just a hopeful figment of my imagination. I've dreamed of a woman like you all my life. Can you be real? It will be enough to know that you exist, that you are real. That will satisfy me, I promise.

Soon, love. Soon.

"What's happening?" Abby demanded from the phone. "What's going on?"

"Some letters came for me, but they were addressed to Maggie," I said, handing the second note to Marcus. "They came to the mailbox I rented for her, when she first moved to town. The letters were forwarded on to her. We're not sure what to make of it."

Marcus folded the letter then put it back in the envelope. "I'll look into this," he said, tucking the missives into his back pocket. "No need to bother the group with them." He met my worried gaze. "No need to worry at all."

"Who's that?" Walt, my father, demanded.

"That's Marcus Sloan," I said in clarification. "I hired him to help me investigate Toby's death and to assist with tracking Maggie's ex's location. I also asked him to—" I stopped, remembering the convoluted scheme in which Marcus had done double research about Tommi's boyfriend. I couldn't remember who knew what.

"To help us with the police," I finished lamely. Billy Armstrong gave me a sharp glance but I believe I kept a bland countenance. "I'm confident Marcus can discern who's sending the letters. Now, should we move on to the Pat The Bastard problem?"

Abby muttered a nasty Italian slur against Pat's parentage. Walt snapped, "Speak English, damn it. Just because your mother taught you those languages it doesn't mean you have to use them."

"How many languages did she teach you?" Marcus asked me in a low voice, squeezing next to me on the hassock.

"Oh, five or six, not counting Rom. Momma taught linguistics at Wellesley."

"And-way ig-pay atin-lay," Robbie said with a grin. " On'tday orgetfay."

I laughed at this reminder of my youth. Maggie and I had always communicated in Pig Latin in order to try to confuse our older brothers. We were appalled to find out they understood every word we said and our 'secret language' wasn't secret after all. "Owhay ouldcay Iway orgetfay?"

Billy Armstrong cleared his throat. "I contacted some friends of mine in Pennsylvania. Apparently Scarlotti was released early because of good behavior."

His words had the effect of sobering us. "What kind of good behavior?" Perry asked, his voice tight and harsh.

Poor Perry. He and his brother were seated on the floor near their mother. I was saddened that two such young men had to be subjected to discussions like this one. They should be out chasing girls and enjoying the summer instead of plotting to make sure their father didn't kill their mother.

"He was a model prisoner," Armstrong said, consulting a PDA. "I checked with the warden and a friend of mine in the D.A.'s office. They both thought the father bought off some people in the jail, to protect his son."

Maggie nodded. "That would make sense. Pat was always mean, but I didn't know how he could survive in jail. But it wouldn't surprise me if Vito did something like that."

"One of the stipulations of his release is that he doesn't leave the state," Armstrong said. "But he's not being monitored, except for weekly visits with his parole officer. He could drive out here if he wanted to and no one would be the wiser."

I thought of Vito, whom I'd just seen the day previously. I glanced at Marcus. He shook his head, negatively. Robbie noticed and raised his eyebrows.

110

Later, I mouthed.

"If he does show up here, we can have him arrested," Armstrong continued. "That would be a parole violation and would be enough to get him tossed back in prison."

"That's a big risk to take," I said. "Do you think Pat would do that? If he does want to see you again, wouldn't it make more sense to try to lure you out to Pennsylvania?"

Maggie swallowed hard. I could see the effort it took. "I know he wants to see me again. He's sent me letters."

"That was against the rules!" Ian said angrily. "He wasn't supposed to have any contact with you. How did he—"

"He sent me letters," Maggie said in a low voice. "To the house. They were unsigned but I know they were from him." She looked at me and I could feel her desperation in what wasn't being articulated. "He got my address somehow."

It was Vito. I knew it. That arrogant old man couldn't bear to think that Maggie and I had bested him and his psychotic son. According to Vito, once a man was married, he was always married. There was no such thing as divorce to him. Divorce meant dishonor. The only way out of marriage was death. Vito ran his family with an iron fist, the same way he ran his trucking business—ruthlessly, with no concern for the well-being of the people involved, and all according to his own medieval standards of righteousness.

Uncle Vanya leaned down toward Ian to murmur something. The boy nodded and sprang to his feet, heading for the kitchen. Vanya waited until Ian was out of hearing then commanded quietly, "Tell us." Age had weathered him like an old tree and he appeared to me to be just as solid and strong.

And just as wise, I thought, grateful for Ian's

absence.

"They were terrible," Maggie whispered. "He said awful things. He's obsessed with me. He wants us to get back together, he wants us all to be a family again." Perry made a disgusted noise. Maggie put her hand on his shoulder. "I know. He's delusional. Prison just gave him the time to solidify what he always felt, that if he can't have me, no one will." Her voice trembled. Robbie took her hand, squeezing it gently.

"Well, it won't happen," Vanya said in a firm, strong voice. "I think we should maybe call in some friends, see if we can't keep an eye out for this bastard. We'll keep an eye on you and your sons," he said to Maggie. *"Kay zhala I suv shay zhala wi o thav,"* he murmured.

Robbie, Aaron and I nodded agreement. 'Where the needle goes, surely the thread will follow.' If Pat were in town, he'd seek out Maggie.

"We'll discuss details over lunch." His voice brooked no argument. Vanya and his 'friends' would handle protection. "Now, Jane, about your husband, God rest his soul."

All eyes turned to me. "Toby was hardly a husband to me," I said. "After all, I thought I divorced him. His second wife probably misses him far more than me."

"That's cynical," Billy Armstrong said.

"I prefer to think of myself as a pragmatist," I said.

"What's the difference?" Marcus asked.

Before I could reply, Robbie said, "A pragmatist is more polite than a cynic."

"That's not strictly true, Robbie," I protested. "A pragmatist is a person who—"

"Jane."

My father's voice stopped me in mid-definition. I recognized that tone of voice. "Sorry, Dad." I smiled at Marcus. "I'll explain later," I whispered.

Robbie rolled his eyes. "Toby was trying to blackmail Jane," he said.

"About what, Aunt Jane?" Perry asked.

"Not exactly," Marcus said. I admired the adroit way he intercepted a potentially embarrassing question. "He told Jane if she wanted a divorce, she'd have to pay for it and pay for him to get out of her life. From what I've been able to gather, his marriage to his current wife wasn't very happy. She hired a detective to check on him because she thought he was cheating on her. When she found out he was already married, she demanded he get a divorce or she'd cut him out of her estate and cut off his allowance."

"He had an allowance?" Abby asked. "For what?"

All of us in the room exchanged glances. "For services rendered," Marcus said dryly. "Anyway, he had to get a divorce from Jane or he was out. But it's beginning to look like Toby wanted out. Of course, it's hard to tell because our main source of information is dead, but from what I can piece together, he was getting ready to leave. All he needed was a nest egg. He wanted Jane to provide that."

Perry was nodding as though this made sense.

"You've done a lot of research," I said, grateful that we didn't have to reveal my covert identity to the boys.

"And I've got more to do, like who would want to kill him. I'm trying to track down the whereabouts of his wife and his stepson at the time of the murder."

"But Robbie and I talked about that," I protested. "We decided it made no sense for them to be involved in his killing."

"No, that's not true," Robbie corrected me. "We talked about the stepson, not the wife."

I opened my mouth to contradict him, but Ian

entered the room at that moment, announcing Sophie required our presence in the dining room, where lunch was now available. We ended the phone conference call with promises to keep Walt and Abby updated on future events.

Conversation over the food centered on practical details such as determining Ian, Perry, and Maggie's schedules for the upcoming week, a discussion of obtaining current photos of Pat in order to circulate them to the local police, and other mundane facts to assist in keeping the Carlson family safe.

Marcus and Billy Armstrong conferred in one corner, comparing notes about something. I wasn't able to eavesdrop because I had to fend off Aunt Sophie, who was attempting to get Marcus alone for a heart-to-heart conversation. I was pleased to see Robbie didn't let Maggie out of his sight for long. I also noticed that Uncle Vanya and Aaron were deep in talk, obviously working out details for their upcoming duties. I felt blessed to have such a willing group of helpers aiding my friend.

After lunch I was carrying dishes toward the kitchen but paused outside the door when I heard two male voices in conversation.

"Jane believes all that crap she writes about in her books about relationships."

It was Robbie. I went into Lurk Mode, which was becoming a reprehensible habit. I pressed anxiously near the door.

"She thinks people can be involved and not fall in love, the way they do in her books. I'd hate to see her hurt. She's very inexperienced." Robbie sounded exasperated.

"Inexperienced?"

Oh, no. I recognized that second voice. Robbie was talking to Marcus.

"I'm reading one of her books," Marcus continued. "I find it hard to believe Jane's as naïve as you seem to think she is. I appreciate the fact you're an older brother who wants to take care of his sister. I have sisters, too, and—"

"It's got nothing to do with me being her brother. Jane hasn't had very many long-term relationships."

Marcus laughed. "If she's had even a tenth of the experiences she mentions in her books, then I don't doubt it. Long-term relationships don't seem to be a problem for her characters."

I felt a qualm at hearing that. He wouldn't expect me to live up to the exploits of my heroine, would he?

"That's what I'm trying to say," Robbie said. "About her experience, I mean." He sounded quite agitated.

I hastened to intervene lest he give away more than he had already. I pushed through the door, smiling at the two men leaning against the counter, the remains of a chicken carcass on the table nearby.

"I think we've had a very useful talk today, don't you?" I asked as I stacked the dishes in the sink. "I believe Maggie will have all the help she needs and I'm confident Marcus can handle those annoying letters."

"I plan to go talk to the clerk at the mail store today," Marcus said, finishing his beer then setting the bottle on the counter. "I didn't get there before they closed last night. We're wrapping up the extra security at the fair, so I'll have more time to handle your case."

He smiled at me. I tingled at the thought of him 'handling me'. "Excellent. I'm sure it's just a fan with an overactive imagination."

Marcus flicked a glance at Robbie, who was watching us with a rather stormy expression. "You don't leave much to the imagination in your books, Jane."

I blushed slightly. "I just try to give my audience what they want."

Marcus looked at his watch. "I'd better be going. Walk me to my car?"

I nodded eagerly, anxious to have a few moments alone with him. I was conscious of Robbie watching us as we left, working through the gauntlet of relatives as we made our way to the front door.

Sophie appeared disappointed, then Vanya leaned over and whispered something to her that caused her to brighten. Marcus must have met with Vanya's approval so that was good enough for her.

It was another warm, breezy day but the angle of light told me our summer was fast drawing to a close. Soon it would be Labor Day and we'd begin our autumnal routines. I felt a sudden pang at the thought of summer ending, but banished it when Marcus drew me toward his car. "I was hoping we'd have a few minutes alone," he said.

"I'm sorry. My family is a bit..."

"Yes, they are." He glanced back at the house then moved so a lilac bush obscured us from the sightlines of those inside. His arms went around me. "One kiss before I go?" he asked, his gaze warm and welcoming.

I twined my arms around his neck and raised my face to his. "Only one?"

His soft laugh preceded a kiss that left me weak in the knees. My whole body felt jolted by an electric current, a current that left me wanting more. When he released me, I staggered. He caressed my arm as I found my balance. "What are you doing tomorrow?" he asked, leaning over to nibble a little kiss along my jaw.

I frantically tried to remember my schedule. "I have to go to school," I murmured. "I need to do some work before classes start."

He drew me to him. I felt the hard, insistent

bulge of a certain portion of his body as he pressed against me. "Maybe I'll see you there. I need to report in, after all. You're my boss." The hot look in his eyes told me exactly what kind of boss he wanted me to be.

"I think you should," I whispered as I pulled his face to mine. "I demand a lot from my employees."

He laughed. "I aim to please."

Chapter 10

I was going to have a passionate interlude with Marcus. He had all but announced it. I was so excited I almost danced back into the house, hard-pressed to act prim and proper as the various relatives said their good-byes. The last to leave was Maggie and the boys. She was effusive with her gratitude. I could tell her mind was relieved at the thought someone would be keeping an eye on her, at least until we knew Pat The Bastard's whereabouts.

Only one large problem remained. Robbie. I had to get him out of the house tomorrow. It was one thing to be flirtatious with Marcus at my place of business, but my campus office would hardly serve as a romantic rendezvous. I needed to get Robbie out of the house in case Marcus and I wanted to come back here. I had to devise a distraction.

"So what were you and Sloan hiding?" he asked as he helped me load the dishwasher.

For an instant I thought he was talking about my upcoming sexual romp. Then I remembered. "Oh. I saw Vito Scarlotti yesterday."

Robbie stared at me in horror, dropping the glass he was holding. Luckily it was plastic. It merely bounced. "What?"

I explained how I was driving on the freeway only to be frightened by the big car. "Now that I consider it, I think it was a car like the police use," I said. "You know, a Crown Victoria or—"

"The car doesn't matter, Jane," Robbie said through clenched teeth. "He almost drove you off the road."

"Oh, no," I assured him. "If he had wanted to run me off the road, the better place to do so would have been at the on-ramp or the exit. That stretch of road there is quite tricky."

"Jane, you're taking this all very lightly."

I straightened up. "I beg your pardon?"

"You seem to be more concerned with Maggie's problems than with your own."

"Maggie's problems are far larger than mine," I retorted.

"I know it seems that way, but your problems—"

"Damn it, Robbie, you don't know what she went through. She almost died because of Pat. She deserves the opportunity to live her life without fear that a maniac will find her, rape her, and get away with it again." I was panting with anger and I'm sure my face was bright red.

"Rape her?" he asked.

"Oh, Robbie, you're so naïve." I felt vindicated in using that phrase when he flinched. "Yes, he raped her and he terrorized her. It started when Ian was a child. She had to live with that for almost ten years because Pat's father was so powerful that if she left, she'd lose the boys, too." I threw up my hands in aggravation. "It happens all the time in the United States, in the world. Women are often frightened into—"

"Jane, Jane." He put his hands on my shoulders, giving me a little shake. "It's okay, honey. I understand. We'll make sure it doesn't happen again." He enfolded me in a strong, warm hug. "We'll make sure."

"I did everything I could to help her, but she didn't even tell me what was going on until years after it started." I was crying now, dampening his shirt. "Then when I tried to help, the authorities and the law—" I pulled away from him to glare up into his dark amber eyes. "You should do something to change those stupid laws."

"I know." He smoothed the hair back away from my face. "I wish you'd told me. I would have helped, Jane."

"You were so upset after... you know, after the Trade Center disaster. And Maggie insisted no one know. Pat has such a horrible temper. She was afraid to put anyone else in harm's way."

"So now you're in harm's way." I started to protest but he overrode me. "It's what I'd expect of you." He dabbed at a tear on my cheek then released me. "Now she has the whole family on her side."

I laughed shakily. "Pat doesn't stand a chance." I turned back to stacking the dishwasher. "But I am so worried about Maggie, there alone with just the boys. I hope you'll make sure Aaron or one of the cousins will stay with her, at least for a few days. I'm so worried about what Pat might do."

"I was thinking I might try to spend some time with them. I already talked with Vanya about it. Aaron will see to it that Maggie and the boys are escorted to and from work. I thought maybe you and I could spend some evenings there."

I could work with that. I decided not to press my luck. "And don't forget Kathy and her husband," I said. "They helped us out before. I'm sure they'll help again. Speaking of which, I need to go to the office tomorrow to get organized for the fall semester. Will you be able to entertain yourself while I'm gone?"

"I'm meeting Billy and a couple of the guys in

his law firm. We're going to play golf, talk some shop, and relax."

"Talk shop?"

Robbie shrugged overly nonchalantly. "Billy mentioned there might be an opening in his firm in a few months. He wondered if I was interested."

"Robbie!" I dropped the silverware basket with a clatter. "Will you move here?"

"I'm considering it," he said with a laugh. "New York just isn't the same anymore. I think it's time I made a change."

"And a certain young lady whom you knew in our youth might have something to do with that?"

"We'll see," was all he'd say.

I went to bed that night with my head full of plans. Tomorrow would be a crucial day in my campaign to get Marcus Sloan into bed. I had to make sure everything was right. I'd shave my legs, choose my nicest lingerie, change the sheets and use those scented sachets I bought. I also needed to steal some time to review a couple of porn videos, in order to make sure I didn't embarrass myself completely when Push Came To Shove.

That reminded me. I'd ordered a new vibrator for research purposes and it should have been shipped by now. I would swing by Mail Box Unlimited tomorrow to check. I snuggled into bed, with only William keeping me company, Ezra having deserted me for my tuna-giving brother.

Tomorrow, I thought drowsily. Tomorrow I would have Marcus Sloan all to myself.

****

I awoke with fevered excitement, went for my run, then almost opened a vein in my haste to get a close shave on my legs in the shower. I chose a loose skirt in beige jewel tones topped by a loose gold blouse, daringly see-through. It was too daringly, in fact. I added a dark brown camisole for decency's sake.

When I emerged from the bedroom, Robbie was chatting on the phone. He raised an eyebrow when he saw me. "Yes, she's fine," he said into the phone. "You missed Aunt Sophie's feast, it was fabulous. It's Abby," he said to me.

"Why is she calling? We just talked to her yesterday."

"She wants to know what I think of your security guard."

"Honestly, you people act like Marcus Sloan is a major fixture in my life. He's just a man I've met who's helping me with some police-related issues."

"Uh-huh," Robbie agreed. "I think she's smitten," he said into the phone.

I could hear the squawking on the other side of the room. "Robbie, don't add fuel to the fire," I warned. "You know how Abby gets about romance issues."

"No, how does Abby get about romance issues?" he asked innocently.

The resulting noise from the phone woke Ezra, who was dozing on Robbie's lap. I beat a hasty retreat, waving good-bye to my brother as he fielded questions from my sister.

I drove to Mail Boxes Unlimited, so euphoric I thought I might float. Life couldn't have been more perfect. Robbie was considering moving here, which would advance my matchmaking efforts considerably. Marcus was attracted to me so I'd finally have the opportunity to experience hot sex with a man I trusted and liked. And Maggie was getting the help she needed and deserved. Everything was perfect...

Except for Toby. I considered his death as I parked the Benz then went into the little storefront business where my illicit mail was received. Who would knife Toby to death? I'll grant you, the man was annoying in the extreme, but so was knifing someone to death. Heavens, talk about extremes! I went to my box and twirled the combination, not surprised to find the large rectangle full. I pulled out a bulky manila envelope I knew would contain letters forwarded to me from my editor, then I pulled out several other fliers, brochures, and other items addressed to "Mail Box Holder." Finally I plucked out the long, narrow package, checking the return address. Yep, that was it, a new sex toy. I'd play with it tonight.

No, wait. I would play with Marcus tonight. I would have no need of sex toys in the foreseeable future. Grinning, I tucked the toy into my briefcase with the other contents of the mailbox then turned to the clerk. His name, *Clyde*, was embroidered in dark blue on his pale blue shirt. He regarded me with mild curiosity on his plain, freckled face.

"Sorry to hear about your legal problems," Clyde said in his slow, measured fashion. I'd known the man for almost five years but had never heard him utter a sentence in anything faster than a dirge-like cadence.

"Legal problems?" I asked, trying to stuff my new sex toy deeper into my briefcase as *The House of Mirth* popped out.

"Man was here asking about your mailbox," he said, leaning on the counter to regard me with placid brown eyes.

His resemblance to a cow was uncanny. I expected to see him chew his cud any minute. "A man, asking about—" Then I remembered. "Oh, yes. A friend of mine was going to check into some...things for me." I wondered what Marcus had found. "I trust you cooperated fully with him and answered his questions?"

Clyde considered my words for a long, thoughtful minute. "Yep, I did."

"Excellent. Anything else for me or is this it?" I gestured to my bulging briefcase.

"Nope. All the mail's out so far." He smiled at me, a slow, engaging grin, much like the ones I saw on dogs when they lie contentedly in the sun.

I pushed away my farmyard imagery, smiling in return. "Thank you, Clyde. I appreciate all your help."

"No problem, Miss Renard." He pronounced my name "Rennurd," but I'd already corrected Clyde a multitude of times prior to this. The poor man just didn't remember. I waved a cavalier goodbye then continued on my way.

Kathy was ensconced behind her desk when I got to TUSP. I peeked beyond her and she shook her head. "Not in," she said. "Crowndorf was here to suck up again, but I guess he left when he saw the boss was gone. And Ted and Grace are here, or they were a while ago. Everybody's trying to look busy with the new kid on the block."

Ted and Grace were married professors who taught British Poets and Contemporary Fiction, respectively. I wasn't surprised that Crowndorf, my nemesis, had put in an appearance. I'd seen his car in the parking lot almost every day I'd been here. He was obviously trying to score points with the new boss.

Kathy gestured to the guest chair next to her desk. "Sit and talk," she commanded, not removing her hands from her keyboard. "I want all the news."

I filled my Bruised Orange mug then settled in for a good gossip. I updated her on the meeting with Robbie and his friend, Mr. Armstrong, which impressed her. "Wait until I tell Mike you know Billy Armstrong," she said excitedly. "Can we get an autograph?"

"I would think so," I said doubtfully, not sure if I should speak for such a celebrity. "He seemed very down-to-earth and reasonable. And listen, he said that there might be a spot for Robbie at his—Mr. Armstrong's—law firm. Just think if Robbie moves here!" Kathy and I smiled at each other smugly. "Robbie's already expressed a great deal of interest in Maggie's welfare. If he moves here, proximity will do the rest. Wedding bells will chime, I'm sure of it."

"When you get an idea in your head, you don't let go," Kathy said admiringly. "But what about the Toby thing? Have they found out who did it?"

"Not to my knowledge." I grabbed my briefcase and stood up. "That reminds me, Marcus may be coming by to see me later today, to give me a progress report."

"Oh, really?" She waggled her eyebrows at me.

I laughed. "If he appears, please direct him to my office."

"You're dressed very nice today, by the way," she said as I prepared to leave.

I glanced down at my skirt. "What, this old thing?"

Her laughter followed me out of the doors and into the hallway. I went to my office where I dumped my briefcase on the guest chair. I opened the package containing the sex toy, examining it to make sure it matched the description. It did in every inch, circumference, and 'realistic feel.' I put it back in the box then tried to secrete it in the bottom desk drawer, but it was full of folders. I settled for sliding the box under the desk, near the front. I pulled folders out of my briefcase and settled down to work.

Anxiety kept me glancing at my clock every twenty minutes or so. Two hours passed thusly when Kathy finally called. "He's on his way," she said in a whisper.

"Who?"

"Marcus Sloan, who else? He's on his way, and he looks yummy today. Oops, gotta go. Talk to you later."

I hung up the phone, wondering what 'yummy' meant. I checked my hair in my pocket mirror, frowning at my riot of red curls. I dabbed on a bit of powder, my heart hammering like a steam engine. Then a knock sounded on my door. "Come in," I called out.

The door opened slowly. Oh, my. Now I knew what yummy meant. Marcus was dressed in very pale blue jeans that just matched his eyes and a tight, dark blue golf shirt that matched the dark blue that rimmed his pupils. He smiled when he saw me. "I came to report," he said, his voice husky.

My moment had arrived. This was it. This was what I'd been planning for three long days. I stood up, my knees trembling. I opened my mouth—and nothing came out.

He locked the door behind him then turned to face me. I gulped at the alert, almost predatory expression in those pale blue eyes. It only took five strides then he was suddenly standing by the desk. "Hello, boss," he said in a low, throaty voice.

I thought my knees would give way. He put his hands on my shoulders, lowered his head, and he kissed me. I slid my arms around him, clinging for dear life. It wasn't until I felt the desk beneath my legs that I realized what was happening. I was sitting on the edge of the desk and Marcus had stepped between my legs, which I had, somehow, wrapped around his hips.

"I've thought about you, Jane," he murmured, nuzzling my neck with his scratchy cheeks.

I sighed with happiness. He smelled marvelous, all warm and a bit sweaty. And he felt fantastic— hard and hot and—"I've thought about you, too," I whispered, running my hands over the taut muscles of his back.

"I have to tell you, it was tough to read that

book you wrote." His expression was like that of a mischievous little boy. "I kept imagining you in place of Tilda, your heroine." He bit softly at my neck. I gasped.

"I'm not really like her," I said, hoping to squash any hopes he had before he could be disappointed. "I'm not an assassin, for one."

He laughed, a low sound, his breath hot on my throat. "I've noticed."

"I don't know how to kill a man five ways or escape into Europe with only a false passport." He moved against me. I could feel an outline of something hard and male press against my center. Good heavens. I'd forgotten how... rigid it could be.

"I'm guessing you know how to kill a man in a few ways that don't involve clothing," he whispered. "Your books certainly read like you know what you're talking about." His body was insistent against me. One of his hands was starting a slow march up my side, slipping and sliding over my blouse.

"Well, I have a vivid imagination," I said desperately, wiggling back.

He took that as an invitation and moved forward. My legs tightened convulsively around him as I strove to keep my precarious balance.

"I don't think you should anticipate that I'm as sophisticated or well-traveled as Tilda."

"I was thinking about other things." His tongue flicked out, tickling me.

I shivered. "In fact, I'm not like her at all."

He slipped a hand under my blouse. It slid up past my waist until he was touching my breast, encased in the silk camisole. As he thumbed my nipple through the fabric, I felt an astonishing wetness begin in my lower body, an occurrence almost embarrassing in its... moistness. "I loved that scene where they had sex in public." His mouth was against my neck, his breath hot on my skin. I felt the large bulge of his erection as he pushed his hips against me. "Care to give it a try?"

His words didn't penetrate for a minute. Then I squeaked, "Here?" I looked around frantically. "In my office?"

He chuckled softly, tugging at the buttons on my blouse until it was open. "Yes, here."

Oh, dear. This was going way, way too fast. I had anticipated a bit of time to get accustomed to the idea of... Oh, dear. He slipped a hand under my skirt, sliding up my thighs. I almost jerked out of his arms as he ran a hard finger over the damp spot on my underwear. "You're wet, Jane," he whispered fiercely. "You're wet and ready, aren't you?"

One finger slid under the elastic of the panty legs and was gently parting my body. I was dizzy with excitement, fear, and... something. "Marcus, I think we should—" I started to try to pull away, but somehow I ended up sliding closer to him. His finger parted me. I felt the most amazing sensation as a hard, callused finger began to flick across my clitoris.

"Let's get rid of some clothes, okay?" he whispered. Without waiting for an answer, he lifted me by putting one hand under my buttocks. He jerked me upward. Before I knew what was happening, my legs had parted and my panties were down around one ankle. He lifted my skirt, pushing it slowly upward, his big hands clasping my thighs as the skirt slid slowly, slowly, slowly up. I leaned back on my hands, not sure what was coming next.

He leaned over me, his hand moving to my...to my...well, to my crotch, let me say it. He parted me and slipped his thumb inside. Oh, God. It felt...amazing, so hard, and insistent and pulsing. I had no control over my body. I was reacting to everything he did. When he lowered his face and gently nudged at my camisole, I lifted it up to give him easier access to my breasts. He moaned, touching me with his hand as he mouthed my nipple through my lacy bra.

I felt a slow, hot unfurling in my gut as he pulsed his fingers in and out of my body. I was on the verge of the first orgasm of my life—or, rather, the first orgasm with another human being in the room. All thoughts of propriety, decorum, and sensible behavior fled. "Marcus, please," I whispered, straining against him. "Please, please."

He laughed softly. "Are you begging?"

"Yes." I leaned back on the desk, not caring what papers went scattering to the floor.

He removed his hand and I groaned aloud. He laughed again. "Just a minute, greedy." He undid his belt buckle and unzipped his jeans, sliding them down his legs.

It was a long time since I'd seen a man in the flesh, as it were, and perhaps my memory was failing me, but he appeared to be more well-endowed than I remembered a man being. I blinked in surprise at the large appendage facing me and once again doubt assailed me. "Marcus, there's something you should know," I whispered.

He stepped between my legs where I was sprawled on the desk, his hands sliding upward to push my legs further apart. "Yes, Jane?" he whispered, leaning over me.

I almost didn't hear the knock on my door because my heart was thudding so loudly. Marcus heard it before I did. His head snapped up just as his penis touched my leg. He and I exchanged desperate looks. The knock sounded again.

"Dr. Renard? Is everything all right?"

Oh, Jesus. It was Dr. Cross, my boss.

Chapter 11

I pushed frantically at Marcus' shoulders. "It's my boss," I whispered. He stepped back, tugging at his clothing. "Hide."

"What?" He looked around the room then at me, incredulous. "What?"

"Hide." I gestured to my old-fashioned desk, a solid hulk of wood. "I'll get rid of him." The leg space under the desk was big enough for Marcus with a little room to spare. "Hide." I kicked my panties off my foot, pushing them under the desk then smoothed down my clothing. I glared at Marcus until he pulled up his trousers.

"We have unfinished business," he whispered, kissing me hard. Then he clambered under the desk, fitting into the small space like a pretzel. I crossed the room to the door, glancing back. There was no sign of anyone. The only sign of a problem was my messy desk, which looked remarkably like it had the last time Dr. Cross was in my office.

I took a deep breath, looked down at myself and re-buttoned my blouse. Then I turned the door lock and pulled open the door. "Dr. Cross. Hello." I wondered if my expression was as bug-eyed as it felt.

My boss' alert dark eyes seemed to zero in on my face. "Dr. Renard, I wondered if you were here. Kathy mentioned you'd come in to work. Do you have a moment?" He was starting to edge past me.

"I was just going to get some coffee," I said, moving to block his passage.

"This won't take a minute." He slipped by me to take the guest chair in front of my desk, looking politely at me as I stood gaping at him from my position at the door.

I closed my mouth with an audible snap and cautiously took my desk chair, not daring to glance down. I crossed my legs at the ankle, trying to tug my skirt down to cover myself. I glimpsed my panties out of the corner of my eye, tantalizingly visible at the side of my desk. I slid my right leg under the desk, hoping to snag the offending lingerie and hide it.

"How can I help you?" I asked politely. I moved my right leg further, tapping at the floor with my sandal.

For answer, Marcus pushed my leg even further, insistently parting me. I felt his fingers begin a slow inching, along my thigh. I gave up on underwear retrieval and tried to close my legs. However, he moved forward so there wasn't enough space with him there. Then I felt his face, warm on my legs, and a gentle licking as he lapped at my inner knee. I almost shot out of my chair at the sensation.

"To be blunt, I was wondering about your publishing record, Dr. Renard. You've only published three articles in the last five years. While the articles themselves were exceptionally good and quite insightful, that's not a great deal of scholarship."

Dr. Cross was regarding me with a polite, attentive look. I struggled to remain seated as Marcus' fingers stole upward, parting my legs until I was totally exposed to him, under the desk. I fought to find a coherent thought. "I've focused more on my teaching performance," I managed to say. "I feel that a person's performance in the classroom is the most important aspect of our work here." A trickle of sweat began to work its way down from my armpit as Marcus found just the right spot with his finger. He began a slow, gentle, pulsing massage. I was powerless to stop him. As though in a dream, my legs parted even wider. I heard a satisfied 'oh' from under the desk. I coughed, hoping to cover the sound.

"That's quite laudable. You do have the highest performance rating of your peers in the department."

I sat still, my hands clasped on the desk in front of me as Marcus proceeded to bring me to the brink of an orgasm. I wanted nothing more than to sink to the floor, lift my skirts, and allow that man to do whatever he wanted to do. Instead I sat with a silly smile on my face, my head tilted, my eyes undoubtedly glazed, as Dr. Cross regarded me with a thoughtful expression.

"I expect if you have a sabbatical next year, you'll be able to work on your scholarship, isn't that right?" he finally asked.

I nodded inanely. "Of course." The words came out as a hoarse, throaty whisper. I coughed. "Of course." I slid down in the chair as Marcus' finger slipped even deeper inside my body. I felt an orgasm start and my eyes widened.

"Well, that's good to know." Dr. Cross bobbed to his feet suddenly.

I gaped up at him. "Yes, it is," I said, wondering what I was agreeing to. I started to sit up straighter but he waved a hand.

"No, that's all right, I can show myself out. You should probably lock the door, though. It's better to be safe, what with the building being mostly empty."

He smiled politely. "I'm looking forward to our faculty meeting on Thursday. See you then."

"Yes, see you then," I said faintly. I watched as he crossed the room to the door, pausing before going out. He glanced at the floor near my desk. I wondered if he saw anything. I held my breath as Marcus increased the pace of his pulsing.

"Nice chatting with you," Dr. Cross said as he closed the door behind him.

I let out my breath in a whoosh of sound when I heard the door click shut. I started to pull away from Marcus, but he emerged from under the desk with his hand still under my skirt. Then he leaned over me, staring down at me, sprawled back in the chair. "On the couch, now," he demanded, jerking me to my feet.

"Marcus, I—"

He crossed the room, locked the door, and had shed his shirt by the time I stumbled to the couch. I sank down, disoriented, as he approached me. I'd almost had an orgasm at least twice in the last twenty minutes. My poor body didn't know what hit it. I hadn't had this much excitement in the past decade. "Marcus, there's something you need to know," I tried again.

"What is it, Jane?" He was staring at me, his pale blue eyes bright and hot.

"There's something I need to tell you." I scooted back on the couch, trying to put distance between us. I could still feel the heat from his body even though a foot separated us. I looked around the room, spying my bright yellow panties, peeking out from under the desk. I closed my eyes in humiliation, wondering if Dr. Cross had noticed.

Marcus looked thoughtful. "I have condoms, if that's what you're worried about."

My eyes snapped open as I gaped at him. Condoms? I hadn't even thought of that. God, I was such a naïve idiot. "No, no, that's fine, I'm sure you're—and I'm—so that's okay and..." I ground to another halt.

"Jane, what is it?"

His voice was tightly controlled, not angry but wary. There was also some concern. It was the concern that almost brought tears to my ears. He must have seen my emotion. "What is it, Jane? What's wrong?"

"There are things you need to know," I said, sliding along the couch until my back rested against the far arm.

Marcus sat down on the middle cushion, one hand resting on my leg. I thanked God I shaved as closely as I did as he moved his hand upward. "You're so silky and smooth," he said in a low voice. "And you smell fantastic." His hand caressed my inner thigh. "What's wrong, Jane? A few minutes ago you didn't care about anything but having sex and now you're acting like you're afraid. Is that it? You're afraid someone else will walk in?" He grinned wickedly. "This time we won't answer the door. We need to finish what we started. I saw that little toy of yours there under the desk. We could put it to good use. I assume you have some batteries around here somewhere?"

"Oh, n-n-no," I stammered. "It's not that. Well, yes, it is that. I'm afraid someone will find us, but that's not what has me most worried." My inherent honesty forced me say, "I have to admit, I find public sex very, very exciting. No, it's not that which has me worried." I pressed back against the couch arm as he lifted my skirt then slid his hand upward.

"What is it then?" He paused, concern obvious in his eyes. "You don't have anything to be afraid of, Jane. I'm healthy and I know you're smart enough to be healthy, too. No one can write like you can and not know about the risks. That's not it, is it?"

"Oh, no, no, that's not it." I was babbling but I couldn't stop. His fingers were creeping along my inner thigh and were just starting to touch me again. I was afraid if he got any closer I'd have an orgasm and wouldn't be able to tell him my shameful secret. He had to know. I might turn out to be a total klutz and not be the woman he wanted. I didn't want to disappoint him. I finally met his eyes. "I'm worried. I'm worried that I won't be right for you. Marcus, I don't want to disappoint you. I'm not very... experienced," I finished in a rush.

He looked perplexed. "Jane, you write those books."

I waved that aside. "I told you, I did research. I have a very, very good imagination. I did a lot of reading in the field beforehand and...I'm just not...experienced. I don't have much firsthand experience. Not much field experience." I nodded significantly at him. "*At all.*"

He absorbed my words. "What are you trying to say?"

"I—um—"

"Jane?" He leaned closer, moving so he was lying alongside me, one hand still tantalizingly close to my...moistness.

"I'm a virgin," I blurted it out then sagged back against the couch. "Well, kind of."

"What?"

The shock on his face would have been comical if it hadn't been tragic. I nodded dumbly.

"But you were married."

"Sort of." I wasn't sure if he was mad or—I couldn't interpret his expression. "Toby and I had sex but just once. Then he slept around so I didn't want to have sex with him because..." I saw Marcus' incredulous expression. "And there were a couple of other guys, but...it's been a long time and.. Marcus, I'm not at all like Tilda. I really don't know anything about...this."

Good Lord, I was crying. I felt like an idiot. I wanted to crawl into a hole and hide. He must think I was the worst kind of tease or, even more horrifying, he must think me a fool. I sniffled and peeked a glance at him.

His eyes were perplexed but compassionate. "It's all right, Jane," he murmured, enfolding me in a gentle hug. I heard the solid thunk of his heart against my ear. It felt so good to be held by him. The hairs on his chest tickled against my cheek, his warmth enfolding me. His muscles were big but gentle. He smelled great, like sweat and some kind of dusty, male smell that was exciting and comforting at the same time. "Here I was worried about whether I could live up to your expectations," he said with a soft laugh.

"Oh, not at all. I just felt you should know in case you were hoping for a, well, for a more experienced person." I took a deep breath. "I'm hoping you can teach me so much, Marcus."

He blew out a long sigh. "Why me?"

"You just seemed right for me." I pulled away to gaze at him. "Don't worry. I won't expect you to get serious about me or romantic or anything like that. I know that men prefer to be unencumbered— footloose and fancy-free, as it were. Just because we're..." I hesitated, searching for the right word, "...intimate doesn't mean I expect you to marry me." I kept my voice light-hearted so he would know I was joking about such a prospect.

"But what if I decide I want to?" he asked, his lips coming close to mine. His voice was teasing, as were his eyes.

"Oh." All breath left me at the thought. "Well, that's negotiable."

"It is, hmm?" He lowered his face. "What are the terms?"

"We can talk about that later, once we've had a chance to audition each other for the role." I gazed into his eyes. "Thank you."

"For what?"

"For not laughing."

"Oh, Jane." His lips were hovering over mine. "I'll never laugh at you."

Our lips met. I slid into a hot, erotic, dark pool of electrifying sensation. His hands were moving over my body. I tugged at his clothing until we were both stretched out, naked, on the couch. He extracted a condom from the pocket of his discarded pants.

"Can I do that?" I asked. I'd purchased condoms, of course, to see how they functioned and had even slid one on a kielbasa sausage to get a sense of its flexibility, but the idea of using one on a real man was exciting.

He handed the little foil packet to me. I hurriedly tore it open, then knelt beside him where he lay on his back, his penis jutting up into the air. I hesitated, looking at him for permission. He just smiled. "Please," he said softly.

"Are you begging?" I teased.

For answer, he pushed his hips upward. His erect penis slid against my hand. I clutched him, amazed at the palpitating thickness, the pulsing and the warmth. "Good Lord, it's so hard," I murmured, running my hand down his length. "Doesn't it hurt to get so hard?"

"Only when I don't get what I want," he said in a harsh voice, his fingers tweaking my nipple.

"Oh, I know what you mean," I murmured. I unrolled the condom along his length, slipping and sliding it downward. When finished, I smoothed it down with my hand. He drew in a breath.

"I think the first time I want to have you under me," he whispered, turning.

"The first time?" I asked, twisting so I was lying next to him.

He gently pushed me onto my back. I opened my legs so he could slide between them. Marcus leaned over me, propped on his elbows. "The first of many," he whispered as he positioned himself at my entrance.

I now had the firsthand experience to add that special *something* to my stories.

I'm sure you'll see the difference in my next book.

****

An hour later, I stretched languidly. I felt amazingly refreshed, sore, sexy, and wanton. Marcus lay beside me, sweat glistening on his body, his hair standing up in little white spikes. "For an inexperienced novice, you did pretty damn good, Jane," he said in a low voice.

"I had a good teacher," I replied, running my foot over his hard, hairy leg.

"I have to tell you, I almost laughed out loud when your boss said you have the highest performance rating of anybody in your department." He idly caressed my breast. "I'd give you the highest rating myself."

"Thank you, sir." I looked up into his laughing eyes. "Seriously, Marcus. Thank you. I'll never forget this."

His hand stilled. "Are you telling me to get lost or something?"

"Oh, no, not at all. It's just...well, I'm not gullible enough to believe that just because you had sex with me, there will be anything permanent." I smiled at him, but it appeared I hadn't assuaged his worries. He still frowned. "What I mean is, no matter how long this..." I searched for a word, finally settling for, "...relationship lasts, I'm grateful to you for giving me the chance to experience something so marvelous, firsthand. Not very many men would be anxious to be associated with an inexperienced spinster like me." I laughed nervously.

"You could say the same about me."

"Hmm?"

"I'm not college educated, I'm a blue-collar sort of guy, I'm not the sort of man a woman like you would want to be seen with."

I glared at him. "Who said that? Honestly, that's the silliest thing I've ever heard. What does it matter what kind of education you have? And—"

Marcus leaned over me, staring into my eyes. "Either you're the dumbest woman on the planet or you're the trickiest one."

"What?" I peered up at him, unsure what I was hearing.

He stared into my eyes until I blushed. He shook his head. "Dumb."

"I beg your pardon?" I struggled to sit up but he pushed me back onto the cushions.

"First of all, I love associating with a spinster like you," he said, his hand slipping lower to massage another portion of my anatomy. "Secondly, I'm grateful to you for the opportunity to experience something so marvelous." His fingers probed into my hot, willing body. "And thirdly..." He smiled, his eyes lighting with that mischievous humor I loved to see. "Thirdly, I sure as hell wish you'd shut up and show me some more tricks that Tilda knows."

"Really?" I was delighted. I was unsure about his recuperative powers, but his appendage was nudging me, so obviously he was up to the task. "I saw this in a film once," I whispered, moving so I straddled him. "I've always wanted to try it."

He did, too.

****

We spent another hour in erotic explorations, delighting each other with new discoveries. When we finally broke apart, my stomach rumbled, signaling the need for sustenance. He laughed when his stomach echoed the noise. "Care to go out for some food?" he asked, nuzzling into my neck then flicking little licks near my ear.

I shivered excitedly. "I think we should. I need to keep my strength up." I touched his turgid penis, now resting, exhausted, on his thigh. "And so do you."

He grinned. "Would fast food suit you?"

"Oh, yes." His penis stirred in my hand, growing firmer as we talked. "The faster the better, I think."

He laughed out loud as he pulled me to my feet, wrapping his arms around me to hug me tightly. "Your wish is my command, boss. There're a couple of places to eat not far from here. Let's go get our strength up."

As we dressed, Marcus tucked my new sex toy into my soft leather briefcase. "For later," he promised. "I'm thinking we should get together tonight and maybe experiment."

I thought of Robbie, wondering how I would manage that. Marcus, though, had the answer, even though it was a grim one. "If he can, your brother— or someone—should probably stay with Maggie Carlson tonight," he said as we walked outside. "I got word from the police in Pittsburgh. Scarlotti hasn't been seen since his release." He led the way to the nearby faculty parking lot. "Why don't you drive? Then you can bring me back to get my car. I have some things to do this afternoon, then I want to be with you tonight, if we can."

I nodded happily. "That sounds good to me." I touched the remote device for my car and the doors unlocked with a solid *clunk*. "Do you think Pat's here?"

Marcus nodded, his face sober. "I'd bet on it."

We slipped into the car. I turned down the

volume on Joe Cocker to prevent Marcus' hearing loss then I followed his directions to a nearby McDonald's. As we entered the establishment, I examined the bright, shining interior. "This will be a culinary adventure for me," I said, peering at the menu glowing above the waitperson who was poised at the cash register. "What's good here?"

Marcus turned to stare at me. "You've never eaten at a McDonald's?"

"I had some french fries once," I said, smiling at the young clerk whose bright earrings embellished his left ear. "Oh, that looks like fun. I'll have that." I pointed to an item on the menu.

"Uh..." The clerk hesitated, his jaw slightly agape. "That's for kids."

"Oh, can't I have it? It sounds like just the right amount of food for me. And it comes with a toy." I smiled at him. "Please?"

He glanced around as though unsure of the rules, then shrugged. "One Happy Meal, coming up. And you?" He glanced at Marcus, who was staring at me as though I'd fallen from another star.

"Number 2 meal," Marcus said, pulling out his wallet to pay. I took the proffered drink cup then examined the beverage machine, finally settling on an iced tea for myself. Our food was prepared very quickly. Marcus took the tray, leading the way to a booth in the corner.

I examined the Happy Meal, intrigued by the toy, apparently a marketing promotion for an upcoming film. I didn't recognize the small superhero, but it wore a cheery blue and red costume emblazoned with a large spider. Its limbs bent in several amazing positions with a flexibility that indicated the athleticism of the tiny hero. I found, to my delight, it was capable of flinging small round pellets—which came in an attached pouch—quite a far distance. I put it away after verifying that it worked properly, thinking I might practice with it later. It promised to be a big hit with my cats.

I tested the food, deciding it was bland but digestible. As I nibbled, I caught Marcus' expression. "What's wrong?" I asked, dabbing a french fry in the ketchup he squirted into a little paper cup and set on the table.

"I don't know if I've ever met anyone quite like you, Jane," he said with a smile.

"Well, we're all unique," I pointed out. I toyed with the fried potato strip, anxious to pursue our previous topic of conversation. "You think Pat's in town?"

Marcus bit with gusto into his rather messy hamburger, chewing for a moment before speaking. "I filled Sam in on what's going on. He promised to pass around Scarlotti's photo and to ask patrol to keep an eye out for the guy. And I gave him your description of the car that almost ran you off the road." His forehead creased in a frown. "I'm worried about you. I'm not convinced it's just Maggie this crazy asshole is after."

"I'm more concerned about Maggie," I assured him. "Pat's obsessed with her."

"Maybe, but—"

"There's nothing we can do about it," I said. "I'll be careful, I promise."

"Well there's only way to make sure you'll be okay." He pointed a french fry at me. "When you go back to work, lock that door. And when you're ready to go, call me. I don't want you alone tonight. I think you should stay with me."

"I have to go home tonight," I protested. "Ezra needs his pill and I have to touch base with Robbie."

Marcus considered that then said, "Call me. I'll escort you there, you can pack a bag, then you're spending the night with me."

"What about Robbie?"

He touched my hand. "Robbie will just have to get used to the idea that you and I are an item, Jane. He's a big kid. I think he'll manage." Then he winked. "If your plans work out, he'll want to spend the night with Maggie, anyway."

"My plans?" I asked innocently.

He smiled warmly at me. "I know a matchmaker when I see one." He held up a hand when I tried to remonstrate. "I was serious. I think someone should be with her. I've got a bad feeling about Pat Scarlotti. I've met his type before. They act first then think later." Marcus shook his head. "We need to stay on our toes."

"I agree." I smiled at him, feeling somewhat shy. "I'd like to spend the evening with you, Marcus." I stopped, not sure how to describe the warm, delightful feeling such a thought gave me.

"What?" he prompted.

"I've enjoyed myself so much," I said in a rush. "I'm looking forward to more."

He picked up my hand, squeezing it gently. "So am I, Jane. Many more, I hope."

I sighed with happiness. Things were going just as I planned.

Chapter 12

I have to admit I accomplished little in the way of scholastic endeavors in the afternoon. After dropping Marcus off at his car, I wandered back to my office, where I locked the door, flopped down in my chair, and daydreamed. Most of the dreams were based on the memory of the amazing hours I spent with him. I hadn't realized that intimate adventures could be so fulfilling, so satisfying. I felt as though not only my body was now experienced, but my heart was, too. This was what it was like to have a real relationship, to have affection mingled with passion, to have passion mixed with respect. It was...

I hesitated to voice it, even in my deepest thoughts.

It was like being in love.

I pushed that notion away. Marcus Sloan wasn't in love with me and I wasn't in love with him. I was, perhaps, infatuated because of the morning we'd spent together, but love? It would take more than a day or two for me to fall in love. It would certainly take longer than that for him. He was an experienced man, one who'd undoubtedly had many lovers and relationships. It was understandable I might mistake passion for love, but Marcus never would. I resolved not to get within a proverbial mile of the topic, lest he think I was striving for something I couldn't have. I didn't want to be considered a grasping, needy female.

My phone rang an hour or so after I sat down and began daydreaming. It was, yet again, Declan Fabersham. "Miss Renard, have you had a chance to talk to the police yet?" he said after a brief, perfunctory identifying phrase.

"No, I haven't. As I told you—"

"I'd like to know what the delay is."

"And I'd like to know how you got this phone number," I snapped, angry he'd shattered my romantic mood.

There was a brief pause. "I had my people research Toby's first wife."

His people. The man sounded like a cheap film mogul. "As I told you, I have no influence with the police."

"Thank you." He hung up without further ado. I fumed briefly then resolved to allow nothing to impair the euphoric feeling that encased me. I settled back to more daydreaming.

At three o'clock, Marcus called. "Ready to go yet?" he asked.

I grew damp just at the sound of his voice. It would have been embarrassing if it hadn't been so exciting. "Yes, I am. I'm not getting much accomplished here."

He laughed softly. "I know the feeling. I keep getting distracted by thoughts of a certain someone." He paused then said, "I haven't felt this way for a long time."

I asked tentatively, "Like what?"

"Oh, you know. Sort of...anticipating."

I heard voices behind him then realized he was speaking in a public place. "I know. I feel exactly the same way."

"I'll be there in a few minutes. Wait for me by your car, okay?"

"Yes. Thank you for watching out for me."

"My pleasure, believe me. I'll see you soon."

I stuffed my poor briefcase full of papers, jamming them on top of the new sex toy. Just as I was leaving, the phone rang. I hesitated, unwilling to be delayed. Then I decided it might be Robbie, or Maggie, so I answered.

It was The Breather. "Have fun today?" he asked in a low, mocking voice.

My euphoric feeling evaporated. "What?" I leaned against the desk, trembling.

"I heard you. I was waiting to talk to you and I heard you. You two should be quieter. These doors aren't soundproof, you know."

Oh. My. God. Someone had been there, eavesdropping? Someone was at my door? What would have happened if Marcus hadn't been there? "Who is this?" I demanded, my voice quavering. "What do you want?"

He gave a low laugh. "You know what I want. I want what he had from you today. And I'll have it soon."

The loud sound of a dial tone filled my head like the buzzing of angry bees. I barely managed to shove the receiver back on the hook. I looked frantically around the office—should I call Marcus? I had no idea where I put his phone number. Should I call the police? What should I do?

Flee. I snatched up my briefcase, clasping it against my chest as I hurtled through the hall, down the stairs and out the door to the parking lot. I sobbed with relief when I saw Marcus, leaning against my Benz. I stumbled to a halt in front of him, tears streaming down my face.

"Jane, what is it?" He put his arms around me

as I dropped my briefcase to the ground. "Honey, what happened, what is it?"

I leaned against him, feeling safe and protected. "Someone called again," I managed to choke out. "He said—" I gulped and said, "He's following me. He was listening outside the door. He said—" I hiccupped then said, "He said he'd have me soon."

"What?"

Poor Marcus. He sounded so bewildered. I pulled away from him, telling him about the previous calls and the one just moments before. He smoothed his hands across my shoulders as I talked. When I finished, he enfolded me in an embrace again, his solid warmth comforting and secure. "It won't happen, Jane," he murmured against my hair as he held me. "Don't worry about it, honey. It won't happen."

"It was so...crude," I said around another hiccup. Crying and hiccupping always went hand in hand with me. It was an embarrassing aspect of my physiology. "I can't believe someone was outside, skulking in the hall, eavesdropping on us."

His arms tightened around me. "We'll take care of it, don't worry."

I pried myself away from him, swiping at the tears cascading down my cheeks. I didn't even want to consider what my appearance might be like. It was probably horrendous. "I can't believe I'm afraid of something so trivial. After what Maggie went through, this is nothing."

Marcus put an arm around my shoulders, steering me toward the Benz. "You have a right to be afraid," he said softly. "That's what perverts rely on, your fear." He gave me a little shake. "He just wasn't counting on having me around."

"You're right. I won't let it frighten me." I retrieved my briefcase, attempting to pry a tissue out without unhinging the entire contents. "Will you follow me home?" I sounded whiney, but I couldn't help myself. That leering voice on the phone unnerved me.

"Yep. Drop me off at my car. I had to park in the visitor's lot. And drive slow enough for me to stay behind you."

I laughed shakily. We drove to the nearby visitor's lot where he got into his Honda. To be honest, I was thankful to have some time alone to compose myself. Marcus must think me a nervous Nellie, prone to vapors and irrational fears. So what if some fool got his kicks from calling me and making nasty innuendos? It was like a teenage prank, one of those "I saw what you did and I know who you are" jokes which so titillated us in our youth and now seemed childish. Still, it bothered me enough that I took the back roads home, avoiding the busy freeway as much as possible. It was more restful to drive on the two-lane county blacktops. Plus it gave me a chance to speed to the roaring blast of Led Zeppelin, something the clogged interstate didn't allow. When we arrived at my house I was renewed and able to put my fears behind me. I noticed that Robbie's rental car, a silver Mustang, was absent.

"That was exciting," Marcus commented as we went into my house.

"What?"

"Our little adventure in law-breaking."

"Oh, that." I waved it away. "It's perfectly safe to go sixty on those roads. And I went through the lights on yellow. That's legal."

Ezra emerged from his nap-spot, demanding his treat. Marcus watched as I stuffed a pill down the calico throat then doled out the noxious smelling Tuna Treats.

"You've got him trained, hmm?" he asked. "Give him a pill, give him a treat."

I dished out an appalling-looking mass of cat

food for William, plunking his dish on the floor next to his brother. "It's debatable who has whom trained." I walked into the sun porch, Marcus following behind.

"You have a nice house but it's too isolated," Marcus said, putting his arms around me.

I leaned back into his solid, masculine strength. "Too isolated for what?"

"To keep an eye on you." He turned me in his arms. "I guess that just means I'll need to stick close to you in order to make sure you're safe." He bent his head toward mine.

We both heard the car at the same time. I glanced out the sun porch window to see Robbie pulling into the driveway. "Here comes big brother," I said with a sigh.

Marcus kissed me quickly. "Let me handle this."

"Marcus, I don't think that's such—" I was talking to empty space. He'd already gone into the kitchen to intercept Robbie. I considered intervening but the warm sun filtering in the room made me drowsy, as did the sight of Ezra, stretched out luxuriously on the floor in a patch of light, bathing. I imagined I felt like him, sated, happy, complete, and smug in the knowledge that more treats would be forthcoming, if I was only patient.

Male voices got louder as they approached the porch. I dropped into a wicker chair and crossed my legs, a sandal dangling off my foot, the picture of the relaxed, happy homeowner. Robbie paused as he came into the room. "Jane, I'd like to talk with you alone," he said without preamble.

I peered behind him to Marcus, who was glaring at Robbie's back. "Of course." I met Marcus' eyes, hoping he could see my emotions in my expression. "Give us a minute, Marcus."

He stared at me for a long moment then nodded, going back out to the kitchen. "Problems, Robbie?" I asked sweetly. My brother sank into a chair next to me. He was disheveled and I belatedly remembered that he had played golf with his cronies. "How did the golf match go?"

Robbie ran a hand over his cropped, springy curls. I noticed with a pang he was gray at the temples. I suddenly wanted, more than anything, to see him happy and settled. Robbie deserved that. I touched his hand. "It's all right."

He smiled ruefully. "I can't help being a brother, Jane. I'm worried you'll be hurt."

"It's part of living," I said. "Part of—" I stopped myself but not before he guessed my intended words.

"Part of loving?" He shook his head. "I don't want him to hurt you. You're so inexperienced, Jane."

I smiled at this gentle assessment of my character. "I trust Marcus, Robbie. You should, too." I sat up straighter in the chair. "Now, on to important things. Marcus?" I called out.

He appeared in the doorway almost immediately. I wondered how much he overheard. I decided not to worry about that. "About Maggie?" I prompted.

Robbie's attention zeroed in on me. "What about her?"

"We feel it's important someone stay with her in the evenings." I dangled my sandal, hoping I looked as though this was an impulsive thought. "It's not enough that the two boys are with her. Pat has made them a target, too. No, we need someone to be there until we can be certain of Pat's whereabouts. Marcus is afraid Pat is on his way here, if not already here. I tend to agree, especially because I saw Vito." I scowled at the memory. "*O lov tai o beng nashti beshen patshasa.*"

Robbie nodded agreement. I translated for Marcus' benefit: "'Neither money nor the devil can remain in peace.' Vito won't have peace because he feels Maggie's dishonored the family." I turned to Robbie. "I don't want her to suffer again, Robbie. It's not fair."

He and Marcus exchanged a long, evaluating stare then Robbie nodded. "As long as you're taken care of, I can take care of Maggie."

I leapt to my feet and hugged him. "Oh, Robbie. Thank you. You don't know what this means to me. I've been so worried about Maggie."

He put a gentle hand over my mouth, silencing me. "Ush-hay. Iway oknay."

"Ou'reyay ethay estbay otherbray away irlgay everway adhay." I hugged him then glanced at Marcus.

His eyes were narrowed in concentration. When he saw my glance, he said sheepishly, "It's been a long time since I spoke Pig Latin. You're the best...brother...a girl...ever had?"

I abandoned Robbie and hugged Marcus. "Exactly! I didn't know you spoke Igpay AtinLay."

He gave a shrug then settled his arm around my shoulder. "Doesn't everybody?" He looked past me to Robbie, who was regarding us with a little smile. "I'll take care of her. I know e'sshay oneway inway away illionmay."

I blushed. One in a million? How sweet.

My brother got to his feet. "I know when I'm not wanted."

I felt guilty. Here Robbie had come out to see me on vacation and I was kicking him out of my house. I started to speak but he laughed. "I'm teasing, Jane. Don't worry about it. Why don't you call Maggie while I shower and make sure it's okay if I see her tonight? I don't want to step in where I'm not wanted."

Marcus chuckled. "Would Jane do that to you?"

"Don't make me answer that," Robbie said as he

left the room. He gestured to me. "Come show me which towels to use."

"You know which ones—" Marcus shoved me and I glared at him. "What?"

"Your brother wants some quiet conversation with you," he said. "Go. I'll explore the kitchen to see if there's any of those pierogies left."

"Oh, yes, there are," I said. "Top shelf in the fridge."

"Go. Let me make dinner." Marcus gestured me off after Robbie, who was striding down the hallway to the bedrooms. "Talk to your brother, honey."

"Oh, all right." I trailed after Robbie to the guest bedroom where he awaited me. "I wish you wouldn't worry so much."

Robbie sank onto the bed. "Jane, your husband has been murdered, a strange man is romancing you, your best friend is being stalked by a maniac, and you're being blackmailed by a fan who thinks you're the hottest erotica writer today."

I opened my mouth to protest but couldn't object to such a succinct summary of my circumstances.

"I have every reason to be worried," he said gently, tugging me to sit next to him on the bed. "The only thing I have any control over is the man who's romancing you. I told you what his brother said. What if it turns out that Marcus Sloan is just using you to relive past memories of an old love?"

Robbie's concern was touching but I had no answers. "I don't know," I said honestly, putting my head on his shoulder. "If he is, there's nothing I can do about it except hope the new memories he has with me will obliterate the old ones he's so fond of. What else can I do?"

He sighed then gave me a brisk squeeze of the shoulders. "I don't know, either. I just hate to see you hurt, that's all."

"Believe me, I'm doing my best to guarantee that

doesn't happen. Marcus and I are just two ships passing in the night. We've had no declarations of love or commitment. This is just a summer fling. Neither of us is getting involved."

"I don't believe you."

I nudged him in the ribs so he released me. "Believe me. Now let me call Maggie to verify your presence would be welcome tonight. I don't know what we'll do if she says she doesn't want you there." He appeared so woebegone I laughed. "I'm sure it won't happen. Go and pretty yourself for your date." I sprang to my feet and headed for the door.

"Jane?"

I glanced over my shoulder at Robbie.

"You know if you need me, I'm here for you."

I nodded, teary. "I know, Robbie. Thanks." I left before he could see my misty eyes. I went to my den. I called Maggie, ascertaining she would be home that evening and would welcome my brother's company.

"Are you sure, Jane?" she asked doubtfully. "Surely he has other things he'd rather do."

"No, he doesn't," I interrupted firmly, alarmed by the sounds erupting from my kitchen. "He doesn't and I am. Please, Maggie. He does so want to help."

"Well, if you're sure he doesn't mind and—"

"Excellent. He'll be there soon. Talk to you later." I hung up the phone then hurried into the kitchen where Marcus was dirtying an amazing amount of pots and pans. "What are you doing?" I asked, standing in the doorway, surveying the carnage.

"Making dinner," he said imperturbably. "Fixing something fit for a queen."

I was flattered but dismayed by the quantity of dishware being employed. "But we could just heat up something in the microwave."

"Here." He thrust a glass of wine into my hands.

"Go set the dining table. We'll eat in there tonight, not the kitchen."

I beat a hasty retreat, going to the dining room to pull out my china plates. I set the table, supervised by William. His head poked up over the edge of the table as he regarded me quizzically, as though to ask why I was disturbing a perfectly good nap spot for something as mundane as food partaking.

Marcus emerged from the kitchen, setting several plates with a flourish on the trivets I hastily set out to prevent the mahogany table from being marred. I inspected the dishes: hot leftover pierogies in some sort of cream sauce, warmed creamed onions, a platter of cold chicken and ham, sliced bread, reheated scalloped potatoes. "A feast," I said admiringly as I lifted my wine in a salute.

"We need to keep our strength up," he said in a low voice as he clicked his beer mug against my glass.

Robbie came into the room, pausing as he saw the repast that was spread out. "I put some aside for you," Marcus said, gesturing toward the kitchen with a jerk of his thumb. "Just a little something to take to Miss Carlson, to show your appreciation to her for letting you be with her this evening."

Robbie ducked into the kitchen, returning with one of my baskets packed with dishes and an impromptu bouquet of flowers sticking out of one end.

"I hope you don't mind," Marcus said to me as he ladled out creamed onions onto my plate. "I just nipped off a few daisies and some other things from the garden."

"I don't mind at all," I said warmly, smiling at Robbie's astonished expression. "It was an excellent idea, Marcus. Thank you."

"Yeah. Thanks," Robbie smiled at me. "You two

have a good evening." He started to sidle toward the door.

"We shall, I'm sure." I bit into the pierogies, sighing as the cream sauce blended with the spicy meat inside. "What is this sauce?" I asked Marcus.

He waved a hand. "Just something I cooked up. An old family recipe." He winked at Robbie. "Fit for a queen."

Robbie laughed. "Glad to know it. You know where to reach me if I'm needed."

I waved him good-bye. The door had barely closed behind him when Marcus said, "I hope you brought your toy home with you. I've been thinking about what we can do with it."

"Really?" I asked, my heart starting to skip an erratic beat.

He smiled slowly. "Yep. I found a great spot out in the garden. Just you, me, a blanket on the grass, some wine and a few size D batteries. I think we could have some fun."

"You know," I said thoughtfully, "when I picked that up, I thought I wouldn't have a need for it. I was hoping to have the real thing to keep me company tonight."

He chuckled. "You will, Jane. Trust me, you will. But I'd like to show you a really, really good time and I'm not sure I'm up to the amount of performances it'll take to make you happy. I don't object to a substitute as long as I get to wield it."

I reached over to touch his hand. "There is no substitute for you, Marcus."

His eyes met mine as he smiled. "Glad to know that."

Chapter 13

The sound of a ringing phone awakened me. I peered blearily at the clock on the bedside table, which read 6:05. I presumed it meant 'a.m.'. The phone rang again. Someone moaned next to me, stirring in bed. I turned onto my side, startled, then remembered. Marcus was with me.

"Where's the light?" he asked, sitting upright.

I switched on the bedside lamp. He blinked in the light, fumbling for something on the floor. His clothing. He plucked a cell phone from a pocket and opened it. "Sloan," he muttered, dragging a hand over his hair.

I evaluated him in the early morning light. His cheeks were heavily stubbled with beard and his hair stood up in little tangled spikes. For a man who'd had a very athletic night, he looked remarkably rested.

"No, I don't think so," he said into the phone. He glanced at me where I lay sprawled on my stomach beside him in the bed. "I doubt if she does." He listened further then said, "Okay. Call me later." He snapped the phone closed then tossed it back on the floor.

"What was that?" I asked as he slipped between

the sheets to settle next to me in the bed.

"Lisa Considine's gone missing." He ran a hand down my arm where it rested outside the sheet. "Sam wanted to know if you might have talked to her lately."

"Lisa...?" Then I remembered. "Toby's other wife?"

Marcus nodded. I was conscious of his alert gaze evaluating me as I spoke. I wasn't sure what to make of that. "I only talked to her that once, at the police station," I said around a yawn. "I don't think she's disposed to be very chummy with me."

He smiled, running his hand under the sheet to touch my breast. "I'd like to be chummy."

"You were very chummy last night," I chided him. He looked contrite until I laughed. "I enjoyed it. But I am the tiniest bit sore today."

He leaned over to kiss me quickly. "I'm sorry. I guess I went a bit overboard."

"Perhaps." I ran my hand down his body, fastening on his burgeoning erection. "How are you today?"

He waggled his eyebrows at me. "Fit as a fiddle and ready to play."

"Hmm." I pushed him onto his back as I tugged down the sheet to view his hardening body. "I think I know just the tune."

As my lips fastened on him, he gasped my name. I smiled smugly. That was just the song I wanted to hear.

****

A couple of hours later we emerged from the shower, all scrubbed and ready to face the day. I was just contemplating my refrigerator and breakfast possibilities when Marcus' cell phone rang again. He smiled apologetically and answered it, one hand still caressing my shoulder as I poured some orange juice.

"No, she hasn't," he said into the phone. He sipped the juice, watching me as I picked up the coffeepot, making occasional comments to the speaker, presumably his brother. Before he hung up, he said, "We'll get there as soon as we can. I need to call her brother first." I heard an angry noise from the phone then Marcus snapped, "Live with it, Sam. See you in an hour." He closed the phone with a snap, jamming it back into his pocket.

He took the coffeepot from me and set it on the counter. "No time for that," he said quietly. "Lisa Considine was found dead on TUSP campus, not far from your office. We need to go to the police station."

Oh my God. That poor woman. Then my stomach sank. First Toby and now his wife were dead. What was going on? "That poor woman," I said. "How did she die?"

He hesitated. "Sam's not sure. He said it looks like natural causes."

"Poor woman," I repeated. "She seemed so young, too. Why are we needed at the police station? Surely her stepson can identify the body." I looked at Marcus.

Instead of answering my question, he asked one of his own. "Can you call Robbie and ask him to meet us there? I don't have Maggie Carlson's number handy." He moved away from me to pick up one of the glasses of juice I poured.

A gentle prodding of suspicion started gathering in my brain. "Marcus, what's wrong? Why should Robbie meet us there?"

He met my eyes but I couldn't read any emotion there. "It might be wise to have your lawyer present."

"What?" I almost choked on my orange juice. "Why? I barely know the woman. Are you implying I killed her? Do you think I would do that? For heaven's sake, when could I have done it? We were together almost the whole time. And you're a cop—or rather an ex-cop. Are you telling me you—you—you did things all night with me and now suspect I'm a killer?" Outrage was making me sputter, as well as my misdirected orange juice.

"The police just want to have everyone involved in your husband's murder questioned." His gaze shifted away. His evasive manner angered me.

"You didn't answer my question, Marcus. Do you think I'm capable of that?"

He wouldn't meet my outraged gaze. "Let's just go talk to the police, Jane."

"Why should we bother? You're acting like a cop right now. I can just give you my statement." I stomped out of the kitchen into the den where my portable phone was located. I pressed Maggie's speed-dial number. Robbie answered with, "Carlson residence."

"Robbie, it's Jane. I need you to meet me at the St. Paul police department. Lisa Considine is dead. They think I did it."

"Jane—" Marcus said from the doorway.

I shot him a venom-filled look. "Please meet me there. Mr. Sloan feels I need a lawyer present." Then I hesitated. "Is Maggie okay? Can you leave?"

"She's fine." I could almost hear the gears whirling in Robbie's brain as we talked. "Someone is coming to drop her and Perry at work. Aaron said someone else would come later, to make sure Ian gets to work okay. I'll meet you in St. Paul. Can you tell me what's going on?"

I glared at Marcus. "I wish I knew. Just meet me there." I slammed down the phone then snatched up my handbag, stuffing in a few personal items from my briefcase. "Let's go," I snapped. "You can follow me to make sure I don't abscond."

"You're being unreasonable," Marcus said as we walked to the front door.

"I'm being unreasonable?" I almost shouted. "For heaven's sake, you almost accused me of murder. You're thinking like a cop, Marcus, not a man—" I shut my mouth quickly, afraid I'd let something slip that would be irretrievable. "Not a man who knows me," I finished.

"I was a cop, Jane, for almost twenty-five years. It's a hard habit to break." He paused by his car, parked behind mine. "Don't blame me for that."

I almost softened at the distressed look in his eyes then stiffened my resolve. The man just spent almost an entire night making love to me. Didn't that count for something? He and I were together almost the entire previous day. There was no way I could kill Lisa Considine. I simply, physically, could not have done it.

I waited for him to back out behind me. I tapped the tiny spider-hero dangling from my rear view mirror, causing it to spin wildly. I knew how he felt. I had tucked his small projectiles into the ashtray and I fleetingly wished they were life-sized so I could lob them at Marcus Sloan as he drove behind me. To calm myself, I slipped Pink Floyd into the CD player. I needed a distraction.

Halfway to town my thoughts finally quieted. I had no reason to be angry with Marcus. As I told Robbie, he and I were just strangers passing in the night. Marcus' willingness to consider my guilt reaffirmed that. I had no right to be hurt or upset. I was just a woman he slept with. I wasn't someone he cared about.

I suddenly remembered the 'lost love,' the elusive Mary whom Sam Sloan had mentioned. I obviously didn't have the status in Marcus' affections that Miss Madison, or Malone, or whatever her name was had. I was just a substitute and a poor one at that.

I swiped at a tear that trickled down my cheek

then turned up the volume on "Comfortably Numb," wishing I were in the state the song described. By the time we got the police station, I had my emotions under control and was icily calm. I had succeeded in putting my entire sexual escapade into perspective. Marcus Sloan was just a man who provided me with a great deal of first-hand research for my books. That was all.

"Jane, I'm sorry if I hurt your feelings," he said as we walked through the parking garage. "I never meant to imply you—"

"Yes, you did," I snapped, cutting off his further apologies. "Too little, too late, Marcus." I maintained a frosty silence as we rode up in the elevator to the fifth floor, where I found Robbie and the large Mr. Armstrong awaiting me. I went into Robbie's embrace willingly, anxious to leave Marcus behind.

Sam Sloan joined us in the elevator foyer with a grim, almost angry, expression on his craggy face. "This way," was all he said, gesturing down the hall. As we started to follow him, he glanced back at Marcus. "Not you."

Marcus stopped abruptly. "What?"

"Not you. We just need to talk to her." Lt. Sloan continued walking. I followed, trailed by Mr. Armstrong and Robbie. I glanced back once. Marcus was standing there, staring at us with an angry expression on his face.

We were escorted into a small room that smelled of body odor and recycled air. Several battered chairs sat around an equally battered table. I noticed metal rings attached to the floor, which struck me as odd. I seated myself with Robbie and Mr. Armstrong on either side of me while Sam Sloan sat across from me.

"I appreciate you coming here to answer questions," Lt. Sloan said. He didn't sound at all appreciative, though. He sounded, as usual, grumpy and angry.

"We're always happy to cooperate with the police," Mr. Armstrong said smoothly. He was impeccably dressed in a three-piece charcoal gray suit with a sedate dark purple tie. The elegant cut of his clothing did nothing to hide his formidable bulk. In fact, it emphasized it.

Lt. Sloan eyed him for an instant then turned his attention back to me. "Where were you yesterday, in the afternoon?"

"And why are you asking?" I demanded.

Mr. Armstrong covered my hand with his, squeezing it gently. "Let me ask the questions, Jane," he said softly. He turned his attention to Lt. Sloan. "Why is that pertinent?"

Lt. Sloan tapped a pencil on the table, apparently deep in thought. "Time of death is placed between noon and four, yesterday afternoon," he finally said.

I started to speak but Mr. Armstrong squeezed my hand again. "And why do we care?"

"We're questioning everyone involved in Toby Considine's death, including your client."

Billy looked at me and nodded. "I was at campus," I said. "I had lunch around one o'clock then I was in my office until three or four."

"Can anyone verify that?" Sloan asked.

I raised my chin defiantly. "I had lunch with your brother then he picked me up later in the afternoon. But no, no one can verify I was in my office the rest of the time." I slid a sidelong glance at Robbie, who looked calm. Reassured, I asked, "Where was Mrs. Considine killed?" Using her married name was the least I could do for the poor woman.

Sloan looked surprised. "We haven't determined that yet."

"I see." I was thinking furiously, considering and

discarding ideas. "Where was she found? Marcus said she was found on campus."

"Jane."

Robbie's voice was very low but it had the effect of shutting me up immediately. He looked at Sloan. "It's a good question. Where was she found? And what was the cause of death?"

Sloan remained still, the pencil poised in mid-tap. "We'd rather not release the information just now."

"It had to be somewhere isolated if she was killed in the afternoon," I pointed out reasonably. "Campus isn't busy at this time of year but there are construction people about." I stopped then said, "Construction—they recently finished renovations to Merrill Hall but now are working at Webster Hall, where we were temporarily housed. Is that it?"

Sam Sloan looked annoyed that I had, perhaps, stumbled on information he and his cronies wished to keep private. "I'm not discussing that at this time."

"I see." Robbie stood up, as did Mr. Armstrong. After a brief hesitation, I joined them. "Then we'll be leaving. When you have reasonable cause to talk to my sister, we'll return."

"Mr. Renard."

Robbie paused. I almost ran into him but stopped myself in time. Mr. Armstrong, behind me, was a very large, hard presence.

Sloan looked at me then at my brother, apparently coming to some decision. "It appears Mrs. Considine was drugged then possibly died of an injection. We found traces of barbiturates in her saliva and a recent needle mark on her arm."

"My fictional assassin, Tilda, has used various drugs in her work," I said. "It's quite easy to obtain information about—"

"Jane."

I once again recognized that fraternal tone of voice. I closed my mouth. Robbie proceeded toward the door. I followed behind.

As I was leaving, Lt. Sloan said, "Miss Renard?"

I looked back at him.

"Leave my brother out of this."

Before Robbie or Mr. Armstrong could stop me, I strode across the room to glare down at the surprised police officer. "Your brother *is* out of this, Lt. Sloan." I whirled and followed my brother and my attorney out of the room.

I brushed by Marcus, standing in the hall. He took one glance at my angry face then went into the room I just left, slamming the door. I started to stalk to the elevators, but Robbie restrained me with a hand on my shoulder. "Wait here," he said quietly, edging me toward a small nook down the hall from the room where I was interrogated. "We'll be right back." Before I could protest, he and Billy Armstrong were gone, talking in low voices.

I leaned against the wall, realizing I was in a phone alcove. Prisoners were probably allowed their one phone call there, I thought, looking at the grimy device. I heard the angry murmur of voices in the room next to me and wondered if Marcus and his brother were arguing again. I considered going into Lurk Mode then decided against it. I wasn't sure I wanted to know what was going on.

I couldn't believe how things had gone awry. Just a few hours ago I was enjoying sex with a man whom I was, admittedly, infatuated with. Now here I was, a suspect in a murder investigation and the man for whom I...harbored feelings considered me a suspect.

The door down the hall opened. I heard Sam Sloan say angrily, "You're letting your feelings get in the way, Marc. She may be a dead ringer for Mary, but she's not an innocent victim like Mary."

Marcus' response was muffled. He was still in the room while Sam must have been standing at the door. I stuffed myself into the little alcove, abandoning my hesitation and sliding into Lurk Mode as though it was second nature to me, which it was fast becoming.

"Oh, yeah?" Sam Sloan's voice was challenging. "She speaks a bunch of different languages, she's educated, she's got red hair, she's smart, she's in a professional job, she's small, she needs your help. How many other ways can she be like Madison? You're full of crap."

"None of that matters!" I heard Marcus shout. Then the door slammed again and both voices were muffled.

I left my lurk location to hurry down the hall, unable to stay there any longer and hear my suspicions confirmed. As I neared the elevator, it opened and Declan Fabersham emerged. The man looked pale, his lithe body drooping with weariness. Even his sun-bleached hair seemed somehow less brilliant than it had just days previously.

"Mr. Fabersham," I said in sympathy. "I'm so sorry for your loss."

He looked perplexed for a moment. "Why are you here?"

"Apparently the officials are discussing your stepmother's death with anyone affiliated with Toby." I had a hard time keeping the scorn out of my voice. It would serve no purpose for me to disclose my true opinion of the intelligence of law enforcement.

"I see." He looked around, appearing lost.

"I believe the investigating people are in that direction." I pointed back the way I'd come as Robbie emerged from a nearby doorway, his face pale.

"We have to go," he said, taking my arm. Mr. Armstrong joined us, looking equally grim.

"What is it? What's wrong?" I twisted, trying to see behind me where the door to the interrogation room was opening. I caught a glimpse of Marcus and Sam Sloan as they came out, still arguing heatedly. Then the elevator arrived. Robbie dragged me inside.

"Maggie and Perry were in a car accident," he said, punching a button angrily. "They're on the way to the hospital."

****

I was in a nightmare and there was no waking up.

Robbie rode with me to the hospital, located near the police station. Mr. Armstrong did not appear there, presumably off on some errand of his own or perhaps to do work for Robbie. I wasn't sure which.

When we got to the hospital it took precious moments to find where the accident victims were being treated. We found them in the emergency area, in a trauma unit. We were unable to obtain any information until a very panicked Ian arrived. He indicated we were part of the family. A large man, introduced as 'Saul, sent by Uncle Vanya,' escorted him.

Once our credentials were established, we settled down to wait. We had a preliminary report that Maggie and Perry were driving on busy 98th Street, a major thoroughfare in Bloomington, where Maggie lived. A car ran a red light and hit them.

"But Aaron was supposed to send someone," Robbie said as he paced the waiting room. He glanced at the guard who had escorted Ian.

Saul nodded. He looked like my idea of a prizefighter, complete with the bulbous nose, large ears, and lack of neck on his hulking shoulders. "We found him. He said when he got there she was already gone."

"Why would she do that?" I asked, bewildered.

Ian spoke up. "Mom got a call from Aaron. He said to go ahead. He said Dad—Pat—was found and we were safe." He looked terrified, angry, and so upset. He also looked far younger than his eighteen years. "I was going to take off, but Saul didn't like it." Ian looked up at the big man, gratitude evident on his youthful face. "We were just getting ready to leave when the hospital called."

I put an arm around my godson's shoulders. "You couldn't have known," I said in consolation. "We just didn't plan for that."

"Shit," Robbie snapped. "She should have called me."

"You were busy with me," I said. "This was all such unfortunate timing."

"I can't believe it's coincidence," Robbie said angrily, resuming his pacing.

I shook my head. "Not coincidence. It's just luck on Pat's part. He probably had someone watching. When you left, he acted spontaneously."

It was almost an hour before a doctor emerged with his report. Perry had a broken leg and ribs, caused when a car hit them on his side. Maggie was badly bruised with a mild concussion. Her air bag had deployed, though, saving her from serious injury. "They were both very lucky," the doctor said, his tired face reflecting his concern. "They were going at a low rate of speed. We'd like to keep Miss Carlson under observation today then she can be released. We'll keep her son for at least two days, possibly longer, depending on how he does." He left after telling us we could visit Maggie very shortly.

Robbie and I exchanged a look. "He planned this," Robbie said in a low voice.

The giant Saul, sitting nearby, nodded. "It splits you up. Makes it harder to guard."

I looked at him in surprise. I hadn't thought him capable of such reasoning. He was right, though.

This accident meant Perry would be in the hospital while Maggie and Ian would, hopefully, soon be home. I immediately made a mental promise they would not be going home alone. If necessary, I would stand guard at their house all night.

Apparently Saul felt as I did. He stood, towering over us. "I got some calls to make." He went out of the waiting room, pulling out a cell phone as he went.

Chapter 14

The day passed in a blur. I called Kathy, informing her of Maggie's status. She came to the hospital at noon, bringing flowers, balloons and an unflagging optimism I found cheering. Maggie was groggy from the drugs but somewhat coherent. I was able to sit with her while Kathy visited. Typical of Maggie, she was concerned about the boys. Kathy and I were able to put her mind at ease, assuring her they were taken care of. When Kathy left I relinquished my seat to Robbie then went to sit with Perry, who had Ian by his bedside.

Dusk was starting to fall before we could take Maggie home, Ian in anxious attendance. Saul had taken up position in Perry's room, where the young man was sleeping after being sedated. Saul informed us that either he or one of his brethren would be on duty at all times. That assurance made it easier for Maggie to go home to get the rest she needed. We left in my Benz, Maggie leaning against Ian in the spacious back seat.

As I drove, I considered what to do. Neither Robbie nor I had heard from Mr. Armstrong during our tenure at the hospital, so I assumed I was not a prime suspect for the murder of Lisa Considine. I didn't expect to hear from or see Marcus again. I had made my feelings clear. He didn't strike me as a man who would be persistent in attempting to rectify any poor impression I might have of him. I remembered, with longing, the repast he set out the previous evening and how attentive he was. Then I gave myself a mental slap on the head, forcing myself back to reality. It was over, it was past, and it was done. Time to move on.

"I'll stay with you for a while then I need to go home," I told Robbie in a low voice. "I need to give Ezra his pill." I glanced in the rear view mirror, taking in Maggie's exhausted form. "I can come back, though, and help."

"I don't want you alone, Jane. After what happened to Maggie and Perry..."

"If it makes you feel better, I'll just dash home, feed the cats, then come back."

He nodded, relieved. "I would feel better. It's one less thing to worry about. What about Sloan?"

I shrugged. "What about him? Like I told you, two ships in the night."

He raised a suspicious eyebrow. "Really? It seemed to me..."

"No, not at all. It was just one of those odd little flings. Nothing important." I kept my voice light and easy. He probably didn't believe me, but he couldn't question me about it at that moment. I pulled into Maggie's driveway, parking next to Robbie's silver Mustang.

I helped get Maggie into the house. She was still groggy. I knew sleep was the best medication she could have. I smoothed her hair back from her bruised face and silently cursed Pat Scarlotti, Vito Scarlotti, and the entire Scarlotti family back through time to their origins, which had undoubtedly been in the deepest corner of Dante's

Inferno.

As I prepared to leave, the ex-boxer Saul pulled into Maggie's driveway, blocking in my car. I stepped outside, prepared to argue with him but he held up a hand. "Orders," he said gruffly. "Aaron is taking over at the hospital and told me to come here. He figured I might be needed."

"You are," Robbie said, emerging from the house behind me. "Jane needs to go to her house. I don't want her going alone."

I started to protest but saw the concern in Robbie's tired eyes. I nodded. "That will be fine." I plucked my purse from the Benz then climbed into the big sedan Saul drove. Waving to Robbie, we sped off.

Thankfully, the massive Saul was an easy conversationalist. All I had to do was issue directions and he seemed happy. Forty minutes later we pulled into my driveway. As I jumped out of the car, he held up a hand that was larger than my head, curls and all. "Let me check the place first, okay?"

"Be my guest." I unlocked the garage door for him then followed him inside, where Ezra greeted us with his usual effusiveness. I performed my medication/treat routine, fed his feline brother then walked back to my den. The message light was blinking madly on my machine. I skimmed through the five messages, all from Marcus.

I'm sorry for the misunderstanding, Jane. Please call me.

Jane, are you there? I'd like to talk. Please call me.

Where are you, Jane? I've tried your office and Maggie's house. We need to talk, honey, call me.

I talked with Sam. They think they know who killed Toby. We need to talk. Call me as soon as you can.

Jane, if you don't call soon, I swear to God I'm going to come out to your house and camp on your doorstep until I see you. Call me, damn it.

"He sounds worried."

I whirled, finding Saul filling the doorway. "That's just how he sounds. I doubt he is concerned."

"I dunno," Saul said as I brushed past him. "Maybe you should call."

"He works for me," I said, going to my bedroom to pack a bag. "Not the other way around." The phone rang again. I picked up on the extension near the bed, forgetting that I wanted to screen my calls. Luckily it wasn't Marcus.

"Dr. Renard?"

I didn't recognize the voice nor did I have caller ID on that phone. "Yes."

"This is Dr. Cross. I want to see you in my office, tomorrow morning at 8:00 a.m."

I stared in shock at the room around me. The room where, last night, I spent a night of passionate sex with Marcus Sloan. It seemed to tilt before my eyes. "I beg your pardon?"

"This is Dr. Cross. My office, tomorrow morning."

Panic started to bubble up in me. "Can you tell me what this is about, Dr. Cross?"

"I think you know. Tomorrow morning. Don't be late." He hung up.

Oh my God. I slid onto the bed, stunned.

Saul crept into the room. "You okay?" he asked.

I shook my head. I was going to be fired. I knew it. My entire career, minor though it was, flashed in front of my eyes. No more leisurely strolls on campus, no more stimulating discussions about American authors with my cronies. No more critiques over coffee and beer at the local bar. There would be no more unstructured time and free summers. What would I do? I wasn't equipped to do any other kind of work. What could I do? I was almost fifty. I would be forced to apply for unemployment and take some mind-crippling job, typing letters or filing papers or—

Now wait. I gave myself a good shake. Wait. He couldn't just fire me. What were his grounds? I was a tenured professor. He couldn't just dismiss me. He had to have some kind of—

Then I remembered.

The underwear. My yellow panties, peeking out from under my desk.

Oh God. What if he heard Marcus and me? What if... Remember that phone call? Someone said they heard us. What if Dr. Cross heard us, too? What if...

What if he was the pervert?

As quickly as the idea slithered into my mind, I pushed it away. Homely, quiet, Freudian Dr. Cross was not my pervert. I may be naïve to the extreme, but I was certain of that. But what if he heard us? We tried to be quiet, but what if someone found out we'd had sex in my office? Good heavens, it was probably illegal. It was certainly unethical. And it might even be immoral.

"You okay?" Saul repeated.

I popped to my feet. "I'm fine." I grabbed a large tote bag from the coat rack in the corner then rifled through my dresser drawers, pulling out lingerie, shorts, and a T-shirt to sleep in. I went to the closet and threw it open, considering my choices. I settled for navy blue slacks, white blouse and matching navy vest for my morning inquisition. I folded them carefully, tucking them into the tote along with navy sandals that were a tad too tight, but which matched perfectly. I would sacrifice podiatric pleasure for style, just this once. I went into the attached bath and tossed makeup into the tote, wondering what I was forgetting.

When I came out, Saul was staring at William,

who was parked at his feet. "He keeps yellin' at me."

I eyed the rotund William, who gave a meow meant to evoke images of starvation, deprivation, and privation. "He merely wants attention. Pet him and he'll be quiet."

Saul leaned over to give William a heavy-handed mashing of his head, which the old cat adored. He purred, flopped onto his back, and stretched. "Whoa, did I hurt him?" Saul asked, concerned.

I stepped over William. "Not at all. He's just ecstatic with joy and weak at the knees." I, too, was weak at the knees but for a different reason. I was going to be fired. I knew it. I would never work in academe again. My name would go on some awful blacklist somewhere and I'd be relegated to a menial teaching post in an obscure backwater college, if I were so lucky to be allowed into a classroom again. I would be forced to teach Intro to Composition and Great American Poets. I would never see a graduate student with a brain again. I'd be relegated to undergraduate hell for the rest of my life.

Maybe Robbie could help.

I dismissed the idea as soon as I considered it. I had no recourse. There was no excuse for having sex in the middle of my office in the middle of the day in the middle of the campus. Nothing Robbie said or did could mitigate such stupidity.

I wandered into the kitchen. I was in flight mode, panicked. Nothing made sense. I dropped the tote bag then pulled open the fridge, pulling out a beer. Then I put it back, picked up the bag, and walked into the sunroom. I stared at the clock. It was almost seven at night. I had a little more than twelve hours to figure out what to do. I took a deep breath. I could do it. I could figure out something. Surely there was some way out of this mess. I had excellent teaching credentials. I could do it. There had to be something I could do.

The phone rang again. I jumped so high I almost tipped over. I blew out a sigh of relief at the caller ID. "Hello, Abby," I said into the receiver.

"Just what the hell is going on out there? I talked to Maria Jenkins, you know her, she used to live down the street from us in Boston? She married that car mogul, what's his name, Heckley? His mother's cousin lives in Maggie's neighborhood. Maria called me and said her mother-in-law's cousin, Carla James, called. She saw Robbie and a bunch of strange people going in and out of Maggie's house. "

"I didn't know you and Maria Jenkins stayed in touch," I said with what I thought was admirable restraint.

Abby made a rude noise. "I stay in touch with all the old gang. Don't try to weasel your way out of this one, Jane Renard. What's going on out there?"

"Maggie and Perry had a car accident."

"I knew it! It's that bastard, isn't it?" She swore fluently in Italian. "I swear to God, someone should break his knees."

Saul lumbered into the room, his new best friend, William, following hopefully behind. "You 'bout ready to go?" Then he saw me on the phone. "Oh, sorry."

"Listen, Abby, I have to go. Call Robbie, he'll give you the scoop." I looked at the giant Saul, my heart sinking. I couldn't go to campus with Saul in tow. I couldn't go to campus with *anyone* in tow, much less a six-foot-six, three hundred pound ex-pugilist with a face like a mashed cauliflower. I had to face my ordeal alone. How was I going to get rid of him?

"Jane, what's going on? What about that security guy you were dating? Is that serious? I told Walt I didn't think it was serious, but—"

"Call Robbie." I babbled Maggie's phone number.

"He's at Maggie's house, she just got out of the hospital. He's staying there to help out."

"The hospital! My God—"

"Call Robbie." I hung up and grabbed my tote bag. I had twelve hours. I'd figure out something. "Yes," I said to Saul, pleased that my voice didn't waver. "I'm ready."

He petted William again, who sagged with pleasure, then we left with Saul glancing back over one shoulder at my portly pet. When we got back to Maggie's house, Robbie met me at the door. "Abby called." He grimaced. "I think I calmed her down. And Marcus Sloan called. He wants to see you. I told him now wasn't a good time."

"Exactly right."

I tried to walk past him, but Robbie put a restraining hand on my arm. "What's going on, Jane? Sloan said they know who killed Toby."

I tried to order my scattered thoughts. "He left me a message about that. Who was it?"

"He didn't say. He wanted to come over and talk in person."

"Well, now is not a good time." I saw the worry in Robbie's eyes. "I'll call him later," I lied. "I'll find out what's going on." As soon as I said the words, a plan blossomed in my mind. I now knew how I would get out of the house without a bodyguard in tow. "I promise."

That seemed to appease Robbie because he stepped aside. I put the first part of my fledgling plan into effect. "I'll sleep downstairs in the family room," I said, hefting my tote bag. "Why don't you take Perry's room? It's closest to Maggie. I'd feel better knowing you were nearby."

He nodded, going back into the living room, where Ian was sitting, having been joined by Saul to watch some loud TV show which involved crashing vehicles. I dashed downstairs to Maggie's family room, a hodgepodge of furniture, masculine athletic equipment and an ancient TV on a tottery stand. I hung up my clothes in the laundry room then sat down on the couch, composing myself.

I was about to make the most important phone call of my life. I had to get my lines right. I rehearsed what I would say, whispering my lines to the framed poster of Eric Clapton playing onstage with Cream. As inspiration went, it was sufficient.

I picked up the phone and dialed Marcus' message line. "Hi, it's Jane. I'm at Maggie's. You can call me on my cell phone." I prayed my voice didn't sound too unsteady.

Within five minutes my phone rang. "Where have you been?" Marcus demanded. "I was getting worried. I couldn't find you at the station when I got done talking to Sam. Where did you go? I wanted to talk to you."

"Maggie had an accident. She and Perry were in the hospital."

There was a long pause. "Jane, I'm sorry. I didn't know. Are they okay?"

The honest concern in his voice almost made my resolve waver. "Yes, or, well, no." I explained what happened. "Robbie and I are going to be here tonight, to help Maggie and Ian. Aaron has someone at the hospital with Perry, just in case."

"God, this is awful. Did you file a police report?"

"I've had enough of police for one day," I shot back then almost slapped myself for sounding so cranky.

He just laughed shakily. "I suppose you have. Jane, I'm sorry about what happened this morning. I didn't mean to—"

I didn't want to hear his excuses. What I *really* wanted to do was quiz him about the lost love in his past, but I didn't dare. I had a plan and I had to execute it. "You said something about Toby. You said they found who killed him."

There was a pause. "Yeah, Sam called me a while ago and told me. It was his wife, Lisa. I mean, his other wife."

I stared at Eric Clapton in confusion. "What? Why would she kill him? She loved him." I tried to remember that night in the bleachers and the figure who talked to Toby. Could that have been his wife? Lisa was tall and slender...it could have been a woman. It was so dark I couldn't tell for sure.

"We're not quite sure since she's—" He stopped.

"She's dead," I supplied. "How do they know it was her?"

"She caught a last minute flight to St. Paul, last Thursday. They found her footprint in the blood, under your husband's chair. They found her fingerprints on the chair back, on the chair next to the one your husband sat in."

It all started to make a convoluted sense. "After she died, they could take her prints and match them," I mused. "Did your brother suspect?"

"When they found out she was in town, yeah, he started to wonder. Sam thinks she was getting worried, wondering if maybe her husband was getting ready to bolt. She followed him, found out he was trying to meet you."

"But how did Toby know I would be at the fair?" I demanded, forgetting my rehearsed script for the moment. "I didn't tell anyone I was going."

"He hired a detective, remember?" Marcus laughed. "You hired your own detective but your husband hired one, too."

"I wish you'd quit calling him my husband," I snapped angrily. "Toby was hardly a husband to me or to anyone."

"Oh, man. I can't seem to do anything right. I'm sorry, Jane."

He sounded so contrite. I *almost* believed him.

"It's all right."

"I want to see you, as soon as possible."

"I can't. Maggie's hurt and we're busy with that."

"I know, I know. But Jane, I want to make sure you understand. I'm sorry if I upset you. I didn't mean to. I've just been a cop for so long it's hard for me to put that aside."

I looked up at Eric, praying for strength. Marcus sounded so sincere. Then I remembered Dr. Cross and my appointment, looming like the Grim Reaper ahead of me. I had to go with my gut instinct and use my rehearsed script. "Marcus, I need some time to consider all this. There's a lot—a lot happening in my life right now. I need some time to think what to do." I took a deep breath, plunging ahead. "I know you've been disappointed with love in your past. I think perhaps I'm not the right person for you to be with."

"I've been—I've—what?"

"So I think it would be best if we just part company. I hope you'll charge me for your time and for..." I stopped myself in time, almost saying *services rendered,* "...for the work you've done for me. But I don't believe I'm the right woman for you. I'm not at all convinced you're the right man for me."

"Jane, what are you talking about?"

"We discussed this, remember? I appreciate the—the—" I silently begged Eric for help. He supplied it, in the form of a quote from a music critic, written in bold type at the bottom of the poster "—truly memorable experience we had. But I know we both feel it's best to remain unencumbered by any emotional attachment and... and..." I was running out of steam, all my carefully rehearsed lines fleeing my beleaguered brain. "So, thank you, Marcus. Please don't call me or try to get in touch with me. It's better this way."

"Are you saying you don't want to see me again?"

The hurt in his voice was unmistakable. I could imagine his expression. It would be perplexed, angry, and woeful. I closed my eyes, trying to banish the image. "Yes," I whispered.

"Why, Jane? I thought..."

"Goodbye, Marcus." I closed the phone, which immediately rang again.

I turned it off. I didn't want to second-guess my decision. I was counting on Marcus's innate politeness and regard for Maggie's woes to keep him away from me tonight, but tomorrow might be another matter. I had to put the rest of my plan into action. I sprang to my feet, tossing my phone back into my bag before going upstairs.

Ian, Saul, and Robbie were sprawled in the living room, munching popcorn and watching a scene on television that appeared to be an autopsy. Then *CSI* flashed on the screen and I relaxed. It was just one of those gruesome detective shows. I gestured to Robbie, who joined me in the hall.

"I talked to Marcus," I said. "They think Lisa Considine killed Toby."

"His other wife?"

I explained Sam Sloan's reasoning. Robbie nodded thoughtfully. "It sounds like they have enough circumstantial evidence. And I guess it makes some sense."

I nodded tiredly, glancing at the staircase. "Is Maggie okay?"

"She's sleeping. Ian or I go up every few minutes to check on her." Robbie rubbed my shoulder. "You look beat. Why don't you get some sleep?"

I yawned theatrically. "I'm picking Marcus up tomorrow morning. We have to go to the police station. His brother wants to talk to me." I ignored Robbie's alarmed expression and hurried on. "No need for you or Billy to be there, it's just a formality. If there's any concern at all, I'll call. Could you ask Saul to move his car? I'll need to get out in the morning."

He nodded reluctantly. "If you're sure. And as long as you're with Sloan..."

I patted his arm in reassurance. "He doesn't live far from here. Not to worry. Good night, Robbie. Thanks for all your help." I waved to Ian, who smiled tiredly in return. "We all appreciate it."

Robbie followed my glance. "They're great kids."

"And they deserve a great father." I kissed him on the cheek. "Think about it." I left before he could reply, going to my couch in the basement. I now had a clear field to drive to TUSP in the morning and deal with my boss.

I settled down for a sleepless night, praying for more inspiration from the guitar god on the wall.

Chapter 15

The day of my execution dawned clear and warm, with a hint of fall in the air. This time of year always held mixed feelings for me: anticipation about returning to class plus some dismay that summer was ending. I steeled myself for the interview ahead, determined not to lose my opportunity to feel that anticipation for years to come.

I barely slept, tossing and turning as I considered my dilemma. When I roused myself and made my morning ablutions, I had a clear plan of attack. I would listen to everything Dr. Cross had to offer then counter his words with reason, logic and calm.

He had no proof I had sex with Marcus. He had no real proof Marcus was even there. True, Kathy directed Marcus to my office, but perhaps he never arrived. There was only suspicion. I could explain away the underwear—a gym bag that spilled on the floor. I could explain any odd noises—a video of *Ethan Frome* I reviewed, thinking I might use it in a class. I had a copy tucked away somewhere on my bookcase. If I recalled correctly, there was a rather steamy scene in there with Liam Neeson and Patricia Arquette.

By the time I left Maggie's house, I was confident I had matters under control. I slid Eric Clapton's *24 Nights* into the CD player, anxious to continue the good karma Eric was obviously sharing with me. I shot off down the freeway invigorated, sure of myself, and ready to take on the world.

I was vigilant as I drove, aware Pat The Bastard might be lurking on any side street or ramp. I saw no suspicious cars and took special care with my driving, only exceeding the speed limit on those stretches of road where I was certain it was safest. As I drove I practiced what I would answer to various hypothetical questions posed by my new boss. When TUSP came into sight, I felt prepared.

I extracted my card key from my overstuffed bag, giving me access to the faculty lot. When I sprang out of the Benz, my little spider-hero did his crazy dance on my mirror. Once again, his antics reflected my attitude: I felt superhero strong and capable of taking on the world. I plucked my Coach briefcase from the seat then strode toward Merrill Hall to do battle with my adversary.

Instead, I had to do battle with a mousy little man who blocked my egress on the sidewalk. He appeared out of nowhere—well, actually from a path that wended its way around the side of the building. I hadn't seen him approach because that area was still deep in morning shadow. I came to a jarring halt, my briefcase once again almost overbalancing me as it bounced against my hip. "Excuse me," I said briskly.

"Dr. Renard?"

I didn't recognize him. He was slightly taller than me, possibly in his thirties with thinning brown hair, black-rimmed glasses, and a rather pale complexion. He wore a dark purple T-shirt with an unfortunate-looking pair of wrinkled beige Bermuda shorts. The black socks and sandals made the ensemble complete. "Yes?" I snuck a glance at my watch then relaxed. I had seven minutes until my appointment.

"I was hoping to talk to you." He stopped, pushing his glasses up with one slender finger and regarding me with an expression of anxiety I associated with needy animals in humane shelters. I was familiar with such looks. It was how I'd become the proud owner of two tragic-looking cats who later turned out to be supercilious despots.

"Obviously." I smiled in encouragement. "And?"

"I was hoping you could help me get in touch with Maggie Carlson."

"Maggie?" I took a hesitant step toward Merrill Hall. "Why do you need to talk to Maggie?"

"I wrote to her but I was afraid to just go see her, out of the blue." He laughed nervously, a rather breathless braying that was most unattractive. "I was hoping you'd help me meet her."

I stopped in mid-step. "You wrote to her?"

He was wringing his hands. I always thought that was a figure of speech, but it wasn't. He was actually wringing his hands. "I work for—with— your brother. He'll vouch for me."

"Robbie?" My voice was rising but I had no control over it. Something was happening here that was unexpected. My frazzled nerves were not responding well.

The poor man's head bobbed like one of those promotional toys given away at baseball games. "Yes, Mr. Renard. We work together. That's how I found out about Maggie." The man blushed a delicate shade of pink that would have been intriguing on a woman but was embarrassing on a man. "I read her books."

I once again called on a benevolent deity to save

me. "What do you mean?"

He must have heard the deadly tone in my voice because he took a step backward. "My name is Edward Johnson. I work in Mr. Renard's legal office in New York. That's where I saw Maggie's book. It was on Mr. Renard's desk and I—" He gulped and I saw his Adam's apple bob unappealingly. "I read it and that's when I—" He stopped again.

"You what?" I demanded.

I would never have thought I could present a menacing façade, but apparently I did. Mr. Johnson backed up again. "I did some research and I found—"

I advanced on him again.

"Her web site."

I stopped. "Her web site?"

His head bobbed again. "I checked the web site registration and found her address."

I tuned him out. The web site. When Tommi set it up for me, I used the Mail Box Unlimited address as the registration address. "But how did you find out about Maggie?" I demanded.

He wrung his hands some more. I resisted the urge to grab them to still their nervous trembling. "I—I—called and—t-t-told the clerk that I was with the postal service and we were i-i-i-investigating—"

"That's illegal!" I advanced on him again. "You lied to the clerk? To Clyde?"

He nodded again. "I just wanted to meet her. I knew Phire Foxe was a pen name. I found out you rented the box and someone else used it, back when the web site was registered. It was obviously a ploy, to hide her real identity. The clerk told me she used it for a time then you took over the use. That's how I found out her name. I googled her. I found a picture of her in the Pittsburgh paper, after that accident. She looked just like I thought she'd look. I thought if I could show her..." He ground to a halt.

"You wanted to be clever," I said through

clenched teeth. This idiot had frightened Maggie nearly to death with his cleverness. "How did you know it wasn't me who needed that box? Why do you think it's Maggie who's the author?"

He stared at me blankly. "What?"

"Why did you assume it was Maggie?"

"She was using it when the web site was set up. It had to be her." He gave me a single, dismissive glance. "Of course."

His evaluation of my feminine attractiveness would have angered me if I weren't already so angry I could barely see straight. "Listen, you—you—" I paused, searching for a suitable word, but for once my knowledge of languages failed me. Nothing was vile enough. "Just because you wanted to impress someone, that's no reason to make dirty phone calls. For heaven's sake, be a man and—"

"What phone calls?"

He sounded confused. I glanced at my watch. "I'm due at an appointment now but when I'm done, I'm going to see what I can do to—"

"I made that appointment."

His smug satisfaction at having tricked me almost tipped me over the precarious edge of civility. "You. Did. What."

This time even *I* heard the menace in my voice. He took another step back but the building prevented him from escaping further. "I had to meet with you, so you could help me. I needed to talk to you in private."

I took a long, steadying breath. "Are you telling me Dr. Cross isn't waiting for me inside this building right now?"

"He may not be waiting, but I am."

I spun so fast my briefcase tipped, spilling out *The Devil's Dictionary*.

Pat Scarlotti was standing behind me.

My first thought was he hadn't changed a bit.

He was perhaps a tad thinner, but he was still tall, dark, and handsome like that Clooney person who was an actor. Prison hadn't affected Pat in the least. I had a fleeting thought that life just wasn't fair. A bastard like Pat Scarlotti spent four years in prison for attempted murder and emerged looking like a damn movie star.

"What do you want, Pat?" I lifted my briefcase, prepared to wield it as an awkward weapon if need be.

Pat smiled but it didn't touch his sultry, dark brown eyes. He wore a supercilious smirk that always annoyed me, as though he knew a secret no one else did and he wasn't going to share. "You know what I want, Jane," he said in his low, cultured voice. He nodded to someone behind me. I spun again, this time losing Ford Maddox Ford's *The Good Soldier*. That was the undoing for my bag. It slid off my shoulder, landing with a resounding *thunk* on the ground at my feet.

Two beefy men emerged from Merrill Hall, blocking any escape there.

"You're crazy, Pat," I said. "What do you think you're going to do, kidnap me? For heaven's sake, it's a public place."

For answer, the two men put pot roast-sized hands on my arms then proceeded to lift me off my feet. "Stop it! You can't do this! Stop it!" I struggled in their grip, my feet making shuffling motions as I sought purchase on the sidewalk. I tried to peer around me but my two captors were huge, blocking any sight of Edward Johnson, the building, or anything but the large black car that waited just a few feet away, parked on the sidewalk with its doors ajar. "Call the police!" I shouted. "Someone call the police!"

I was unceremoniously stuffed into the back seat of the car where I sprawled, half-on, half-off the seat, finally straightening up to make a grab for the door handle.

Vito Scarlotti put a restraining hand on my arm just as his son got in the car behind me. I twisted, trying to get away.

Something sweet was pressed against my face and I gagged.

****

I awoke with a raging headache and an urgent need to vomit. I tried to sit up but was restrained. I choked. Someone said, "Aw, shit, she's getting sick."

I was pushed, harshly, onto my side. A small stream of bile dribbled out of my mouth. My stomach convulsed and a bit more bile dribbled out. Someone put a straw in my mouth and I sipped cautiously. Cool water rushed down my throat, soothing the worst of the upset.

It was then I realized I couldn't see anything. I attempted to touch my eyes but my hands were bound. "Oh, for heaven's sake," I muttered.

Someone laughed.

"Who's there?" I tried again to sit up. This time I was allowed to move. In fact, someone even propped me up, pushing me on the shoulder until I was upright. The hand remained on my shoulder for longer than necessary, making me cringe. It was very disconcerting to be blind like this and not know who was with me.

"It's good to see you again, Jane."

I moved my head, seeking the source of the voice. I realized my eyes were covered with some kind of cloth in addition to the fact my hands were bound. I reached out with my foot, feeling only a solid surface. Therefore I was either on the floor or on some other long object. It didn't feel unduly hard but also wasn't soft, like a bed, so I suspected I was sitting on something on the floor. I wiggled my legs. At least my feet weren't bound. If I could get a chance, perhaps I could make a dash for it. "Pat?"

"In the flesh."

Someone laughed again quite nearby, a guttural, low laugh that reminded me of the awful voice on the phone. "What do you want, Pat?"

"I always thought you were smarter than that, Jane. You know what I want."

There was movement near me. Air swirled nearby then a scent of something sweaty and somewhat unpleasant, like sour body odor. I tried to move away but when I did, I touched something or someone near me. I jerked away.

"Now, now. Bill is just keeping you company."

That person laughed again. I shivered involuntarily. "Why did you go to campus without your escort, Jane?" Pat asked.

I raised my head, facing in what I thought was the correct direction. "None of your damn business, Pat." I realized I should have lied, claiming to have someone following me. I frantically tried to devise a ploy to trick him, but nothing came to mind. "If you think you can use me to get Maggie, you're mistaken. My brother Robbie is with her. He won't let anything happen to her."

I could almost feel the tension increase in the room. "Your brother Robbie?" he asked.

Pat's voice was cold, harsh, and rage-filled. I remembered a call he made to me once, when he shouted and hurled disgusting threats over the phone line. This was like that time. I shivered again but stiffened my resolve. This monster wouldn't have Maggie again. "Yes," I said firmly. "Robbie has taken it on himself to help provide Maggie with protection. And we're on to your tricks. I've hired a detective and he's been investigating you. We knew you were in town. And that stupid stunt your father pulled put us on our guard. Honestly, Pat, trying to run me off the road. That was so foolish."

"Thank you, Jane." I heard a vague 'click' noise then someone chuckled nearby.

"For what?" I turned my head this way and that, seeking him.

"For providing me with what I need." I heard movement, the sound of feet on a rough floor surface. "Lock her in and come with me."

"I thought you said we could—"

"Not now." Pat's voice was clipped and commanding. "Later."

The person next to me got up with an audible grunt. I was conscious of cold seeping through my clothes. I surmised I was on the floor, possibly in a basement given the damp smell in the air. Several sets of feet made a clumping noise, as though they were climbing bare wood steps. A door opened and closed somewhere, a slight breezing rippling across my face.

"Hello?" I called out cautiously. I heard what I recognized as a lock turning then footsteps receding.

It felt as if I was alone. I raised my arms and touched my face. My supposition was correct. Some sort of mask loosely covered my face. I plucked at it but was unable to move it, much less remove it. While covering me with a black mesh, it also allowed a bit of light through as well as air. It must have been fabric of some kind, perhaps tied at the back of my head or behind my neck. My hands, although bound in front, prevented me from getting my arms behind my head. I lacked the manual dexterity to maneuver my hands to the side, tilt my head, and investigate whatever held my mask in place. I gave up on that goal as impossible. Instead I managed to clamber to my feet, tripping over the foamy mat that I sat on.

I 'examined' my surroundings, touching my way around a space that had rough concrete blocks as its primary building component. A basement, I decided.

I felt some pipes, both hot and cold, along one end. In a corner near a pile of lumber I also touched something feathery and sticky. Jerking my hands away, I guessed it was a spider web. That led to all sorts of unpleasant imaginings conjured by science fiction movies seen in my youth and my predilection for reading J.R.R. Tolkien as a child. I hastened away from the web lest Shelob be lurking there.

A few minutes later my foot kicked something on the floor. I discovered a staircase, leading upward. I considered ascending but decided discretion was the better part of valor. I continued my cautious exploration without discovering any weapon or item of use. I did find one door, but I couldn't get it to open. There was a dead bolt but I wasn't able to turn it because it appeared stuck. Or perhaps it had a locking device of some type on it. If I had the use of my eyes, I might have discerned it. I gave up on the door and continued my exploration, returning to the foamy mattress from whence I had set out.

I sank to the floor after first ascertaining it was spider web-free. The basement did not smell unduly moldy so I was hoping it was relatively clean and new. I decided what I couldn't see wouldn't hurt me so I pushed my fears aside. I had to focus on getting out of there, not on potential arachnids or other multi-legged creatures who were probably more afraid of me than I was of them.

I don't know how long I sat, deep in thought, when I became aware of a tapping noise. I raised my head, peering around, trying to determine where the noise originated.

"Here." A voice came to me, very soft.

I looked up.

"Yes." The word was almost hissed. I got to my feet, leaning against the wall then peering up and behind me.

"To your right, a few steps," the voice directed.

I moved to my right, keeping my back pressed against the wall.

"Up here."

Up where? I raised my head and saw what appeared to be a brighter rectangle of light above me. Ah. A window. "Who's there?" I whispered.

"Marcus."

I almost fainted. "Not," I said in disbelief. "Why should I believe you?"

There was a pause. "We spent Monday night near a hibiscus bush. I have the scratches on my butt to prove it."

"Marcus!" I almost shouted with excitement.

"Hush."

"Oh." I suddenly remembered my precarious predicament. "How did you get here?"

"I followed you from Maggie's house but I couldn't park in the faculty lot without a card key. I had to walk to your office."

"But how—"

"You dropped your briefcase. I've got the Benz. Listen, how many are there?"

"How should I know, I have a blindfold on." Honestly, was he as blind as I was? "Get me out of here. Where is here, by the way?"

"You're in a house in Victoria, about an hour west of the Cities. It's in one of those new subdivisions, with big houses all spaced far apart. Scarlotti is probably renting it. There're four or five cars in the driveway."

"Where did you—?"

"No time, Jane. I've called the police. Sam's on his way."

A burst of gratitude rushed through me at the thought of grumpy Sam Sloan coming to the rescue. "Okay, what should I do?" I heard the sound of voices behind me, getting louder. "Someone's coming." I reached up on my tiptoes, flailing about to try to reach the window.

"It's okay, honey. I'm here. It's okay. Hang on."

Easy for him to say. I was stuck in a basement, blindfolded, and tied up. I had no idea where my captors were or what would happen. I fumbled back to my previous spot, dropping onto the foamy mattress just as I heard the door open and loud voices.

"He said we could," one man said.

"He said later," another answered.

"It is later."

I heard footsteps clunking down the steps. Oh dear. It was probably the two beefy guards, the ones I sensed earlier. They were coming to move me on Pat's orders. I started to struggle to my feet when I sensed a presence in front of me.

"No need to get up," he said in a low voice. "You're just gonna be on your back in a minute anyway."

A heavy hand landed on my shoulder and pushed me back to the floor.

Chapter 16

I barely had time to think much less fight. A big hand covered my mouth, pressing the cloth down. I was suddenly gasping and choking.

"Don't try screaming," he whispered in my ear, his breath hot and moist. "No one will hear. Scarlotti is busy with his wife."

Dear God. Maggie was there? How had she been lured there? What was happening? I twisted, trying to get away but only succeeded in wedging myself even more firmly under the big man's body. He pressed on me, making my breath expel in a long, gasping *whoosh*.

Someone was groping my breasts. It wasn't the one on top of me. That one still had a hand on my mouth and his other hand had my bound hands upright, pushed against the floor, over my head. I wasn't sure how many there were. I heard two voices but what if there were more? What if there were three or four or...? Hands were squeezing my breasts, tearing at my blouse. Cold air prickled my skin. My bra was painfully jerked up. A big hand came down on my breast and squeezed, hard. I cried out, kicking.

It was insane. I didn't know what to do. Who did I fight? I couldn't see anything. I was in a black fog, figures hazy through the cloth. I realized, with sickening clarity, it was a perfect situation for them. They could rape me and I couldn't identify them. The only other people around were their cronies. I was trapped in this basement. They could do anything they wanted to me. And they could do it as long as they wanted.

The one manhandling my breast was pinching my nipple. I groaned.

"She loves it," the one on top of me said. He surged against me, grinding his erection into my crotch, prying my legs open with a well-placed knee. "She loves it. We'll take turns with her. I get her first then you can have her. Then we'll make her suck us off." He laughed, grinding and pulsing against me. Hands were on my pants, tearing at the button and zipper. I twisted, trying to get away from the groping hands, the probing body, the hard, cruel erection pressing on me.

"What was that?"

The one who was chewing on my breast raised his head. I sighed in relief at the cessation of pain, trying to take advantage of the moment by rolling. I had heard nothing, but I prayed it was Marcus, or maybe Sam Sloan. At that moment I would have welcomed Shelob as a rescuer.

The one on top of me obviously didn't believe his companion. He twisted my arms. I cried out again as my muscles started to spasm. My knees jerked up in an attempt to protect myself. I hit some part of his anatomy hard.

"Bitch," he growled. My hands were suddenly free, but it didn't help me. He was holding me down by sitting on my thighs, tearing at my lower clothing with both of his hands. The one holding my breast was still there, still pinching me.

"There's somebody out there," he whispered.

"Bullshit." My pants were being dragged down as the man scooted back, still pinning my legs. I struggled with him, hitting the other one next to me as I attempted to grab my clothing to pull it back on. I was starting to give in to panic. I didn't know what to do. Any self-defense lessons I once learned had long vanished. Any research I did for my books was obliterated by my panic. I was in primal mode, terrified.

"There's somebody out there. I'm telling you."

The one next to me surged to his feet, stepping on my arm in the process. I yelled at the stunning pain when his heel ground into my elbow. The one on my legs was prying a hand between my thighs, forcing my knees apart even though my pants were only halfway off. He was moving, fumbling with his pants. I could feel it against me, feel his hands moving. I wiggled even more, struggling as hard as I could to sit up, trying to edge back, away from him.

Something slammed into the side of my head. I dropped back to my shoulders, stunned. Stars danced in front of my eyes and all breath left me. I lay there, limp, as he tugged at my pants, yanking and pulling.

Someone yelled. I couldn't understand the words. My ears were ringing. An odd, metallic taste was in my mouth. The man on my thighs was cursing in a low, angry voice. He jerked me upright by my bra, the elastic band digging cruelly into my skin. "Get up, you bitch."

I was weak, unable to respond. He pulled me to my feet, holding me around the waist as I lolled on his arm, like a life-sized Raggedy Ann doll with her clothing torn off. He jerked at my pants. I struggled with him, thinking he meant to tear them off. But he was pulling them up even as he dragged me with him. I tried to peer through the black mask but I couldn't see anything. My head hurt and I was conscious of cold air on my skin. I knew I was almost naked. I wanted to do something to cover myself but I couldn't. All I could do was hang over his arm like some kind of rubbery toy.

"Put her down!"

Oh, I heard that. I raised my head groggily. I was very, very cold. In fact, I was starting to shiver. The man holding me hoisted me in front of him, both arms going around me. It was repellent to feel his hairy arms against my bare skin. I fought against nausea at the thought of him touching me. I lolled forward, his arms digging into my breasts. He put one hand under my chin, jerking my head back viciously until I was facing forward.

"You don't have a shot," he growled, his mouth close to my ear.

I tried to wiggle but I was still hazy, not able to see anything.

"Jane, listen to me!"

I tried. I really did. The man holding me jerked me around. I realized he was taking slow steps backward. I wondered where we were going. I remembered the door I encountered earlier. Perhaps it was an exit.

"Jane, can you hear me?"

I wiggled my bound hands to indicate I wasn't totally insensible.

"Ain-jay!"

Oh, for cryin' out loud. It was Marcus and he was using code. Didn't he know I was stupid with pain and barely conscious? I dragged my feet, making the big man slide me along like a limp sack of heavy, soggy noodles. I wiggled my hands again.

"Ump-jay eft-lay!"

It took a precious second for my mind to process the words. As soon as I did, I jerked hard to the left. When the man's arms loosened in startled surprise, I pushed off with as much strength as was possible, flying away as a huge noise exploded into the space. Something hot hit me on my bare chest then I collided with a hard, sharp object, going down in a tangle of arms, legs, torn clothing and...wood. Lumber collided all around me and over me. I threw my arms up to protect my head then held my breath, waiting to be impaled, raped, or shot.

Voices shouted. Feet thudded above me. I cowered in my lumber cocoon, curling into a fetal little ball, panting like an animal that's escaped a predator. I started to close my eyes, just wanting the whole thing to be over, the whole thing to finish so I could go home, relax, take a bath and put it behind me.

Someone tore away the lumber covering me. I screamed, scrabbling into the pile of lumber, trying to pull it over me, to hide me.

"It's okay, it's okay," someone kept saying. "You'll be okay."

"It's not her blood," I heard someone say. "Get a medic here."

"It's okay, Jane. I'm here."

Someone touched the mask. I screamed again, beating at the hands that touched me.

"It's me, Jane. It's me, it's Marcus."

I started to sob, still trying to get away from the hands. Something soft was tossed over me. I grabbed it, tugging it tight. Then the mask was pulled off so I could see again. I blinked in the light streaming in from a window, staring up into Marcus' pale, frightened face.

"What took you so long?" I demanded. Then, true to form, I proceeded to cry and hiccup myself into hysteria.

****

It took almost thirty minutes before I stopped shivering and was calm enough to sit, drink a cup of water, and think coherently. The men in the ambulance van gave me a smock-like garment to wear to replace my grimy blouse and torn trousers. It was quite short, but as fashion went, it covered me decently. I was so happy to be free of that awful basement I didn't regret the loss of a $70 outfit from Marshall Field's. I noticed some police personnel put the ruined clothing into a sack. Remembering my few viewings of crime shows, I surmised they would analyze it for various unsavory stains. I decided they could burn the items when they finished their processing.

I did, indeed, have a coating of blood on my chest, splattered there by the thug who'd tried the hardest to rape me. A bullet in his shoulder was small payment for the terror and pain he put me through. I restrained myself and didn't gloat at this sign of divine retribution, which came in the form of Marcus Sloan.

He was talking with his brother, several other police-looking people, Robbie, and my attorney, Billy Armstrong. I don't know how Mr. Armstrong got there, but there he was, hopefully defending my interests. I was too tired to care. I lay propped up on a gurney, watching as Pat Scarlotti and his infamous father were led away in handcuffs to a squad car with the guards who escaped harm. The thug, Bill, who attacked me and been injured by Marcus, had already been whisked away in an ambulance. Anxious neighbors queued beyond the yellow crime tape, watching avidly.

One woman in particular was waving whenever I glanced her way. She appeared so anxious I finally pushed myself upright and tottered off the gurney, meandering toward her through the crowd. I was probably an amazing sight in my blue sack-like gown, blue sandals, and hair that had been bagged and showed the effects of static cling.

"Thank God you're okay," the woman said, thrusting something at me.

I peered at it, confused. It was a cell phone. I put it to my ear. "Hello?"

"Oh my God, what happened?"

I pulled the phone away and stared at it. This was surreal. "Abby?"

"Maggie called me and told me what was happening after Robbie ran out to kill Pat."

"After Robbie—"

"So when Maggie told me you were in Victoria, I called Delbert Mooney. You remember him. He went to college with me. He had such a crush on me in junior year. He married a girl who lived in North Dakota. I remember her family lived somewhere west of the Cities. So he called his cousin and she..."

I tuned out the explanation. Trust Abby to have spies in every corner of the metro. "I'm fine," I interrupted. "Why was Robbie killing..." I stopped when I saw Robbie, Billy Armstrong, and Marcus all turn to look at me. I waved the cell phone. "It's Abby," I called out.

Robbie rolled his eyes and shook his head. Marcus strode over to me, plucked the phone from my hand and said into it, "Jane is busy right now. She'll call you later." He listened for a minute. "Yes, I am. Yes, I did. No, I won't. Good-bye, Abby." He handed the phone back to the woman in the crowd then steered me toward the small group of my male protectors who were huddled together.

"What did you tell Abby?" I asked, stumbling slightly.

"I told her that yes, I was your security guard, yes, I rescued you, and no, I wasn't going to break your heart."

I didn't have time to respond to this odd recitation because we had reached my sibling and my attorney. "Why were you coming here to kill

Pat?" I asked, leaning into the arm Robbie put around me.

"Pat had a tape recorder in the basement when you and he were talking," Marcus said before Robbie could reply. "He called Maggie and planned to use the recording to convince her he had you. But she wasn't there. She went to the hospital to be with Perry. His brother, Ian, took the call." Marcus glanced at Robbie. "Smart kid. He played along with Scarlotti, pretended to want to get his mother and father back together. He got his father to say where he was."

"Oh, my, he is a smart boy," I agreed. "To do all that after what he's been through." I hugged Robbie with my arm draped around his waist. "I told you, he deserves a good father. I can't believe that arrogant bastard would think Ian would think—"

"Anyway," Marcus interrupted, "Ian told Robbie and—"

"But where was Saul?" One good interruption deserved another. "He was supposed to be on guard duty. He wouldn't have left his post."

Marcus gave me an aggravated glance. "He went to the hospital with Maggie, leaving your brother with Ian." At this point Marcus turned his exasperation on Robbie. "And your brother decided to save the day. Just what the hell did you think you were going to do?"

Robbie was unrepentant. "I hadn't decided yet. I figured I'd develop a plan on the drive over here."

Marcus shook his head and returned his attention to me. "He's your brother, all right. So Ian called Billy Armstrong, who called Sam, who I already called."

Billy Armstrong rumbled, "I followed Robbie. You know the rest."

"But..." I had so many questions I didn't know where to start. "What about Pat? Why did he think

Maggie would come? And why did Vito let him do it?"

"It was perfect," Marcus said. "Talk about luck. You handed him the chance." I tried to protest but he wasn't to be stopped. "He had no idea you were going to leave or I would follow. He saw you and decided to take a chance."

"But what was his purpose?"

"Payback," Robbie said grimly. "He'd use you to get Maggie and he'd let his guards—" He stopped, his eyes sympathetic.

I shuddered but forced myself to ask, "But what about Maggie? What could he do? They're divorced. She'll never go back to him. The boys are grown and he can't..." I had a sudden thought. "Not his own children. Not even Pat is that monstrous, is he?"

"We're not sure," Marcus said. "But one of Vito's guards said the old man was disgusted with his grandchildren. There was no love there, at all. He said if anything happened to them, it wouldn't bother him. So maybe Pat was planning to use that as a threat against Maggie."

"Oh, Lord." I was suddenly ill. "Was that little pervert a part of it? Edward Johnson?"

"Edward Johnson?" Robbie interrupted. "What's my paralegal doing here?"

"That guy I saw?" Marcus asked. "Man, he took off running when Pat grabbed you."

"But what's he doing here in Minnesota? Jane? Are you sure it was him?"

I barely heard him. I was starting to fade out, my adrenaline having given way to exhaustion. Then I remembered something Marcus said. "Perry! What's wrong? Is he okay?"

"Fever," Robbie said, his voice grim. "The doctor said it's not unusual, but Maggie is worried, she wanted to be with him."

"Of course." I looked down at my unattractive

attire. "Would someone please drive me home so I can change, then I'll join her?"

All three men regarded me with doubt clear in their expressions. "Don't you think you should go home, maybe go with the doctor and get checked?" Billy said.

"For what? I was hit on the head but I'm fine now. I wasn't..." I stopped, choking on the word. Robbie squeezed my shoulders in understanding. "Marcus stopped them before..." I stopped again, afraid to voice the words. It was foolish, I know, but I felt if I didn't voice what had happened, I could erase the memory. Or at least I could keep the memory of those prying fingers and greedy bites at bay.

"I wish I'd gotten there sooner," Marcus said in a low, ominous voice.

I was surprised to see guilt in his eyes. "Nonsense," I said with as much vigor as I could muster. "It worked out fine. Just fine. Now I need to be with Maggie." I smoothed down my impromptu dress, which had a habit of riding up to reveal far too much of my somewhat plump thighs. "After I change."

Sam Sloan approached us, striding through the crowd with another grim-faced police officer at his side. Marcus met them and they talked in low voices, Billy Armstrong leaning near to listen. He said something to the other men and they all nodded. Billy rejoined us. "I'm going to take you home to get changed, then we'll go to the Scott County Sheriff's Office, where you can make your statement. Then we'll go to the hospital." He glanced at Marcus, still talking with Sam Sloan. "A police officer will come with us."

"I already made a statement," I protested. "To Sam and Marcus."

"I know," Billy said, his dark face sympathetic

and calm. "But this is a formality. You need go to the office so they can get a signed statement."

I nodded in understanding. The Sheriff's Office wasn't too far from my house. I was grateful I wouldn't have to drive all over Timbuktu in order to do my civic duty. "What about Marcus? Will he—?" Will he what? Come with me? Meet me? What was I going to ask? I shook my head, bemused.

"He needs to make a statement, too." Billy put a huge, gentle hand on my arm, starting to lead me away. "He shot a man."

"But I'm his alibi," I said. "I mean, I know why he shot the man. He shouldn't get in trouble because of that."

"He's not in trouble," Billy said soothingly. "It's just a formality. He'll go to the station with another officer. It's not Sam's jurisdiction so we want to make sure everything is done by the book. We don't want any press reports of favoritism or anything."

"Oh." I gazed longingly at Marcus, who was talking with the other men.

"I'll take your car, meet you at the hospital," Robbie said. "Go with Billy now, okay?"

"What about that man? That Edward person?" I asked.

"We'll talk about it, later, Jane. Go with Billy."

I wanted to go to Marcus and talk to him, but now was not the time. "All right," I said reluctantly. I took Billy Armstrong's proffered arm, walking next to his solid, secure bulk to the perimeter of the taped-off area. Marcus turned and watched me. I raised a hand in farewell. "Thank you," I whispered.

He smiled. I thought it was a sad smile. Then he nodded before turning back to his conversation. I got into the big sedan, settling back in the comfortable seats with a sigh. As we drove away, the hot August sun streamed into the car, warming me. I glanced at the clock, amazed to see it was only noon. It felt as though a lifetime had passed. I eased my too-tight shoes off with a sigh and closed my eyes.

The minute I did, I was suffocated, as though that big man was sitting on me, holding me down. I jerked upright with a strangled sob.

Billy's voice was compassionate. "It'll take a while, but you'll get over it."

He spoke with a surety that was as reassuring as it was dismaying. "Have you represented women who...?"

He nodded, his big hands clenching and unclenching on the steering wheel. "My sister went through a rape. That's why I was so willing to help Maggie." He smiled at me. "And you. Don't worry, Jane. You'll be able to put it behind you."

I wiped at a tear trickling down my cheek. I wanted to believe him. I just found Marcus and passion. I didn't want to lose them so soon.

The problem was, I wasn't sure if I would ever get the chance to find them again.

Chapter 17

Three hours later I was hugging Maggie at Perry's bedside, Ian and Robbie watching. "It's over," I told her through my tears. "Pat's in jail again and so is his father."

She hugged me so tightly I almost lost my breath. "I know," she said. "Robbie told me. Jane, I'm so sorry for what happened. I got you in such trouble. If it not for me, none of this would—"

"Hush," I said firmly, pulling away from her. "How's Perry doing?" I looked down at the sleeping boy. Then I noticed he had a faint beard. Perry was a man now, not a boy

"He's better. The doctors said it's common to have a fever like this. I was afraid it might be an infection but it's not."

I touched Perry's hand. He was so like Pat with his clean, chiseled face. The main difference was in his eyes, which were now closed. He had Maggie's guileless, dark blue eyes. And his heart, I thought. He didn't have a trace of Pat Scarlotti's evil anywhere in his soul.

I looked around as Kathy Sylvester came into the room. "I heard what happened," she whispered, drawing me aside slightly. "Are you okay?"

"Who told you?" I self-consciously touched the bruise on my forehead where the massive guard struck me.

"It was on the news." Her eyes were as big as platters. "Jim Crowndorf came into the office and told us about it."

I groaned out loud. This was all I needed. My biggest nemesis now had ample ammunition for his campaign for the chair of Full Professor. My sabbatical was vanishing before my eyes like the proverbial polar bear in a snowstorm.

"They said on the news someone was shot and you were assaulted."

"I didn't think they could release that news unless I signed a paper or something." I considered contacting Billy Armstrong, who dropped me at the hospital after my statement-giving. I wondered if he would file a lawsuit for me. Then I dismissed the notion. The news was bound to get out sooner or later. "I was attacked," I corrected. "Not assaulted. I mean, not in the clinical sense of the term. I suppose, technically, I was assaulted but not *assaulted,* if you know what I mean."

"Are you okay?" Kathy touched my shoulder.

"Yes, no harm done. Just a bruise or two." I tried to smile but my lip quivered. She enfolded me in a hug to her ample bosom. "I'm-m-m-m f-f-f-f-i-n-n-e," I stuttered as I wept on her shoulder.

"Who got shot?" she asked when I could get my breath.

"The man who assaulted me." I dabbed at my tears with the tissue Maggie handed me. "Marcus shot him."

"In the nuts, I hope," Kathy said forcefully.

Ian and Robbie both looked uncomfortable at this declaration. I shook my head. "In the shoulder. It was enough to incapacitate him so I could escape from his..." I glanced at Ian and said, "...attempts."

Maggie, Kathy, and I engaged in a group hug, sisters united in a common revulsion. When we were calm, Kathy and I slipped out of the room to talk where we wouldn't bother the sleeping Perry. I updated her on all that happened, to many exclamations and the interruption of occasional questions. As Robbie and Maggie came out to join us, I turned to him and said, "I was just telling Kathy about that odd little man. Who is he?"

Robbie ran a hand over his red curls, cropped short and springy. "Edward Johnson is a paralegal in my office. He left on vacation this week."

I vaguely remembered Robbie mentioning something about that when I initially contacted him about my troubles with Toby. Good heavens. Toby and Lisa. I forgot about them. And I probably would again as I turned my attention to Robbie, who was explaining.

"He told me he was going to South Carolina to visit relatives. What did he look like?"

I described the benign, nervous man with the unfortunate fashion sense. Robbie nodded glumly. "That's Edward. Why did he come here?" Then he stopped, his face flooding with color. "Oh, no. It couldn't be."

He was so embarrassed I glanced at Maggie, not sure if I wanted any dark secrets revealed in front of the woman whom I was hoping would soon become my sister-in-law. "What?" I asked cautiously.

"I had one of your books on my desk," Robbie said in a quiet voice, leading us away from Perry's hospital door. He blushed, glancing at Maggie. "It was *Pleasure Principal*."

Ooh. One of my hotter ones. I received four flames for that one in the *Erotica Review* and a lava lamp icon from *Romancing the Morn*, another monthly review magazine. I glanced at Maggie to see how she was taking this. I was startled to see her hide a grin after giving Robbie what could only be described as a frank, lustful glance. Luckily he didn't see, otherwise I'm sure it would have flustered the poor man into stuttering incomprehensibility.

"Edward asked where I got it and I sort of laughed it off." Robbie blushed again when I gave him a narrow-eyed glare. "It's a lawyer's office, Jane. Come on, give me a break. It doesn't look too good to have an erotic romance sitting around. I bought it that day and, well, anyway, I said I got it from a friend who knew the author. He and I sort of... well, you know, guys, we..." He stammered to a halt. I waited, knowing Robbie would eventually divulge the story. His innate honesty would force him to admit any culpability on his part. "He asked to borrow it and I said he could. Later, when he returned it, he said he thought it was great. He wished he could meet the author. I mentioned that my sister... knew the author so maybe I could get him a signed copy."

I started nodding before he stopped talking. It made sense. "So this Edward starts to research me, Phire Foxe. He finds the mailbox number associated with the web site. He finds it was registered to me but Maggie was getting mail there." I stopped. "Wait a minute. How did he find that out?"

Robbie once again ran his hand through his hair, a sure sign of agitation. I was certain if a family pet had been handy, the poor creature would have been stuffed full of food given Robbie's propensity for distraction.

"It's a legal office, Jane," Maggie said. She slipped her arm through Robbie's. He appeared startled but grateful. "The man probably came up with some legal-looking paper and served it on the poor clerk."

I remembered Clyde-the-clerk's comment about

my 'legal troubles.' I assumed it was Marcus talking to him, but perhaps it was this Edward character.

"It's kind of cool you incited such lust in this guy so he came all the way out here to meet you," Kathy commented, eyeing Robbie, Maggie, and their twined arms with interest.

"Cool is not the term I'd use. I suppose he broke some laws." I turned to Robbie, who was struggling to appear nonchalant about Maggie clinging to him.

"Well, maybe, but..."

"He frightened Maggie," I protested when I saw Robbie's rueful expression. "And he sort of stalked her or he would have if he could."

Maggie's hand slid down Robbie's arm and took his hand. "I think he's had a big enough scare, don't you?" she said. "He saw Pat grab you and probably thought his life was in danger, too. When he finds out I'm not the romance diva he thinks I am..."

Robbie leaned over and whispered something. Maggie blushed. Kathy and I exchanged gleeful looks. "I'll consider it," I said graciously, starting to edge away. "Let's get coffee." I nudged Kathy. "Do you want anything?" I asked Robbie and Maggie.

"Besides a private room and some time to have fun?" Kathy muttered.

I shushed her and we left since no apparent answer was forthcoming from my bemused brother or my smug friend. As we went down the hall toward the cafeteria, Kathy said, "Your ploy worked for your brother. What happened with that security guy? The one who saved your life? Are you going to fall gratefully into his arms?"

My heart ached at the thought. I wasn't sure how I felt. Grateful, certainly. Concerned that shots had once again been exchanged in the rescue of a woman he presumably cared for. Uncertain about how he felt. "Not sure," I said with as much casualness as I could evince. "For now I just want to relax and enjoy being safe."

"Enjoy it while you can," she said cheerfully. "Don't forget the faculty meeting tomorrow." She grabbed a tray, making a beeline for the pie selection in the cafeteria's buffet line. "Ten o'clock in the department conference room. Be there and be ready to think on your feet. I'm sure Jim Crowndorf will be gunning for you. Oh, look. French silk pie. My favorite. Want some?"

I nodded weak agreement. I decided I might as well fatten myself for the slaughter.

We parted company thereafter, Kathy to go back to work and I to return home, the genial Saul in tow. Robbie insisted on a guard, at least until he could join me later. I protested, knowing he and Maggie wanted time together, but Robbie prevailed. "I'll be home later, after supper," he said, kissing me on the cheek. "You've had a rough day. I want to be there for you. Maggie understands."

I was too tired to argue. I drove home, Saul filling my passenger seat. We paused long enough to go to a Burger King, which Saul asserted had far superior fare to MacDonald's. Their toys, however, were not as charming as my small spider-hero. I had a choice between a dancing teacup and a singing teapot. I settled on the dancer, which was wound with a small key. It was amusing but rather spastic in its antics. It bobbled on a small spring contraption, shaking and jerking while emitting a high-pitched sound. I earmarked it as a possible cat toy.

When we got home, Ezra informed me he needed his treat, so I dealt with him while Saul and his new best buddy, William, went in search of cat food. After doling out the goods, I sagged with relief onto the couch on the sun porch, grateful to be home and safe. I tentatively closed my eyes. When horrid nightmares didn't ensue, I relaxed fully. Within minutes I was in a deep, fitful doze, more a light nap than true sleep. I heard Saul come into the room then ponderously tiptoe out. Ezra settled on the couch above me, exhaling tuna breath then soon emitting a throaty snore.

The phone rang soon after I lay down, startling me into wakefulness. I answered, feeling groggy and disoriented.

"Miss Renard," the peremptory voice stated.

I sighed. Abrupt conversations with Declan Fabersham were becoming common in my once boring life. "Mr. Fabersham, this is not a good time for me to talk." I yawned, anxious to resume my napping.

"Why was I questioned in relation to the death of my stepmother?"

I looked up at Ezra, who was upside down and balanced precariously on the back of my couch, basking in warm sunlight. "I have no idea," I said. "I presume because everyone affiliated with Toby was questioned."

"It makes no sense."

His voice sounded upset. I could understand that. I was upset to be questioned, too. He was even more intimately acquainted with the woman, so the police were probably more suspicious of him. I decided to allow my disdain for the police to be evidenced. "I agree," I said warmly. "I'm afraid the law enforcement officials in this town have a very poor opinion of those people who are innocent bystanders. I wouldn't let it bother you unduly."

"Do you think so?"

I was flattered he thought I had such sophisticated knowledge of police procedures. I always considered myself a somewhat commonplace person, except, of course, for my predilection for penning steamy prose which was a secret shared by very few. "I believe so," I reassured him. "It's been my experience the police tend to check the easiest possible places first then expand inquires when that fails. Don't worry."

"There's one other thing."

I sighed. Why was there always 'one other thing' with people like this? "Yes?"

"Lisa told me Toby gave you something of value. She wanted to get it back. I believe she was going to campus to talk to you. Did you and she talk?"

Something of value? What could Toby have had in mind? "No, I haven't talked to your stepmother since I met her in the police station. What could Toby have given me?"

"Thank you."

He hung up abruptly. What an odd conversation. Well, at least he was polite. I snuggled on to the couch, rubbing Ezra's tummy and receiving a satisfying purr in return. I allowed it to lull me back to my nap.

Two hours later I stirred, feeling refreshed. Ezra had deserted me, probably for the people who were speaking outside on the deck. I went to my bathroom and tidied myself, scrubbing my face and hands, anxious to remove any memory of that noxious guard's touch. Then I went to the kitchen to pour a glass of wine before opening the sliding door to join Robbie and Saul.

They were lounging, beers in hand, on my wooden deck overlooking the woods behind the house. The two cats were near their appointed guardians, William near Saul the head-masher, and Ezra near Robbie, the tuna-giver. Each cat alternately watched their new friends and the cheese plate with the attentiveness of lions stalking antelope on the veldt. I curled up in the rope swing chair that hung from an overhanging hook, easing into its cozy confines.

"Did you sleep good?" Robbie asked.

I nodded. "It was just what I needed." I took a sip of wine. This part of the house faced north and was in cool shadow. The riot of flowers from my small garden sent various scents to us on the gentle breeze.

"Marcus came to the hospital," Robbie said, picking at his beer label. Ezra perked up, obviously recognizing the signs of distraction and thus an impending food possibility. He had learned Robbie's habits quickly.

"Did everything go well for him? When he gave his statement? He didn't get into any trouble, did he?"

"No, not at all. I mean, there's always a certain amount of paperwork involved whenever someone uses a firearm."

Saul nodded wisely. "Yeah, lots of bullshit." Then he grimaced. "Sorry. I meant to say crap."

"Oh, that's fine," I assured him. "No need to watch your language around me. I'm an English teacher. I've heard it all." I sipped some more. "I hope he'll be okay."

"You should call him." Robbie nudged my rope swing with his foot, making me twirl in my cocoon.

"Yeah," Saul agreed, a rumbling belch issuing from his massive chest. "Oops. Sorry. Call him. He seems like a right guy."

A right guy? I puzzled over that expression for a moment. Saul must have seen my confusion. "He's a stand-up guy."

I nodded, afraid I'd get more incomprehensible explanations if I didn't pretend a certain acquaintance with his slang. "I know."

"So you'll call him?" Robbie pressed.

"Perhaps," I said evasively.

We all heard a car pulling into the driveway. "That'll be my ride," Saul said, making movements to heave himself to his feet.

"It's just Aaron." Robbie gestured to him to remain seated. "He'll come in."

Sure enough, a minute or two later, my somewhat-cousin Aaron came out onto the deck, followed by Uncle Vanya and Aaron's brother Daniel. The men plucked beers from the cooler that sat between Robbie and Saul, took the remaining seats, and proceeded to rehash the day's events, skimming delicately over my near-rape with Vanya, pronouncing, "What happened to Janie shouldn't happen to a pig much less a beautiful woman who was raised right and is so gentle she wouldn't hurt a fly. But at least the bastards were handled by Janie's friend, *zhan le Devlesa tai sastimasa.*"

The other men rumbled an agreement. I translated for Saul. "May he go with God and in good health." Saul nodded approval.

Uncle Vanya leaned over and tapped me on the leg. "Your Aunt Sophie will be sending your rescuer a little token of her esteem. Tell him to expect a visit sometime soon."

I nodded, knowing this meant a feast would soon be arriving on Marcus' doorstep.

"I talked to your father, who, although not Rom, still has a father's concern at heart. I've told him his girl will be taken care of. Thank God I'm able to tell him I've seen her with my own eyes and she's fine."

I made a mental note to call Walt at the earliest possible moment to reassure him of my safety and health.

"And I also told your father that should you decide to marry this man who saved you that you would have the blessing of the family. This Sloan seems like a good man. Men I know and trust have said he's acted correctly throughout all of this."

I stared at Uncle Vanya, alarmed. "Uncle, Marcus and I have no intention of marrying. He did, most kindly, rescue me, but that's all."

The old man held up a hand and I fell silent. "I'm saying, should you decide..."

I laughed. "It takes two to make such a decision."

He grinned and winked. "A man knows these things. Sometimes, a woman has to be forthright. Sometimes a man doesn't know what he really wants to do."

I sipped my wine to give myself an opportunity to compose an answer. "I appreciate your support, Uncle, and the support of the boys." I nodded to 'the boys,' who nodded in return. "And should such a thing occur, I'll remember your words."

He beamed at me. "Good." Some unspoken message was passed. He and the boys got to their feet, Saul joining them. William looked up, dismayed at losing his friend. Robbie and I walked with the men to the front door.

"Saul, thank you so much for all your help," I told him as we paused outside near the World's Biggest SUV. I put my arms around the big man, or rather, tried to encircle him.

He patted me on the shoulder. "Glad to help." He peered past me to the house, where William sat on the front stoop in a ray of sunlight, regarding us with a woebegone expression. "Nice cat."

"If you'd like to find a cat for yourself, just call me," I said, touching his arm in commiseration. "I'd be happy to go to the local humane society with you and help you find the appropriate animal."

He brightened. "Really? I never had a pet. I might like that. Thanks."

Robbie and I waved good-bye as the troops left. He draped an arm over my shoulder and we turned back to the house. "Vanya is right, you know," he said quietly. "Marcus is a good man. You could do worse than marry him."

"Marry?" I pulled away, alarmed. "Marriage has

never even been mentioned in my presence. Heavens, Robbie, a second date has never even been mentioned." Then I blushed. "Even a first date, for that matter."

Robbie chuckled. *"Stanki nashti chi arakenpe manushen shai."*

I knew the expression well. 'Mountains do not meet, but people do.' My brother was telling me to meet Marcus halfway. "I know, Robbie," I murmured, disheartened. "But is there a possible future? I have no idea how he feels about me, and, to be honest, I don't know how I feel about him."

"Just give yourself a chance, Jane," he counseled. "Never walk away from love. It's too precious a gift."

"Well, if it's offered, perhaps I'll partake," I said, trying to lighten the mood. We went to the deck and picked up our drinks. We were just settling back in our respective seats when the portable phone on the table next to Robbie rang. He answered, his eyes going to me. "Sure," he said. He handed me the phone.

"It's Marcus." He raised his beer. "Time to partake, Jane."

He slipped away before I could tell him I didn't want to take the call. I took a long, steadying breath and prepared to face the truth.

Chapter 18

"How are you doing?"

The concern in Marcus' voice was evident. I swallowed around a suddenly large lump in my throat. "I'm fine," I managed to croak. "A bit bruised."

"Jane, I'm sorry. I didn't know they'd hurt you. When I saw you...when I saw what they'd done—Jane, I'm—"

"It's okay," I assured him. "Please. There was no real harm done. I was just frightened. Well, and bruised. When he tore my bra he—" I stopped, not wanting to go into details. "I'll be right as rain in a day or so."

There was a long, awkward silence. Then Marcus laughed uncomfortably. "I don't know what to say."

"I know. I feel the same way." I watched as William snagged a piece of cheese off the plate. He carried it off triumphantly, acting as though he'd stalked and brought down a full-grown cow after a long, arduous chase. "Marcus, there's something I have to ask you." I could sense his wariness. I hurried on before he could say anything. "It's about a woman you knew. I heard you and your brother talking about her. Marcus, are you still in love with her?"

"What?"

"Are you still in love with Mary Madison?" There. The words were out. I felt better for having said them but apprehensive about his answer.

He paused. I held my breath. "I don't know," he finally said.

I was swamped by disappointment. I had hoped for a vehement *of course not*. I didn't want his wishy-washy declaration of *unsure*.

"I don't know if I was ever in love with her," he continued.

Now that was odd. From the way his brother talked, this was a Major Event in Marcus' life. "You don't know?" I asked incredulously.

"Why are you asking about Mary?"

I wracked my brain for a suitable lie but settled for the truth. "I'm under the impression I'm very like her."

He didn't answer immediately. "It's true, you are sort of like her. She's got a bunch of college degrees and knows a few languages."

"And she has red hair," I said, rubbing salt into my wounds.

"Who told you that?"

"Your brother. I overheard you talking about it."

Marcus hesitated so long I wasn't sure if he was still there. "She's not you, Jane. I'm not confusing the two of you."

Bitterness at my plight made me say, "That's a relief. I'd hate to have you call out in the middle of a passionate moment and use the wrong name."

"Jane, that's unfair. Mary and I were never..." He stopped. "We weren't that close."

"Are we? Are we that close?" I was horrified at the jealous words that popped out of my mouth but I couldn't seem to help myself. I was hurt, angry, and upset. And why? I tugged on my curls, trying to initiate some sort of intelligence in a brain that had apparently lost all rational thought. Marcus and I had simply had sex. We hadn't declared an ever-lasting allegiance, a desire to be together for all time. All we'd had was sex, pure and simple.

"I hoped we were." His voice was very quiet. "But it's starting to sound like maybe you're having second thoughts. You were pretty quick to get angry at me the other day. It sounds like you're starting to back away."

I was quick to anger? I begged to differ but I knew it would do no good to quibble about that. "I told you what I thought, Marcus," I said. My voice reflected my obvious attempt to keep my temper under control. "It wasn't very pleasant to have someone who I cared for, someone with whom I was intimate, be suspicious of me. I was angered you didn't trust me. I was upset you thought so little of me."

"Well, I guess I know how it feels," he said in a low voice. "I'm feeling that way now."

I stared at the now-empty cheese plate in shocked outrage. How dare he compare the two events! Being accused of murder and being accused of mental infidelity had little to do with each other. "The two are hardly the same," I said stiffly.

"Really? Doesn't it all have to do with trust?"

"They aren't the same," I repeated stubbornly.

"It's starting to sound like maybe you don't want to see me again."

All the anger drained out of me. My stomach ached with a fierceness that was painful. I wanted to start the whole conversation over again. I wanted to go back to step one and replay everything. Instead, I said, "I'm not sure."

"Oh." The word seemed pulled out of him. "I

understand. I just wanted to make sure you were okay. I'm glad there's no lasting problems or—Anyway, I'm glad you're okay."

"Marcus, maybe I—"

"I'll probably have to see you when Scarlotti goes to trial," he hurried on.

Have to see me? He made it sound like he'd be going to the guillotine. "Perhaps."

"Okay. Well..."

I longed to say something, *anything*, that would make things right, but words escaped me. All intelligence seemed to have fled.

"Good-bye, Jane."

He hung up before I could speak.

Robbie came out onto the deck, obviously having been lurking just inside the door. Eavesdropping was, apparently, a family trait. He took one look at my face and said, "Aw, shit. What happened?"

I set the phone down, picked up my glass, and threw it as hard as I could into the woods behind the house. It shattered with a satisfying *crack* against a tree. "You were right," I said, my voice unsteady. "He's still in love with someone else."

"Oh, Jane, I'm sorry." He sat down next to me and took my hand in his. "I'm sorry, honey. I know how you cared for him."

I hiccupped. "I'm fine, Robbie. Just fine. As I keep telling you, Marcus Sloan was just a ship that passed in the night. This isn't some romance novel. There's not always a happily ever after." I mustered a brief smile. "Now it's time to get on with my life. I have a faculty meeting tomorrow that I need to prepare for." I stood up, grateful that my legs would hold me.

He still gripped my hand. "Are you sure, Phire?"

I gave our joined hands a little shake. He released me. "Certain, Roberto. Thank you."

His gaze followed me as I walked into the house.

I fled to the safety of my bedroom where I collapsed on the bed for a good, long cry. I lay there for what felt like an eternity, replaying the conversation with Marcus in my mind. I longed to find some magic words that would make it all right, but there were none. What I told Robbie was true. There aren't happy endings. I staggered to the bathroom, made my evening toilette then fell into an exhausted sleep, happily unpunctuated by nightmares.

When I awoke in the morning, a terrible sight greeted me in the mirror. I had a large bruise on my forehead that covered part of the side of my face. My breasts had bruises around the nipples and underneath, where my bra band had been. And my thighs were bruised where the thug tried to pry my legs apart. I shuddered and went into the shower, anxious to wash away an imagined feel of groping hands.

I had an awkward time dressing because I couldn't wear a bra without a great deal of pain and the only camisoles I had were either in the laundry or the wrong color. I settled for going bra-less, for once thankful I had a somewhat petite bosom and thus wouldn't bounce my way through the most important faculty meeting of my life. I chose a loose dark gray linen skirt, dark blue blouse and loose gray over-vest to hide my under-nakedness, wincing as I pulled on a pair of matching sandals. My poor feet had yet to recover from my stylish choice of the day before.

I had a moment of panic when I couldn't find my Coach bag then remembered I left it in the car, where Marcus dropped it the day before after absconding with my car in pursuit of Pat Scarlotti. My stomach burned when I thought of Marcus. I decided to follow the philosophy of one of the bitchiest heroines of all time, Scarlett O'Hara, and think about it tomorrow. Today I had to worry about my career.

I bid adieu to Robbie, who was reading the newspaper in the sunroom. "Do you want some company? A driver?" he asked, concerned.

"No, I'll be fine. I'm just going to this meeting then I'll come back home. What are your plans for the day?"

"I have to meet with Billy." He grinned mischievously at me. "I may need a place to stay until I can find an apartment."

It took a moment for understanding to soak into my tired mind. "You're going to do it? Move here?"

He nodded. "I'm hoping to. I have to do some more interviews, but I think it'll be possible. Would you mind having company for a time until I get settled?"

I gave him a hearty hug and a resounding kiss, which made him squirm like a teenager. "I'd love it," I declared. "Although I'll have to fight Maggie for your attention."

"You think so?"

I ruffled his hair. "I'm sure of it. Thank you, Robbie. You've made my day."

He gave me a little shove. "You go knock 'em on their ass." The phone at his elbow rang. He glanced at the caller ID. "Go, get out while you can. It's Abby."

I laughed and scurried away.

When I got to the Benz I had to adjust the seat settings and mirror from what Marcus used on the previous day. Again, I felt that pang when I remembered him. I looked at my little spider-hero, who dangled from my mirror. I superstitiously removed him then stuffed him into my skirt pocket. I had the feeling I would need some superhero support today.

TUSP was starting to show signs of bustling activity, but it would still be several days before the complete influx of students began. I parked in the faculty lot and hurried into the building, going to my office to drop off my bag. I took a moment to verify my appearance in the mirror in the ladies' room before proceeding to the main floor to join my peers who were gathering in the conference room adjacent to the department chair's office.

Kathy's eyes widened. "Man, that's a beaut," she said, eyeing my bruise. Then she glanced over her shoulder at the conference room. "Better get in there, they're all here. Crowndorf is here and he's armed with newspapers."

"Oh, no." I hurried into the room, almost skidding to a stop when I saw all my department peers were assembled, various specialists in Western Fiction, Film Studies, Shakespeare, Chaucer, Renaissance Poetry, British poetry, all weighty, serious, scholarly subjects. All ten of my colleagues sat there, chatting and drinking coffee as Jim Crowndorf leaned over the oval table, his pudgy face angry and his red polka-dot bowtie askew with his agitation.

"It's outrageous," Crowndorf said. He looked up at me, his pale gray eyes snapping with righteous indignation and poorly concealed glee. "Is this true?" He stabbed a finger at the newspaper. "Is it true you write—" He seemed to lose the power of speech.

"Why don't we all sit down?" Dr. Cross suggested mildly. "Dr. Renard, are you well enough to be here today? It looks like you sustained a rather bad injury."

Several other voices murmured consoling words. I swallowed hard. "I'm fine," I said with an assurance I didn't feel. I sank into a chair, Scott Welty (Film Studies) on one side and Robert Sanderson (Western fiction) on the other. Jim Crowndorf took a chair at the end of the oval table. Kathy came in and set my Bruised Orange mug in front of me, filled with coffee. I whispered a *Thank you*. She winked and left.

Jim waggled an accusing finger at the newspaper in the middle of the conference table. "This story says Jane writes—"

"What?" I asked faintly. I hadn't had a chance to review the media. I cleared my throat and tried to go on the offensive. "What are you saying?"

"The newspaper mentioned one of the suspects in your case, a Vito Scarlotti, accused you of writing romance novels." Dr. Cross regarded me with polite interest.

Oh, God. Trust Vito Scarlotti to do a thorough background check on anyone who interfered with his precious son. I had no doubt the son of a bitch probably made bail, held a press conference, then flew back to Pittsburgh with his psychotic son in tow, leaving a trail of innuendo behind him.

"Romance novels!" Jim Crowndorf almost lunged across the table in his effort to snare a newspaper. "They aren't romance novels, they're these—these—"

"Pornographic books?" Rebecca Winston asked. She was seated opposite me, a tiny white-haired woman dressed in her habitual faded denim jumper with a colored T-shirt underneath. Today it was a brilliant red color, matching her nail polish. "Oh. I'm sorry, dear. I believe they call it erotica now. In my day, we called it soft porn."

Dead silence descended on the room. I stared at her, my eyes wide.

"Exactly." Jim pounced. "And it besmirches the reputation of—"

"Of course, let's not forget *Candide*," Robert Sanderson said thoughtfully. "And *Leaves of Grass*. I think at one time even *The Arabian Nights* was banned as pornographic."

"And *Lolita*," Lillian Jones commented. "And *Fanny Hill, My Secret Life*, and *Moll Flanders*." She looked around the table. "Was *Tom Jones* banned? I can't remember."

"And *Madame Bovary*," Scott Welty said. "That was banned in its day."

"Then there's *Ulysses*," Grace Ann Cavanaugh said.

"And who can forget *Lady Chatterley?*" her husband, Ted, said. He shook his head. "Lawrence was persecuted for that and *Women in Love* and—"

"Jane's book hardly fall into the category of great literature," Crowndorf snapped.

Rebecca tapped one stiletto-like blood red nail on the tabletop. "You write about stranger sex, don't you, dear?" she asked in her modulated, soft voice. Her sharp hazel eyes seemed to glow with laughter as she regarded me.

I gave up on my original hope of concealing my secret identity. I could almost feel the little superhero in my pocket chuckle at my guileless naiveté. "Yes, I do," I mumbled.

"Well, there you are," Rebecca said. "The zipless fuck. *Fear of Flying*. Erica Jong."

"Who can forget the fuss that book made?" Scott said. "People acted as though sex with total strangers hasn't been around since the beginning of time."

"And don't forget *The White Hotel*," Ted added. "It came out about the same time. Good God, that book was hot."

"This kind of discussion of femininity and sexuality inevitably leads us to Kate Chopin," Margaret Trueheart said. She was our Feminist Fiction leader. "*The Golden Notebook*. Another banned book."

"And, of course, Virginia Wolff," Grace Ann interjected.

Jim Crowndorf gasped. "Jane's pornographic books are not to be compared to Virginia Wolff."

No one listened. This was a group of academics who had the bit between their teeth. They were going to gallop to the finish line no matter what he said. "There've been a lot of supposedly pornographic books on the banned list," Scott said. "I never quite understood *Of Mice and Men*."

"It was the glove," Ted said. "That was creepy. What's-his-name always wore the glove to keep his hand soft."

"Really?" Rebecca looked thoughtful. "I always thought there might be a homosexual relationship between Lenny and—" She waved her hand. "You know, what's-his-name."

"Just like Jim and Huck," Robert said. The so-called homosexual relationship between Twain's two characters was a pet peeve of his.

Several people made loud noises. "That old chestnut," Scott said in disgust. "A few critics can't be bothered to learn dialect so they call a relationship they don't understand subversive or immoral. Twain is laughing his ass off, wherever he is now." He grinned at me. "I would guess he would have more fun in hell, but he probably ended up in heaven."

"And speaking of subversive, don't forget Ayn Rand," Margaret said.

Someone groaned out loud. Rand was a favorite of Margaret's.

"That's not the p-p-p-point!" Jim looked like he might have a fit. I eyed him askance. He was starting to foam slightly at the mouth. "We're discussing whether pornographic books should be associated with—"

"They're quite good, dear," Rebecca said, her quiet voice cutting across Jim's stutter with the effect of a klaxon in the fog. Another silence descended on the room.

"You've read them?" I asked in a small voice. I

wanted to slide under the table.

Rebecca nodded, white hair wisping like a halo. "I liked *Deck the Halls*." She chuckled. "Your depiction of the building after hours was dead on."

"I liked *Fun in the Fields*," Scott said. "I remember parties like that when I was young and we had keggers in the cornfield."

I turned to him. "You've read my—"

Several heads bobbed around the table.

"You all knew?"

Heads bobbed again.

"How?"

"I caught Kathy reading one at lunch and made her tell," Rebecca said. "Then I mentioned it to Margaret."

"And I mentioned it to Scott."

"And I mentioned it to Grace and Ted."

"And we—"

Dr. Cross held up a hand. "Suffice it to say, we knew, Jane." He smiled benignly at me. "I, of course, was given all the facts by my predecessor, who also knew."

"In fact, Ted and I thought we'd try our hand at a novel," Grace Ann said in her sweet, cultured Southern voice. "I think we'll stick with straight murder mysteries, though. Perhaps something in the cozy line, although I would love to try one of those slasher books that are so popular now. We'll avoid the romance line since you seem to have a lock on the erotica."

I looked around the room at the smiling faces, tears starting to trickle down my cheeks. "You don't mind?"

"Well, I most certainly do!" Jim shouted.

"Oh, shut up," Scott said. "As you well know, Renaissance fiction is chock full of pornography. The only thing that keeps it from being banned is it's verbose, boring, and studied by esoteric assholes like you." He beamed at me, his homely face creasing. "Ignore him, Jane, he's just jealous."

"But—but—" I turned to Dr. Cross. "It's okay?"

"It's not exactly the visibility I was hoping for, but erotica is a fast-growing field of popular fiction which will probably, at some point, be studied academically. It might be useful to have an instructor who's well versed in the field."

Jim was making noises like a strangled fish. I looked at him with concern. What a newspaper headline that would make! *Erotic writer kills colleague in English Department faculty meeting.*

"What about having sex in the office?" he sputtered. "Surely that's—"

"I beg your pardon." Dr. Cross' voice lowered the temperature in the room to autumnal proportions. "What are you suggesting?"

All eyes turned to Jim Crowndorf. He said haughtily, "These doors aren't soundproof, you know."

I turned slowly to face him. "What did you say?" Jim's face turned a mottled shade of red. "It was you," I accused. "It was you who said that."

He stared at me, panicked. I recognized the knowledge in his eyes. He was the pervert who'd called me. But why? If he didn't know I wrote erotica, then why did he bother me with those stupid phone calls? I assumed the calls had to do with my writing but—

In an instant, pieces of the puzzle clicked into place. Crowndorf was always around when I was. Kathy mentioned he was lurking around the halls. What if Crowndorf had a crush on me or thought he could... I stared into his eyes. His facial color changed from red to fire engine red.

I was right. And he knew I knew.

He jumped to his feet. "I refuse to be insulted like this." His voice was high, wavering. "This is ridiculous." He started to make a break for the door.

"Dr. Crowndorf, please sit down," Dr. Cross said patiently. "We aren't done discussing the things that—"

"I'm done," he croaked. "I don't feel well. I'm— I—have to—I'm—" He bolted for the door.

I jumped to my feet and started after him.

"Dr. Renard."

I paused. Dr. Cross was regarding me with bright, curious dark eyes. "Have a seat," he said placidly. "You can chat with Dr. Crowndorf later."

I looked at Crowndorf, who had stopped by the door that led out of the room. I narrowed my eyes and glared at him. "I saw what you did and I know who you are," I said in a low, threatening voice.

He blanched, jerked the door open, and fled.

I sat down, took a deep breath then clasped my hands on the table in front of me. "I'm sorry, Dr. Cross. You were saying?"

Scott Welty started to laugh.

Chapter 19

The remainder of the meeting was anti-climactic. We discussed how to handle the press ("ignore them," Rebecca advised. "Play them," Scott advised). In the end, Dr. Cross decided to issue a statement, which we all helped draft:

Dr. Jane Renard, a respected member of the English faculty at The University of St. Paul, was attacked while defending a family friend but fortunately was not seriously injured. Dr. Renard, known for her academic research in American fiction of the late 19th century, also is a best-selling author, writing under a pen name, as is usual for many writers in popular fiction today. The English department lauds Dr. Renard for her desire to help her friend and wishes her a speedy recovery in anticipation of a busy Fall Semester.

"That's an understatement," Scott said wryly. "You'll probably be inundated with undergrads who want to take your classes."

"William Dean Howells isn't that fascinating," I protested.

He grinned. "But you are."

"I trust you'll be working on your academic

scholarship and your research on American authors," Dr. Cross said as the meeting broke up.

I nodded vigorously. "Of course." I didn't want our press statement to be a lie. I'd start a new scholarly paper immediately.

"And I believe we may want to postpone our discussion about the Full Professorship, at least at this time."

I stifled my disappointment. "Of course."

"However, given the trauma you've had recently, I believe a short sabbatical, for one semester, might be in order. I'll see what I can do with the Winter Term schedule. Perhaps we can free up some time for you to recuperate and work on your next article." He smiled at me.

I smiled gratefully in return. "Thank you. For everything."

"I look forward to an interesting year, Dr. Renard." He went into his office.

I sank down in the chair next to Kathy's desk. "Did you hear?" I whispered.

She nodded to the phone on her desk. "I had it set to *conference* while you guys were in there," she said in affirmation. "I heard every word. What was that bit with Crowndorf?"

"I think he—" I stopped as Scott, Rebecca, and others came over to the desk. "I'll tell you later." I looked up at my peers. "I can't tell you how much it means to me to have your support. Thank you so much."

They all started talking at once, as was typical for a group of academics. We moved our conversation to the hall, then to a nearby pasta parlor for lunch as we revisited the meeting, discussing all the implications in every detail. It was several hours and several glasses of wine later before I returned to my office, sank down, and contemplated what happened.

I so wanted to call Marcus and tell him I found out who the Phone Pervert was. I picked up the phone then put it down several times, not sure what to say to initiate such a conversation. What would he think? Should I call him? Shouldn't I?

I realized I was accomplishing nothing sitting in my office. With a sigh, I gathered my briefcase and went to the Benz. As I drove home, I thought about calling Marcus, rehearsing possible conversational openings in my mind. Nothing seemed right, however. We hadn't parted on the best of terms. It seemed too contrived for me to be calling him after our dismissive phone discussion of the day before.

I did battle with my pride and insecurity all the way home, coming to no conclusion about the correct course of action. Robbie's rented Mustang was nowhere in sight so I assumed he was with Maggie. But as I pulled in my driveway, I saw a late model S-type Jaguar parked near the driveway verge, affording me just enough room to park the Benz. I touched my garage door opener, wondering who was visiting. As I did, a man appeared, walking around the side of the house where he had obviously been ascertaining whether I was at home or not. As he approached I recognized Declan Fabersham.

Today he was dressed like a model for one of those Ralph Lauren ads: crisp dark blue shorts, soft, fitted light blue shirt and wearing loafers with no socks. His tousled, sun-bleached hair was swept back from his tanned face and his lithe, athletic body seemed to glow with good health. He had the type of craggy good looks Robert Redford had in the Great Gatsby, before he aged and become rather creased. Fabersham looked like an aging preppie.

He looked like a very worried aging preppie. I could see the tension in the angle of his shoulders and the jerky, inelegant way he moved. His unexpected visit annoyed me. Here I was, fresh from my triumph over the despicable Jim Crowndorf. I wanted to rest on my laurels, drink some wine, and work up my courage to call Marcus. I did not want to converse with a haughty man who had an over-inflated idea of his own worth. Then I remembered the death of Lisa, his stepmother, and tempered my impatience. After all, the man was a stranger in town. Presumably he just wanted to chat with someone he knew, even though we were barely acquainted.

"Mr. Fabersham," I said as he neared the car and peered to look inside. "What a surprise." I tried to inject warmth into my tone but wasn't sure if my impatience showed through.

"Miss Renard, I was hoping we could talk before I leave town." He stepped back, waiting for me to pull into my garage. His action was peremptory, as though I was keeping him from some vital appointment.

Inwardly fuming, I pulled the Benz in and got out, reaching for my briefcase stored in the back footwell. As I did, Mr. Fabersham came into the garage and waited for me near the stairs leading into the kitchen.

Something about his actions perturbed me. I wasn't comfortable inviting a strange man into my home. Perhaps it was a residue of yesterday morning's attack by the guards hired by Pat Scarlotti. Fabersham appeared anxious to get into my house. It may have been typical of his thoughtless, casual impatience or perhaps some other motive was at work.

"You're leaving town?" I dallied, delaying the need to invite him in by setting the briefcase on the hood of the Benz then pretending to search inside for something of importance.

"Yes, in a few hours."

I live in Chaska, which is located as far from the

airport as one could get and still be considered in the Twin Cities metropolitan area. If he needed to talk to me, a phone call would have been far more efficient. "You should be going to the airport soon, then," I pointed out. "Traffic at this time of day is quite congested, especially around the airport. And you need to leave ample time to pass through the different security checks."

"I realize that. I just need a few minutes of your time."

His voice was clipped and angry. I couldn't think of any reasonable explanation to remain standing in the garage, so I reluctantly led the way up the steps. "I'm going out soon," I lied. "My brother will be coming home to pick me up."

"Your brother?"

He sounded shocked or... I couldn't quite put my finger on a word to describe the surprise in his voice.

"Yes, my brother. He's visiting in town and is staying with me. I suspect he'll be home any moment since he and I are going out." I was making up my story as I went but Fabersham appeared to believe me. He followed me through my little mudroom into the kitchen.

As we entered, Ezra approached with his usual urgent request for his treat. Fabersham took a step backward at the sight of the rotund cat stalking toward us, clamorously vocalizing his demands. "What's that?"

"That's a cat," I said with some asperity.

"Why's it making so much noise?"

I almost asked, *"why are you?"* but the social behavior instilled in me by my mother overrode my desire to be rude. "He's given a treat at this time every day, when I get home from work," I explained, putting my briefcase down on the counter. As I did, I knocked against the little teacup toy I received when Saul and I went to the Burger King restaurant. It started to roll toward the edge. I scooped it up, stuffing it into my skirt pocket with my spider-hero in order to avoid teacup injury. I went to the cupboard to get Ezra's pill and treat.

Fabersham followed me, almost treading on my heels in his closeness.

"Mr. Fabersham, is there something I can help you with?" I asked, pushing past him to get at the cat dishes and the noxious Tuna Treat in the can.

"I was hoping you could tell me what you found out from the police."

I looked at him in surprise. "I beg your pardon?" I forced the medication down Ezra's throat then dished up the tuna, holding my breath so the fishy fumes wouldn't reach me.

Fabersham was too close to avoid it. Plus he didn't have the benefit of previous experience with the noisome cat food. He stepped back in alarm, almost treading on Ezra, who hissed and scurried away.

"For heaven's sake," I said in exasperation. "Let me feed my cat." I put the dish down. Ezra approached cautiously, eyeing Fabersham's expensive-looking loafers with trepidation. Finally deciding it was safe, the rotund cat settled down with a happy sigh.

I knew what to expect next. William came out, howling his dismay at being ignored. Fabersham looked like he'd have a tantrum. I dished out food for my other feline companion then turned to my unwanted guest. "Now why are you here?"

"I told you, the police questioned me about Lisa's death. I'd like to know why."

I resisted the impulse to say *perhaps because they suspect you.* I had the feeling if I said that, the man would have an apoplectic fit. "Why would you think I'd know about police procedures?"

"You've been questioned all along about Toby's

death and about Lisa's."

I was starting to get very annoyed. "Of course I was questioned," I snapped. "I was married to Toby and Toby was married to your stepmother. It only stands to reason I'd be questioned." I started to edge away from him but he didn't take the hint. He followed me, too close within my personal space. It was uncomfortable. "I didn't find out anything from the police. I haven't talked to the police about your stepmother's death since the day she was found. I've been rather busy with other matters."

"What? What other matters?"

He took a step closer to me. I stepped back, alarmed. He was tall and towered over me. Luckily I had good proximity sense, thus avoiding the cats. "Don't you read a newspaper? I was attacked yesterday, a man was shot—" The blank look on his face was my answer. "Really, Mr. Fabersham, there are other things occurring in the world than those that affect you."

I hurried away, toward the sunroom, but Fabersham stepped in front of me, blocking my exit from the kitchen. He didn't appear to have heard my words. He returned to his previous complaint. "You've been talking to the police all along," he said in a low, angry voice. "What have you found out?"

This was getting somewhat frightening. "Why do you think I've been talking to the police?" I asked, glancing around the kitchen for anything that might be used as a defensive weapon should I need one. My knife rack was on the other side of the room, my toaster was securely plugged in, and the only other object that might conceivably be wielded was a cutting board the size of a paperback book. Where was a good missile launcher when you needed it?

"I saw you at the station. And you're dating that cop."

"He's not a cop and we're not dating." The words

came out forcefully, probably because of my agitation over my fractured relationship with Marcus.

Apparently my vehemence surprised Fabersham because he took a step back. I took advantage of his distraction to step to the patio door. I glanced out at the deck, praying for some sort of weapon—a garden hoe, a razor-sharp pair of shears, an open container of toxic weed killer. All I saw was a discarded beer bottle, around which several drunken bees were hovering, and the portable phone, which Robbie left there. "Why are you concerned, Mr. Fabersham?" I turned, trying to block his view of the deck and the phone, in plain sight.

"Lisa was killed near your office, at Watson Hall," he stated. "It stands to reason they'd be talking to you."

"You didn't answer my question," I said. "Why are you so concerned?" Then his words penetrated. To my knowledge, Sam Sloan did not release the information about where the body was found. I surmised it had something to do with the construction site at Watson Hall, but Sloan didn't confirm or deny. How did Fabersham know? I tried to formulate a method to glean that information without tipping my hand. "Besides, you must be mistaken. My office isn't in Watson Hall."

The stunned surprise on his face alerted me I made a grievous error. "What?"

"Well, if you've ever been on campus you'd know my office is not in Watson Hall." I glanced at the patio door, almost cursing out loud when I saw it was locked. Damn that Robbie and his conscientiousness! There was no way I could flick the lock, open the door, and get outside. Well, perhaps boldness would do. I put a hand on the door. "Excuse me," I said as firmly as I could. "My brother left a bottle out there."

The malevolent look he directed at me was

chilling. "I don't care," he said in a voice that quavered. "The sign said the English department was in Watson Hall."

"What sign?" I flipped up the little locking mechanism then put a hand on the patio door handle. I started to inch the door open.

"The one on campus."

The cats, done gobbling their gourmet feasts, meandered toward us. William plunked himself near the door, peering up at me imperiously. I slid open the patio door, thankful for a reasonable excuse to escape from Fabersham's nearness. At least outside there was more room to maneuver. I slid open the screen and prepared to step outside as William wiggled his chubby bottom, anxious to leap into the great outdoors.

Fabersham put a hand on the doorframe, very near my head. "Where do you think you're going?" he asked in a low voice.

I was mildly concerned before. I was frightened now. "Out." I ducked under his outstretched arm, emerging onto the deck.

William chose that moment to attempt a graceful sidestep of the clumsy humans who were blocking his egress to the outer world. He slipped past, narrowly avoiding Fabersham, who stepped back with a muttered curse, startled at the calico apparition at his feet. I used that moment to bend over, kick the discarded bottle, pluck up the portable phone and whirl around, my hand holding the phone away from him. The folds of my skirt swirled. I was able to slip the phone into my pocket. I bent over for the beer bottle I kicked.

Fabersham jerked my arm. I cried out in surprise, almost stumbling. "Leave it," he snapped. "What did you tell the police?"

"About what?" I demanded.

"Don't play games with me." The muscles in his

neck stood out in sharp relief. His dark brown eyes were unreadable but I knew he was appallingly angry.

"I don't know what you're talking about." I struggled briefly, trying to release his grip but my actions were in vain. He had me in a hold that precluded movement on my part.

"Lisa came to see you. What did you talk about?"

"What?"

My honest surprise seemed to startle him. His grip loosened so I was able to pull away. I took a step back, almost skidding on the discarded beer bottle.

"She told me she was going to see you that afternoon," Fabersham said. He looked around desperately, as though unsure of how we'd moved to my deck facing the woods behind my house. I slipped a hand into my pocket, hoping to somehow ascertain, by touch, which of the many protuberances on the phone was the "Rocket Dial" button that would summon 911 emergency personnel.

I chose the wrong pocket.

I almost screamed in anger. My hand was now holding the little teacup, which as a weapon posed no threat to anyone except possibly ants and other tiny insects when it did its little stomping dance. "Your stepmother didn't come to see me," I said. "Or, if she did, I wasn't there. I wasn't in my office the entire time. Perhaps she came and I was gone. But if she went to Webster Hall, I wasn't there. Our offices have moved back to Merrill, you see. So I wasn't in my old office in Webster—my temporary office, that is—but I was in my permanent office in Merrill Hall. But I wasn't there all afternoon."

My flood of verbiage seemed to bewilder him. Good. I was pleased to see he was as confused as I was.

"She was coming to see you. About Toby."

"Toby's dead." I was truly confused now.

"She wanted to know how much Toby told you. Toby told her that he was going to leave an important document with someone he trusted."

"Well, that wouldn't be me," I said, edging toward the three steps leading to the yard below. If he noticed, he gave no sign. "Toby didn't trust me."

"She thought he did. She thought that's why Toby was coming to St. Paul. To see you."

I threw up my hands in supposed exasperation and took two more steps toward freedom. "Toby was coming here to see me to blackmail me."

"Blackmail you?" Fabersham shook his head. "That makes no sense. He was blackmailing us." He reached behind him, pulling something out of a back pocket. I realized that he had never had his back to me the entire time he was in my house. I now knew why.

He held a gun.

Chapter 20

I swear, my first thought was, *he has to be kidding*. Why did he think he could shoot me and get away with it? Then I saw his odd, crazed eyes and those thoughts fled. The man was insane with fear. "Blackmail?" I croaked, my throat suddenly parched.

"About us." His hand wobbled but the gun remained fixed on me. I had seen a gun once, when I went to a gun range and asked to examine various models for research for a book. The owner, a paunchy little man with bad skin, appeared amused by this request. He spent a happy afternoon regaling me with tales that I suspected were fictitious but which were interesting nonetheless.

I didn't remember those guns being as big as the one in Fabersham's hand. "Us?" I asked, sounding like a parrot.

"Lisa and I."

Oh, Lord. This was bad. He was telling me far too much. I backed away from him, now standing in front of the three low steps that led down to my yard, the woods behind my house, and the river far below. "I don't understand." I didn't want him to talk, but I didn't know what else to do.

"Lisa married Toby as a front. My father—he was a real bastard. The way he set it up, if she and I married, the trust fund reverted to a local hospital."

He explained it as though it was the most natural thing in the world. Perhaps in his world, the world of Ralph Lauren people with Money (capital M), it was. I almost dislocated my eyes, if such a thing was possible, trying to discern how close I was to the steps. "But what about Toby?" I asked inanely. "Why did you..." I couldn't voice the words.

"Kill him? I didn't."

I almost sagged with relief. Had he admitted guilt, I would know I was doomed.

"Lisa did. I just helped."

Oh God. I was doomed.

"It was easy to kill him. You saw how dark it was there." Fabersham shook his head, as though decrying the sad lack of lighting at the venue. "He wasn't expecting it from her. That's why she did it. If I was there, he'd know something was up. But he didn't expect violence from Lisa."

"But why? Why not just go on as you were? She could pretend to be happily married to Toby while you and she could..." I choked, trying to find a delicate way to phrase it, "...continue your relationship."

"Toby wanted out. Lisa gave him money to shut him up but it wasn't enough. He wanted his freedom. That wasn't going to work."

"Then just find another husband!" I threw up my hands in exasperation, almost overbalancing. "I'm sure there are plenty of gigolos who would love the opportunity."

He gave me a *gee, what a moron look*. I recognized it. My undergraduates leveled it at me when I asked about the music that always sounded as if it was oozing from the little appendages stuck into their ears.

"There was talk, at the club, about us. Everything was starting to fall apart. If she got divorced, she'd have to give Toby money and that would eat into the fund. This way, we could get rid of him, get rid of the blackmail threat, then the grieving widow could move away from the home that held so many memories. We'd find another man and set him up."

"But why?" Oh, this made no sense. "Why not just have a clandestine affair?"

"We wanted to have a baby. Or, she did." The disdainful expression on his face told me what an excellent father he'd be. Not. "We needed a husband. If she was single and got pregnant and if it could be proved the baby was mine, the trust fund would be dissolved." He smiled crookedly. "My father didn't trust us."

Good God, everything in my life was revolving around issues of trust. Tommi didn't trust Joe, I didn't trust Marcus, Marcus didn't trust me, Declan Fabersham's father didn't trust him. I shook the distracting thought away, struggling to find a way out of my predicament.

It was Ezra, my elderly feline companion, who came to my rescue.

Spying us all on the deck, Ezra decided to meander out to join the group. Declan Fabersham had his back to the door which led into the kitchen. Ezra sat down behind Fabersham and proceeded to initiate a thorough bathing. Seeing a pair of stationary vertical objects handy, the old cat decided to avail himself of their proximity to facilitate his balance. He leaned against Fabersham's bare legs.

The man jumped at least a foot in the air, cursing and shouting. I fled, leaping down the three steps to the small grassy verge then crashing into the woods beyond. I had a brief frightened thought for my poor cats, left to fend for themselves. My last glimpse of them was of vanishing tails as both cats reacted to Fabersham's thrashings. I prayed their innate feline intelligence would stand them in good stead.

I went through the first line of trees, thick pines lining the top of the hill's bluff which stood sentinel tall above the next stand of trees, some scrub oaks and maple saplings. I thrashed through them, narrowly avoiding the broken glass caused by my fit of temper the previous day. Behind one impressive oak, balanced precariously on the slope, was a small declivity where I put out bread, apples, and various foodstuffs for the possums, groundhogs, and other inoffensive mammals. I hunkered down, avoiding the mushy remains of one such feast. I pulled out the portable phone and pressed Rocket Dial. In a breathless whisper, I described my predicament (*man with gun, stalking me, at my house, in the woods*). It seemed to take forever, but the calm woman on the other end of the line finally assured me help was on its way.

I heard Fabersham crashing through the undergrowth.

I stuffed the phone back in my pocket. It would be at least ten minutes until anyone could get to my house. Marcus was right. I was too isolated. I peered around for anything that would serve as a defensive projectile, knife, or bludgeon. All that met my inspection were downed branches, my rickety bird feeder full of sunflower seeds, and the remains of a fence, long rotted. There was nothing I could use.

I huddled in my little nest, listening as Fabersham entered the woods. I patted my other pocket to ascertain if I had retained my car keys. Perhaps I could use the 'panic button' to make the Benz's klaxon alarm go off. No keys. All I had was a tiny teacup and spider-hero. I pulled them out and stared at them, fear washing through me.

Panic was starting to take over. A man with a gun was trying to find me. He didn't need to get close to me to kill me. This wasn't like the other day, when a man grabbed me with personal assault in mind. This new threat, this man, could stand there, yards away, and still kill me. I had to find some way to hide long enough for the emergency personnel to get here. I clung to my little toys, feeling like a trapped animal with no recourse. I made a silent promise, to whatever deity was listening, that if I got out of this I would re-double my support for gun control laws. It seemed the least I could do.

The little spider-hero dug into my hand. I wished with all my might for a real superhero to appear. He regarded me, small and capable. An idea glimmered in my brain. To my right, about thirty feet away, was a solid-appearing flat piece of earth that jutted out from the hillside, approximately six feet square. I was below this area and could see the washout underneath where erosion had taken its toll. Only a third of that area was truly on solid ground. The rest was suspended in space, over a steep gully etched out of the hill, over a latticework of tree roots. If I could entice Fabersham to creep out onto that spot...

I looked down the hill then up to the bird feeder. Sunflower seed shells littered the ground. I reached out and dug up a handful of hulls, putting them in my skirt pocket with the phone. I backed down the hill, moving to the right. Luckily Fabersham was making so much noise he didn't hear my progress. When I was below the washout, I took out the little teacup. I assessed my situation, eyeing my escape route.

I put the little dancer on a downed log, flipped the small activation switch then I scuttled away, hiding under the washout. The small teacup began its erratic *stomp stomp stomp*, bobbing and weaving on the old log while emitting a high-pitched *whee whee* noise. I pulled my ammunition from my pocket, piling it up like small cannonballs. Then I got out my spider-hero and waited.

I heard Fabersham approaching the tinny *thump* that echoed on the log. I knew the little dancer couldn't sustain its balance for too much longer. As soon as I sensed Fabersham above me, I put a sunflower hull into my spider-hero's throwing arm and let loose, down the hill toward a pile of down trees not far away. The hull made a satisfying *tick* sound. I repeated the gesture again, praying Fabersham would walk onto the outcropping to investigate the noise.

I heard cautious footsteps above me. I held my breath as I picked up a hull and tossed it into the dead leaves on the ground ahead of me.

Cold air seemed to wash over me. The hair on the back of my neck prickled. He was near. I could feel him. I held my breath. I had to time this perfectly.

He stepped forward.

I tossed another hull, followed by a spider-hero hull tossed far into the woods.

He stepped further forward.

I put a hand on a tree root above me, pulling with all my might. The sensation of Fabersham, just scant inches away, was almost palpable. I jerked cautiously.

Nothing happened for one long, heart-stopping moment. I switched my efforts to another, smaller root, tugging like a demented handler pulling on a recalcitrant animal.

Coldness washed through me. He was near, so very near.

Fabersham stepped forward, peering over the edge.

Our eyes met.

He raised the gun.

The ground gave way.

I clung to the root as earth, man, and small saplings crashed into the hill, tumbling in a cascade down the steep slope. I hazarded one glance behind me to ascertain a body was flipping, ass over teakettle, down the incline. Then I scrambled up the hill with my small spider-hero still in hand, tearing my skirt in my haste to get away. I attained the summit but promptly lost my balance and fell down. Pushing to my feet, I crashed into the bird feeder, almost knocking myself unconscious. I then raced around the side of the house and was captured by a pair of strong, masculine arms.

I started to scream, kicking and fighting. It took two large police officers to calm me long enough for me to point, somewhat incoherently, to my hillside. Then I collapsed on my deck, sobbing and hiccupping.

That's where Robbie found me when he came home, thirty minutes later.

As the mighty Saul said, there is an amazing amount of bullshit that goes on when one is dealing with the police, especially when a firearm is involved. At some point, Robbie called Sam Sloan and Billy Armstrong. I told my story perhaps a dozen times, breaking down and weeping again when I described how Ezra saved my life and bemoaning the loss of my cats, whom no one had found. Had I known they were sleeping on my bed, I would have been reassured but I didn't discover that until some hours later.

Declan Fabersham was retrieved from the bottom of my hill, close to the fast-flowing Minnesota River. He had a broken arm and several cracked ribs, which I felt was only fair. I decided to keep my promise to the deity about the gun control protests, having been given proof that there is justice in the world.

Hours later, Sam Sloan, Billy, Robbie, and I sat at my kitchen table, drinking coffee. Well, they were drinking coffee. I was swilling wine like there was no tomorrow. My spider-hero sat in a spot of honor in the middle of the table and my dancing teacup, rescued by the police crime scene people, sat nearby, grimy but still capable of gyrating. I vowed to find them suitable trophy cases at the first possible opportunity.

"I'm not sure I understand it," I said for possibly the third time. I lost count, due to the quantity of wine I was consuming. "Lisa and Declan were lovers. She married Toby in order to make it look good. Toby figured it out." I snorted with laughter. "I'm just glad Toby got what he deserved. Oh, no, I don't mean dying," I said hastily at Sloan's shocked look. "But somebody finally used him instead of him using them." I hiccupped and sipped my wine. "Toby decides to blackmail them. And then...?"

"We think what happened is, she told Toby she found out he was still married. She demanded he come here and agree to a divorce." Sam Sloan looked confused but I didn't blame him. I was confused, too. I was almost certain it wasn't just a wine confusion. "They wanted to deal with him out of town. They followed him, found out where he was going to meet you."

"That letter sat in your mailbox and it wasn't sealed," Robbie pointed out. "They probably read it, knew he'd be there. It was a perfect spot to kill him. You were there and suspicion would fall on you."

"But why did Lisa come to see me at the campus?" I touched my little teacup, which gave a tiny spastic shake in return, as though anxious to repeat its performance. "And who killed her?"

"We found traces of the drug given to her in a glass in her hotel room." When I would have spoken,

Sam held up a hand. "It had Declan's fingerprints on it. I think he went with her. When they got to campus, Lisa was groggy and disoriented. Declan took her to the construction site. It was noon and no one was around. There are a lot of places where two people could stand, out of sight. He told her they were going to your office, to talk to you about what Toby had given you. She died of an embolism. It can be caused easily."

"Ah." I nodded. I'd researched this for a book. "If one injects air into a vein, it causes an embolism which acts immediately."

"Yep. It would only take a minute to inject her. She died instantly. He would inherit the entire trust fund."

I shook my head. "Robbie and I checked. She was going to give it to Save The Whales."

"Manatee," Robbie corrected.

"Nope." Sam Sloan shook his head adamantly. "We checked the will. Everything went to her stepson. It was why he seduced her in the first place. He figured they'd just get married and he'd get his hands on the money. He didn't know his father put that clause in the will."

I remembered the maze of dry wall and twisting corridors that were in place during the renovation. Sam was right. There were any number of nooks where two people could hide. "He did it? He killed her?" Oh, that poor woman. Every man in her life betrayed her. Her first husband didn't trust her and made that will, Toby betrayed her, and the man she ultimately loved, Declan Fabersham, betrayed her. The poor woman.

"We think so. Then he tried to find out what your husband sent you."

"But I don't have anything—" I stopped. "Oh."

"What?" Sloan demanded.

"I haven't read through the mail I got at my

mail box address. Maybe it's there." I hurried into the den and snatched up the letters I tossed there days ago. I shuffled through them, returning to the kitchen, triumphant. "Here." I thrust it at Robbie, but Sam Sloan intercepted it. He handled it with a handkerchief, slipping a penknife under the seal then opening the one folded page. He read the missive then pulled a plastic bag from his pocket to put the letter inside. Only then were we allowed to view it.

Janie: You're my insurance policy, baby. If something happens to me, go to tobylovesjane.com. *You know the password, gypsy queen. You'll see something interesting there. Thanks. I hope you don't hate me too much.*

Robbie and Billy were already hurrying to the den and my desktop computer. "Password?" Robbie called over his shoulder.

"Gadjo." It was the Rom word for a non-gypsy. I used it as a term of endearment, so long ago. "Toby loves Jane?" I asked. "What a joke."

"I guess there's all kinds of love in the world," Sam Sloan said in a thoughtful voice. "I need to tell you something about Marc."

"Don't," I interrupted. "I'm not owed any explanations."

"He told me what you talked about on the phone," Sloan said with a determined expression. "I was wrong. Yeah, he was interested in Mary, but it never came to anything. He loves you, Jane. I know he does. I was just pissed off that he—" Sam shook his head as though trying to straighten out his thoughts. "I don't know. I guess I'm just envious or something. Don't be mad at him, okay? Give it a chance."

"Jane! Come in here and see this!"

I was spared having to answer Marcus's brother. I joined my brother in the den to read the incriminating evidence my late husband decided to share with me.

But of course, you've read all about that, right? It made the national news when it came out about the insider trading and all that fuss. Who would think Toby was such a sneaky little bastard?

I should have known.

****

The next night Robbie insisted we keep 'our date' and go to the State Fair.

I really didn't want to. I had bad memories of that grandstand and what happened there. But he was determinedly cheerful, pointing out we had the tickets plus he bought tickets for Maggie, Ian, Kathy, and her husband, Mike. Perry was still in the hospital, but would be released on Sunday so we planned a party for Labor Day Monday to celebrate. Billy and his wife Jodie would attend, as would some of my colleagues from school. I was thinking of calling Marcus and inviting him, which would only be fitting because he helped solve our problems. I hadn't worked up the courage yet to do so.

"Tonight will be the start of our weekend of celebrating," Robbie said as he drove us to the fairground where we parked in the "Giraffe" lot. "All the things you were worried about have been solved. Pat and his father were extradited to Pennsylvania, your late husband's murderer has been caught and the guy who was writing the fan letters has been found."

"What happened to him?" I asked as we joined other fairgoers entering the grounds.

He grinned. "Edward and I had a long talk. I pointed out that the woman he thinks of as Phire Foxe is the woman I plan to marry—someday," he added quickly when he saw my gleeful look. "And I'm responsible for Edward's performance reviews, so it might be safer if he finds another author on which to expend his...energy."

"Well, that should solve that problem. Thank you for dealing with it, Robbie."

"It was my fault, in a way. I didn't think he'd get so..." He glanced at me. "I suppose I still think of you as my baby sister and not as a steamy author."

I nudged him. "That's okay. I forgive you. And what about Pat? Are we truly done with him and his damn father?"

Robbie faltered, the anger evident in his face. "Yes, we're done with him. They screwed up big time by pulling that stunt out here. Scarlotti's money won't help them. Billy will make sure of that. Pat broke the law by coming to Minnesota, Vito broke the law by grabbing you, and that son of a bitch who mauled you—"

I put a restraining hand on his clenched fist. "It's okay, Robbie." I thought of the formidable Mr. Armstrong. I had no doubt Vito and Pat would have a very hard time of it indeed. It was a cheering thought. Then I remembered poor Toby and was depressed again. "What a pity things couldn't have worked out so well for Toby."

"It's not your fault, Jane. If Toby had just played along, he'd still be alive today. He was greedy."

I nodded sadly. "I know. But it's still so..." I tried to put into words what emotions I was feeling. "It's all such a waste. Lisa loved Declan. He loved the money. Toby didn't love anyone. It was all such a waste."

"I told you once that when love is given, you need to take a chance." He led the way into the grandstand after handing our tickets to the young man at the turnstile.

"You should talk," I remonstrated. "I almost had to throw you into Maggie's arms."

The person in question was in the handicapped section, waving to us. Robbie waved in return. "And

I'm glad you did. I just wish you could be as happy."

I shrugged, hoping to appear nonchalant. "Someday my prince will come."

He paused. "If he does, will you welcome him? If Marcus came to you, would you welcome him?"

I tried to sort through my confused feelings as people walked around us. I was conscious of Maggie and the others, watching us curiously. "Yes," I admitted. "In fact, I've been trying to think of how to initiate contact in a way that doesn't, well, you know, it doesn't—"

Robbie shook his head. "Don't worry about pride." He grinned, young and carefree. "*Te xav ka to biav.*"

I laughed. "No, may I eat at *your* wedding." I nudged him up to the stands and the people waiting for us. "And soon, I hope."

We took the seats that were saved for us, Robbie sitting next to Maggie and putting an arm around her as though it was the most natural thing in the world. They were so good together, with her perky, tousled good looks and his tall, protective handsomeness. Having the specter of Pat removed had lightened everyone's countenance and mood. We were a festive group as we got our beer and waited for the show to begin.

The host soon emerged, his huge image visible on the large screens flanking the small stage. Like the ZZ Top concert, the crowd was mainly in the bleachers with a few select chairs on the track for those who had paid a higher ticket price.

To my delight Princess Kay and her court were in the front row, this time dressed in evening gowns and tiaras. Then I realized this was the final night of the fair. They would close the doors on the Dairy Barn at eleven p.m., a ceremonial event that marked the end of the Great Minnesota Get-Together. I felt a gentle tug of melancholy at the thought.

The show that night seemed to reflect my mood. Garrison Keillor's *Prairie Home Companion* radio show was a staple of public broadcasting and had been on the air for several decades. It was an eclectic mix of songs, skits, and witty monologues, all interspersed with Midwestern humor. I thought it would be an amusing end to Robbie's vacation and a fitting beginning to a new school year.

Tonight, though, the focus seemed to be on nostalgia, with a wistful romantic theme. The songs reflected this, mournful tunes about lost love and times gone by. I kept glancing down to the track, where poor Toby sat just a week earlier. A week ago I met Marcus for the first time. A week ago my life changed forever. It was depressing and a little frightening to realize what an effect one man made in my life. I wondered where he was. Was he still helping with Security? I watched the various guards walking around but didn't recognize his distinctive bodybuilder's physique and his spiky white hair.

I considered what Robbie said. I knew he was right. I should swallow my pride, call Marcus, and apologize. He apologized to me, after all. I did owe him an apology. And the picnic was a perfect venue.

By the time we reached the break at the one-hour mark, I decided I would call Marcus in the morning to ask him to our celebratory picnic. It was at this point in the radio show that the host took messages from the audience and read them to the crowd. Because this was a live radio show, these were always funny or endearing little missives to loved ones around the country who were listening. It was also the signal for the audience to stand up and stretch. The messages being read were a background noise as I got up from my spot near the aisle and moved in place, glad for the respite from the hard metal chair.

Charlie, I miss you and will be home soon, Love,

Jack.

I have seen a pork chop on a stick, a woman carved out of butter, and a pig that is so big it puts a sumo wrestler to shame. I guess my life is complete. Love, Sandy.

Margie, please make sure I turned off the coffeepot. I think I must have or I would have heard by now that the house burned down. But please check anyway, signed, Karl.

Having a great time, glad I'm not there, signed Bobby from Sacramento

I regarded Maggie, who remained seated, and Robbie, next to her. "Come on, you two," I teased. "Unwrap yourselves long enough to take a break."

"And here's a special announcement. In fact, it's so special I'm turning over the microphone so the sender can do it."

Only the stage was lit, with the rest of the area in semi-darkness. The side screens showed a man walking across the stage. I recognized that distinctive walk and that white hair. He took the microphone and looked directly at me. "Ain-jay, I'mway orrysay. Ancay Iway auditionway orfay atthay arriagemay objay?"

The buzz from the audience almost drowned out his words. I struggled to interpret what I was hearing, my mouth agape. Marcus stared directly at me.

"Ain-jay, I-way ovelay ou-yay. Ancay Iway auditionway orfay arriagemay?" He nodded to the host and handed him the microphone then strode to the side of the stage. I was paralyzed with amazement as the spotlight swung wildly, following Marcus as he raced down the stage steps, across the racetrack and up the stairs to the grandstand until he stood in the aisle directly below me.

Marcus gazed at me. "Jane," he called out. "I'm sorry. Can I audition for that marriage job?" He started walking up the stairs, his eyes intent on mine.

The crowd around me hushed. I took a hesitant step downward. "Marcus?"

"What do you say, Jane? Can I?" He stopped, his eyes worried.

I had no hesitation in the least. "Es-yay," I called out. I catapulted down the stairs to stand in front of him.

Behind me I heard a cell phone ringing. Robbie said, laughing, "It's Abby. She was listening to the show on the air. What should I tell her?"

I leaned into the safety of Marcus' arms. "Tell her I said yes!" I gazed into Marcus' eyes. "I told you. There is no substitute for you."

"And I told you—" His lips hovered over mine. "You're one in a million, Jane Renard."

A word about the author...

I was born in a small town in Iowa, and have traveled extensively in the U.S. and overseas, finally ending up back in the Midwest where I'm married to a glass artist who spends a lot of time in the studio, making amazingly beautiful things. We have assorted animals who live with us and who make regular appearances in my books under various pseudonyms (they know who they are).

In 2003, I read my first romance novel and immediately decided this was the genre for me. But there was a problem: the books I read all featured young heroines, interested in starting a family and having babies. So I started writing romantic suspense (with an occasional side trip into paranormal fantasy) about older women, with some age on' em, who are interested in men and sex and having a good relationship (which may or may not include a marriage). I hope you enjoy reading about them as much as I enjoy writing about them.

Contact JL at jaye@jayellwilson.com
Visit JL at www.jayellwilson.com

Thank you for purchasing
this Wild Rose Press publication.
For other wonderful stories of romance,
please visit our on-line bookstore at
www.thewildrosepress.com

For questions or more information,
contact us at
info@thewildrosepress.com

The Wild Rose Press
www.TheWildRosePress.com